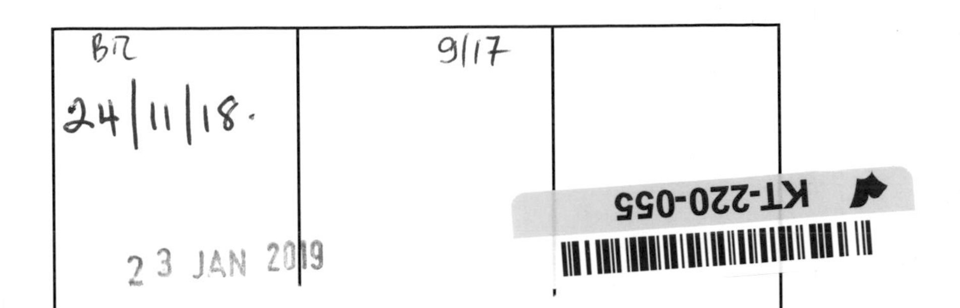
BR
24/11/18.
9/17
23 JAN 2019
KT-220-055

9030 00005 6720 0

The Red-Haired Woman

ALSO BY ORHAN PAMUK

A Strangeness in My Mind

Silent House

The Naïve and the Sentimental Novelist

The Museum of Innocence

Other Colours

Istanbul

Snow

My Name Is Red

The New Life

The Black Book

The White Castle

THE RED-HAIRED WOMAN

ORHAN PAMUK

Translated from the Turkish by Ekin Oklap

FABER & FABER

First published in the UK in 2017
by Faber & Faber Ltd
Bloomsbury House
74–77 Great Russell Street
London WC1B 3DA

First published in the United States in 2017
by Alfred A. Knopf, a division of Penguin Random House LLC, New York,
and in Canada by Knopf Canada, a division of
Penguin Random House Limited, Toronto

Printed and bound in the UK by CPI Group (UK) Ltd, Croydon CR0 4YY

Originally published in Turkey as *Kırmızı Saçlı Kadın*
by Yapı Kredi Yayınları, Istanbul, in 2016.

A CIP record for this book is available from the British Library

ISBN 978–0–571–33029–4

to Aslı

Oedipus, the murderer of his father, the husband of his mother, Oedipus, the interpreter of the riddle of the Sphinx! What does the mysterious triad of these deeds of destiny tell us? There is a primitive popular belief, especially in Persia, that a wise Magian can be born only of incest.

—NIETZSCHE, *The Birth of Tragedy*

OEDIPUS: Where would a trace of this old crime be found?

—SOPHOCLES, *Oedipus the King*

As a fatherless son, so a sonless father will be embraced by none.

—FERDOWSI, *Shahnameh*

• PART I •

1

I HAD WANTED TO BE A WRITER. But after the events I am about to describe, I studied engineering geology and became a building contractor. Even so, readers shouldn't conclude from my telling the story now that it is over, that I've put it all behind me. The more I remember, the deeper I fall into it. Perhaps you, too, will follow, lured by the enigma of fathers and sons.

In 1984, we lived in a small apartment deep in Beşiktaş, near the nineteenth-century Ottoman Ihlamur Palace. My father had a little pharmacy called Hayat, meaning "Life." Once a week, it stayed open all night, and my father took the late shift. On those evenings, I'd bring him his dinner. I liked to spend time there, breathing in the medicinal smells while my father, a tall, slim, handsome figure, had his meal by the cash register. Almost thirty years have passed, but even at forty-five I still love the smell of those old pharmacies lined with wooden drawers and cupboards.

The Life Pharmacy wasn't particularly busy. My father would while away the nights with one of those small portable television sets so popular back then. Sometimes his leftist friends would stop by, and I would arrive to find them talking in low tones. They always changed the subject at the sight of me, remarking how I was just as handsome and charming as he was, asking what year was I in, whether I liked school, what I wanted to be when I grew up.

My father was obviously uncomfortable when I ran into his political friends, so I never stayed too long when they dropped by. At the first chance, I'd take his empty dinner box and walk back home under the plane trees and the pale streetlights. I learned never to tell my mother about seeing Father's leftist friends at the shop. That would only get her angry at the lot of them and worried that my father might be getting into trouble and about to disappear once again.

But my parents' quarrels were not all about politics. They used to go through long periods when they barely said a word to each other. Perhaps they didn't love each other. I suspected that my father was attracted to other women, and that many other women were attracted to him. Sometimes my mother hinted openly at the existence of a mistress, so that even I understood. My parents' squabbles were so upsetting that I willed myself not to remember or think about them.

It was an ordinary autumn evening the last time I brought my father his dinner at the pharmacy. I had just started high school. I found him watching the news on TV. While he ate at the counter, I served a customer who needed aspirin, and another who bought vitamin-C tablets and antibiotics. I put the money in the old-fashioned till, whose drawer shut with a pleasant tinkling sound. After he'd eaten, on the way out, I took one last glance back at my father; he smiled and waved at me, standing in the doorway.

5

He never came home the next morning. My mother told me when I got back from school that afternoon, her eyes still puffy from crying. Had my father been picked up at the pharmacy and taken to the Political Affairs Bureau? They'd have tortured him there with bastinado and electric shocks. It wouldn't have been the first time.

Years ago, soldiers had first come for him the night after the military coup. My mother was devastated. She told me that my father was a hero, that I should be proud of him; and until his release, she took over the night shifts, together with his assistant Macit. Sometimes I'd wear Macit's white coat myself—though at the time I was of course planning to be a scientist when I grew up, as my father had wanted, not some pharmacist's assistant.

When my father again disappeared seven or eight years after that, it was different. Upon his return, after almost two years, my mother seemed not to care that he had been taken away, interrogated, and tortured. She was furious at him. "What did he expect?" she said.

So, too, after my father's final disappearance, my mother seemed resigned, made no mention of Macit, or of what was to become of the pharmacy. That's what made me think that my father didn't always disappear for the same reason. But what is this thing we call thinking, anyway?

By then I'd already learned that thoughts sometimes come to us in words, and sometimes in images. There were some thoughts—such as a memory of running under the pouring rain, and how it felt—that I couldn't even begin to put into words . . . Yet their image was clear in my mind. And there were other things that I could describe in words but were otherwise impossible to visualize: black light, my mother's death, infinity.

Perhaps I was still a child, and so able to dispel unwanted thoughts. But sometimes it was the other way around, and I would find myself with an image or a word that I could not get out of my head.

My father didn't contact us for a long time. There were moments when I couldn't remember what he looked like. It felt as if the lights had gone out and everything around me had vanished. One night, I walked alone toward the Ihlamur Palace. The Life Pharmacy was bolted shut with a heavy black padlock, as if closed forever. A mist drifted out from the gardens of the palace.

Sometime later, my mother told me that neither my father's money nor the pharmacy was enough for us to live on. I myself had no expenses other than movie tickets, kebab sandwiches, and comic books. I used to walk to Kabataş High School and back. I had friends who trafficked in used comic books for sale or loan. But I didn't want to spend my weekends as they did, waiting patiently for customers in the backstreets and by the back doors of cinemas in Beşiktaş.

I spent the summer of 1985 helping out at a bookstore called Deniz on the main shopping street of Beşiktaş. My job consisted mainly of chasing off would-be thieves, most of whom were students. Every now and then, Mr. Deniz would drive with me to Çağaloğlu to replenish his stock. The boss grew fond of me: he noticed how I remembered all the authors' and publishers' names, and he let me borrow his books to read at home. I read a lot that summer: children's books, Jules Verne's *Journey to the Center of the Earth,* Edgar Allan Poe's stories, poetry books, historical novels about the adventures of Ottoman warriors, and a book about dreams. One passage in this latter book would change my life forever.

When Mr. Deniz's writer friends came by the shop, the boss started introducing me as an aspiring writer. By then I had started harboring this dream and foolishly confessed it to him in an unguarded moment. Under his influence, I soon began to take it seriously.

2

One day after school, led by some instinct to the wardrobe and drawers in my parents' bedroom, I discovered that my father's shirts and all his other belongings were gone. Only his smell of tobacco and cologne still lingered in the room. My mother and I never spoke of him, and his image was already fading from my mind.

My mother and I were becoming fast friends, though that didn't prevent her from treating my decision to become a writer as a joke. First, I had to make sure I was admitted to a good university. To prepare for the entrance exams, I needed to make enough money for cram school, but my mother was dissatisfied with what the bookseller was paying me. The summer after I finished my second year of high school, we moved from Istanbul to Gebze. We were to stay with my maternal aunt and her husband in Gebze, living as guests in the extension they had built in their garden. My aunt's husband was to give me a job, and

I calculated that if I spent the first half of the summer at it, by the end of July I could resume work at the Deniz Bookstore in Beşiktaş while attending cram school. Mr. Deniz knew how sad I was not to be living in Beşiktaş anymore; he said I could spend the night at the bookstore whenever I wanted to.

My aunt's husband had arranged for me to guard his cherry and peach orchard on the outskirts of Gebze. When I saw my post, a rickety table under a gazebo, I took it to mean I'd have plenty of time to sit around and read. But I was wrong. It was cherry season: flocks of loud, audacious crows swarmed over the trees, and gangs of kids and the construction workers from the site next door were constantly trying to steal the produce.

In the garden next to the orchard, a well was being dug. I would go over sometimes to watch the welldigger work with his spade and pickax while two apprentices lifted and removed the earth their master had dug out.

The apprentices cranked the two handles attached to a wooden windlass, which creaked pleasantly as they hauled up bucketfuls of dirt and tipped them over into a handcart. The younger one, who was about my age, would go off to unload the handcart as the older, taller apprentice would yell, "Here it comes!," sending the bucket back down to the welldigger.

During the day, the welldigger rarely emerged. The first time I saw him, he was on his lunch break having a cigarette. He was tall, slender, and handsome, like my father. But unlike my naturally calm and cheerful father, the welldigger was irascible. He frequently scolded his apprentices. I thought it might embarrass them to be seen getting told off, so I steered clear of the well when the master was out.

One day in mid-June, I heard the sounds of joyful shouting and gunshots coming from their direction and went to take a look. Water had sprung from the well, and upon hearing the good news, the owner of the plot, a man from Rize, had come over to celebrate, gleefully firing his gun into the sky. There was an alluring smell of gunpowder in the air. As was customary, the landowner distributed tips and gifts to the welldigger and his apprentices. The well would allow him to realize the various construction projects he had planned for his land; the city's water network had yet to reach the outskirts of Gebze.

I never heard the master shouting at his apprentices in the days that followed. Bags of cement and some iron rods arrived on a horse-drawn cart one afternoon, and the master welldigger set about lining the well with concrete before covering it with a metal lid. I spent a lot more time with the crew now that they were in such a good mood.

One day I walked over to the well thinking there was no one there. Master Mahmut appeared from among the cherry and olive trees, holding a part from the electric motor he'd installed to power the pump.

"You seem curious about this work, young man!"

I thought of those people in Jules Verne's novel who went in one end of the world and came out the other side.

"I'm going to dig another well on the outskirts of Küçükçekmece. These two boys are leaving me. Shall I take you along instead?"

Seeing that I was hesitant, he explained that if he did his job right, a welldigger's apprentice could earn four times as much as an orchard watchman. We'd be done in ten days, and I'd be home in no time.

"I will never allow it!" said my mother when I got home that evening. "You will not be a welldigger. You're going to university."

But by then the thought of earning quick money had taken root in my mind. I kept telling my mother that I could earn in two weeks what I'd make at my aunt's husband's orchard in two months, leaving me with plenty of time to prepare for the university exams, go to cram school, and read all the books I wanted to read. I even threatened my poor mother:

"If you don't let me go, I'll run away," I said.

"If the boy wants to work hard and make his own money, don't knock the wind out of his sails," said my aunt's husband. "Let me ask around and find out who this welldigger is."

My aunt's husband, who was a lawyer, arranged a meeting at his offices in the town hall with my mother and the welldigger. In my absence, the three of them agreed that there would be a second apprentice who would go down into the well so I wouldn't have to. My aunt's husband informed me what my daily wages would be. I packed some shirts and the pair of rubber-soled shoes I wore for gym class into my father's old valise.

On the day of my departure, it was raining, and the time to meet the pickup truck that was to take me to the job site seemed never to arrive. My mother cried several times as we waited in our one-room guesthouse with the leaky roof. Wouldn't I change my mind? She would miss me terribly. Granted, we were poor now, but it needn't have come to this.

Clutching my valise, and affecting the same defiant expression I saw on my father's face when he was put on trial, I walked out of the house, saying teasingly: "Don't worry, I will never go down into the well."

The pickup was waiting in the empty lot behind the towering old mosque. Master Mahmut, cigarette in hand, observed my approach with a smile, assessing my clothes, the way I walked, and my bag, like a schoolteacher.

"Get in, it's time to go," he said. I sat between him and the driver sent by Hayri Bey, the businessman who had commissioned the well. We drove for an hour in silence.

As we crossed the Bosphorus Bridge, I looked to my left at Istanbul, toward Kabataş High School, to see if I could recognize any buildings in Beşiktaş.

"Don't worry, it won't take long," said Master Mahmut. "You'll be back in time for cram school."

I was pleased that my mother and my aunt's husband had already told him my concerns; it made me feel I could trust him. Once we'd gone over the bridge, we got stuck in one of Istanbul's traffic jams, so that by the time we were outside the city, the sun was already setting, blinding us with its searing rays.

I say we were leaving the city, but I wouldn't want this to confuse my readers. In those days, the population of Istanbul was not fifteen million, as it is now, but five. As soon as you passed the old city walls, the houses became fewer, smaller, and poorer, and the landscape was dotted with factories, gas stations, and the odd hotel.

We followed the railway tracks for a while, veering off as darkness fell. We'd already passed Büyükçekmece Lake. I saw a few cypress trees, cemeteries, concrete walls, empty tracts . . . But most of the time I could see nothing at all, and no matter how hard I tried, I couldn't figure out where we were. We saw the orange glow from windows of families sitting down for dinner, and we saw neon-lit factories. We drove up a hill. Lightning struck in the distance, lighting up the sky, but nothing seemed to illuminate the lonely lands we were passing through. Sometimes a mysterious light would reveal endless stretches of wasteland, the bare, uninhabited earth, but in a moment I'd lose sight of it all again in the darkness.

Finally, we stopped somewhere in that emptiness. I could see neither light, nor lamp, nor house, so I thought perhaps the old pickup had broken down.

"Give me a hand, let's unload this," said Master Mahmut.

There were blocks of wood, the components of a windlass, pots and pans, tools and equipment stuffed into rough plastic bags, and two mattresses bound together with rope. The driver took off saying,

"Good luck and God be with you," and when I realized the extent of the darkness surrounding us, I became nervous. There was lightning again somewhere far off, but the sky behind us was clear, and the stars shone with all their brilliance. Farther still, I could make out the lights of Istanbul reflecting off the clouds like a yellow fog.

The ground was still damp from the rain, and there were scattered wet patches. We searched that flat expanse for a dry spot and brought our belongings there.

Master Mahmut started pitching our tent with the wooden poles. But he couldn't do it. The ropes that needed pulling and the little pegs that had to be driven into the ground were all lost in the night, and a dark dread had wound itself around my soul. "Pull on this, not there," Master Mahmut called out blindly.

We heard an owl hooting. I wondered whether it was necessary to put up the tent, since the rain had stopped, but I respected Master Mahmut's determination. The heavy, musty cloth wouldn't stay in place but kept folding over itself and us, like the night.

By the time we managed to put the tent up and unroll our mattresses, it was long past midnight. The summer rain clouds gave way to a radiant starlit night. The chirping of a nearby cricket soothed me. I lay down on one of the mattresses and fell asleep immediately.

3

When I woke, I was alone in the tent. A bee was buzzing. I got up and stepped outside. The sun was already so high that the light hurt my eyes.

I was standing on a vast plateau. On my left, to the southeast, the land stretched downhill toward Istanbul. There were cornfields in the distance, light green and pale yellow; there were fields of wheat, too, but also barren land, rocky and dry. I could see a town nearby with houses and a mosque, but there was a hill obstructing the view, so I couldn't be sure how big the settlement was.

Where was Master Mahmut? The wind carried the sound of a bugle call, and I realized that the grayish buildings behind the town must be a military garrison. Beyond that, far away, was a row of purple mountains. For a moment, the whole world seemed to take on the silent quality of memory. I was pleased to be here, ready to make my own living, far from Istanbul, far from anyone.

A train whistled through the flat expanse between the town and the garrison. It seemed to be heading in the direction of Europe. It crept toward our empty section of the plateau before snaking gently away and stopping at the station.

I spotted Master Mahmut coming back from the town. He followed the road initially, but soon he was taking shortcuts, walking through wheat fields and barren patches.

“I got us some water,” he said. “Come on, then, make me some tea.”

While I was busy brewing tea on the portable gas burner, the landowner, Hayri Bey, arrived in his pickup, which had ferried us here the night before. A young man, slightly older than me, jumped off from the back. From their exchange I learned that the second apprentice, the one from Gebze, had pulled out at the last minute, so this young man, a worker of Hayri Bey's named Ali, would join us instead, descending into the well as needed.

Master Mahmut and Hayri Bey walked up and down the plot for a long time. Utterly bare in places, in others covered with rocks and grass, it was in all more than two and a half acres. A gentle breeze was blowing from their direction, and even when they'd reached the farthest corner of the plot, we could still hear them arguing. I edged closer to where they were. Hayri Bey, a textile merchant, wanted to build up a fabric-washing-and-dyeing factory here. There was much demand for these services from the big exporters of ready-to-wear clothing, but the process required large amounts of water.

This land, which had neither water nor an electricity supply, had cost Hayri Bey almost nothing. If we managed to find water, he would reward us handsomely. His politician friends would arrange for power lines to be brought in. Hayri Bey would then build a modern factory complex—he'd already shown us the plans—with dye works, washing rooms, warehouses, a smart office building, and even a cafeteria. Master Mahmut followed Hayri Bey's aspirations with sympathy and interest, but in truth, like me, he was mostly focused on the gifts and the money that had been promised us if we found water.

"May God be with you, may His strength flow through your arms, and His sight open your eyes," said Hayri Bey, like an Ottoman general sending his troops off on some heroic mission. As the pickup drove out of sight, he leaned out the window and waved at us.

That night Master Mahmut's snoring kept me up, so I lay my head down outside the tent. I couldn't see the lights of the town; the sky was dark blue, but the glow of the stars seemed to turn the universe a golden hue. And here we were, perched on a colossal orange suspended in space, trying to fall asleep in the darkness. Did it seem right that, rather than reaching up toward the gleam of the stars, we had resolved to burrow into the ground on which we slept?

4

SOIL PROBES had yet to become widely available back then. For centuries, welldiggers had looked for groundwater and divined where to dig guided by instinct alone. Master Mahmut was well acquainted with the elaborate orations delivered by some of these garrulous old masters. But when they picked up a forked rod and traipsed up and down a plot of land reciting prayers and whispering incantations, he dismissed their antics. Still, he knew himself to be among the last practitioners of an art that had existed for thousands of years. So he approached his work with humility. "You must look for dark, damp black soil," he told me. "You must find the lower stretches of the land, the gravelly, rocky patches, the sloping ups and downs, the shady parts, and feel the water beneath." He was eager to teach me how it worked. "Where you see trees and vegetation, the soil will be dark and damp, understood? But look carefully, and don't let yourself be fooled."

17

For earth was made up of many layers, just like the celestial sphere, which had seven. (Some nights I would look up at the stars and feel the dark world beneath us.) Two meters of rich black earth might conceal a loamy, impermeable, bone-dry layer of wretched soil or sand underneath. To work out where to dig for water as they paced the ground, the old masters had to decipher the language of the soil, of the grass, insects, and birds, and detect the signs of rock or clay underfoot.

These particular skills led some of the old welldiggers to become convinced that, like the shamans of Central Asia, they, too, were in possession of supernatural powers and the gift of extrasensory perception, allowing them to commune with subterranean gods and jinn. I remember as a child hearing my father laugh at such tales, but those hoping for cheap ways to find water wanted to believe them. I remember people in the poorer neighborhoods of Beşiktaş turning to this divination when deciding where to dig a well in their gardens. I myself had seen that when welldiggers crouched among the creepers and pecking hens in those back gardens, listening to the soil, old men and middle-aged ladies would treat them with the same reverence usually reserved for the doctor putting his ear to their sick baby's chest.

"We should be done in two weeks at most, God willing. I'll find water ten or twelve meters down," said Master Mahmut on that first day.

He could speak more freely with me than he could with Ali, who was the landowner's man. I liked that and came to feel that this well was our shared project.

The next morning, Master Mahmut chose the place where he would dig. It was not remotely where the landowner's factory plans had envisaged it. It was in a completely different place, in another part of the plot.

As a result of his political activities, my father had been in the habit of keeping secrets, so whenever he did anything important, he never involved me or asked what I thought. But Master Mahmut held forth in detail on the challenges of this land and freely shared with me his reasoning as he puzzled over where to dig. This was immensely gratifying and drew me to him. Still, when the time came to decide, his thoughts turned inward again, and he eventually chose the spot without consulting me or explaining anything. That's when I first became aware of the sway Master Mahmut now held over me, and so even as I enjoyed the affection and intimacy he showed me (such as I'd never felt from my father), I began resenting him for it.

Master Mahmut broke the surface of the earth at his chosen spot. But why, after all that walking and deliberation, had he chosen this particular place? How was it different from any other? If we kept digging there with that pickax, were we sure to find water eventually? I wanted to ask him all these questions, but I knew that I couldn't. I was a child; he was neither my friend nor my father, but my master. Only I saw in him a father.

He took a piece of rope and tied the spade to one end and a sharp nail to the other. The rope was one meter long, he told us. A stone wall wouldn't do down there; he would have to line the well with concrete. The concrete wall would have to be between twenty and twenty-five centimeters thick. Keeping the rope taut, he traced a circle two meters in diameter, scoring the ground with the nail while holding the spade at the center. Ali and I carefully joined the marks, and the circle appeared.

"The circle of a well must be drawn very precisely," said Master Mahmut. "Any mistakes, any straight edges along the curve, and the whole thing will collapse!"

It was the first I'd heard about the fearful prospect of a well collapsing. We set to work inside the circle. With a pickax, I helped Master Mahmut dig, and when I wasn't doing that, I carried the loosened earth over to Ali's handcart. But the two of us together could barely keep up with Master Mahmut. "If you don't fill the cart up so much, I can unload it and come back quicker," said Ali, struggling to catch his breath. The two of us soon grew tired and slowed down, but Master Mahmut's pickax continued to swing relentlessly, and soon the pieces of rock he'd dislodged began to accumulate by the well. Whenever the pile grew too large, he'd drop his tools and have a cigarette under an olive tree as he waited for us to catch up. A couple of hours into our first day, my fellow apprentice and I had already realized that the best we could do was try and keep up with Master Mahmut and follow his instructions promptly and unquestioningly.

Digging all day under the blazing sun exhausted me. I fell into bed straight after sunset, unable even to eat a bowl of lentil soup. Gripping the pickax had left my hands blistered, and the back of my neck was sunburned.

"You'll get used to it, little gentleman, you'll get used to it," said Master Mahmut, his eyes fixed on the small television he struggled to get reception on.

He may have been teasing me for being too delicate for manual labor, but it made me glad to hear him call me "little gentleman." Those two words told me that Master Mahmut knew my family was educated city folk, which meant he would look out for me as a father and not burden me with the heavier tasks. They made me feel that he cared about me and took an interest in my life.

5

THE SETTLEMENT was fifteen minutes on foot from our well. It was the town of Öngören, population 6,200, according to the blue sign with enormous white letters marking the entrance. After two days of ceaseless digging, two meters, we took a break on the second afternoon and went down to Öngören to acquire more supplies.

Ali took us to the town carpenter first. Having dug past two meters, we could no longer shovel out the earth by hand, so like all welldiggers, we had to build a windlass. Master Mahmut had brought some lumber in the landowner's pickup, but it wasn't enough. When he explained who we were and what we were up to, the inquisitive carpenter said, "Oh, you mean that land up there!"

Over the following days, whenever we went down to the town from "that land up there," Master Mahmut made a point of dropping by the carpenter; the grocer, who sold cigarettes; the bespectacled tobacconist; and the ironmonger, who stayed open late. After digging all day, I relished going to Öngören with Master Mahmut for an evening stroll by his side, or to sit in the shade of the cypress and pine trees on some little bench, or at a table outside some coffeehouse, on the stoop of some shop, or in the train station.

It was Öngören's misfortune to be overrun by soldiers. An infantry battalion had been stationed there during World War II to defend Istanbul against German attacks via the Balkans, and Russian attacks via Bulgaria. That purpose, like the battalion itself, was soon forgotten. But forty years later, the unit was still the town's greatest source of income, and its curse.

Most of the shops in the town center sold postcards, socks, telephone tokens, and beer to soldiers on day passes. The stretch known among locals as Diners' Lane was lined with various eateries and kebab shops, also catering to the military clientele. Surrounding them were pastry shops and coffeehouses that would be jammed with soldiers during the day—especially on weekends—but in the evenings, when these places emptied out, a completely different side of Öngören emerged. The gendarmes, who patrolled the area vigilantly, would have to pacify carousing infantrymen and break up fistfights among privates, in addition to restoring the peace disturbed by boisterous civilians or by the music halls when the entertainment got too loud.

Thirty years ago, back when the garrison was even larger, a few hotels had opened to accommodate military families and other visitors, but transport links with Istanbul had since improved, and now these places stood mostly vacant. Showing us around town on that first day, Ali explained that some of them had been converted into semisecret brothels. These were all to be found in the Station Square. We took an immediate liking to this square, which boasted a small statue of Atatürk; the Star Patisserie, with its thriving ice-cream trade; a post office; and the Rumelian Coffeehouse—the entire scene lit by the golden-orange glow of the streetlamps.

On a street leading to the station was a depot for construction vehicles, where, Ali told us, his father was employed as a night watchman by one of Hayri Bey's relatives. Late in the afternoon, Ali also took us to a blacksmith. Master Mahmut used the money Hayri Bey had advanced him to buy timber and metal clamps with which to bind together the various parts of the windlass. He also bought four bags of cement, a trowel, nails, and some more rope. This wasn't what he would use to lower himself into the well. That far-sturdier rope was back at our camp, wrapped around the spool for the windlass we'd brought from Gebze.

We loaded all of our purchases onto a horse-drawn cart someone at the blacksmith's had summoned for us. As the cart's metal wheels made an unholy racket against the flagstones, I thought of how these days here were numbered, how I would soon be back with my mother in Gebze and, not long thereafter, in Istanbul. Walking alongside the cart, I sometimes found myself abreast of the horse, looking into his dark, tired eyes and thinking he must be terribly old.

When we reached the Station Square, a door opened. A middle-aged woman in blue jeans stepped out onto the street. She looked over her shoulder, calling sternly, "Hurry up, will you?"

As the horse and I reached the open doorway, two more figures emerged: first, a man, maybe five or six years older than I was, and then a tall, red-haired woman who might have been his elder sister. There was something unusual, and very alluring, about this woman. Maybe the lady in jeans was the mother of this red-haired woman and her little brother.

"I'll go get it," the lovely red-haired woman called out to her mother before disappearing inside again.

But just as she was stepping back into the house, she glanced at me and the elderly horse behind me. A melancholy smile formed on her perfectly curved lips, as if she'd seen something unusual in me or the horse. She was tall, her smile unexpectedly sweet and tender.

"Come on, then!" her mother called out to her while the four of us—Master Mahmut, his two apprentices, and the horse—walked past. The mother looked annoyed at the Red-Haired Woman and paid us no heed.

Once the laden cart had rolled outside of Öngören and its flagstones, the noise of the wheels died down. When we had reached our plateau at the top of the slope, I felt as if we'd arrived at a different world altogether.

The clouds had dispersed, the sun was out, and even our mostly barren patch of ground seemed filled with color. Noisy black crows hopped onto the road that snaked between the cornfields, spreading their wings and taking off as soon as they saw us. The purple peaks toward the Black Sea had assumed a strange blue shade, and the rare clumps of trees among the drab, jaundiced plots in the plains behind the mountains seemed particularly green. Our land up here, the whole of creation, the pale houses in the distance, the quivering poplars, and the winding train tracks—it was all beautiful, and a part of me knew that the reason I felt this way was that beautiful red-haired woman I had just seen standing in the doorway of her house.

I hadn't even gotten a proper look at her face. Why had she been arguing with her mother? Her whole demeanor had struck me as her red hair gleamed uncannily in the light. For a moment, she looked at me as if she already knew me, as if to ask what I was doing there. In that moment when we caught each other's eye, it was as if we were both trying to summon, perhaps even to question, an ancient memory.

I looked at the stars and tried to picture her face as I drifted off to sleep.

6

THE NEXT MORNING, our fourth day on the job, we used the equipment brought from Gebze and the wood and the other materials purchased in Öngören to build a windlass. It had a tapering crank at either end and a large drum around which the rope was spooled, and the axis nestled into two X-shaped wooden rests. There was also a rough plank on which to set the bucket once we'd pulled it up from the well. With surprising deftness, Master Mahmut drew a detailed pencil sketch of the machine so that I could see how it was to be assembled.

Down in the hole, Master Mahmut would shovel earth into the bucket, and once it was full, Ali and I would hoist it up on the windlass. The bucket was larger than a pail for water, and much heavier when filled to capacity with dirt and rocks, so that even working in tandem, the two of us would struggle to haul it up. It also took a lot

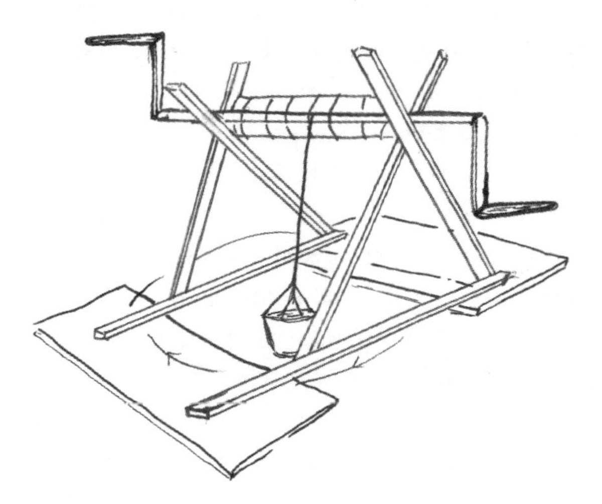

of strength and not a little skill to rest the bucket on the plank and slacken the rope enough to unhook it. Every time we managed that feat without a hiccup, Ali and I would glance at each other as if to say *Mission accomplished,* and breathe a sigh of relief.

We would then frantically rake some of the debris out of the bucket and into the handcart, until the bucket was light enough that we could lift it outright and tip what remained straight into the cart. I would lower the empty bucket carefully back into the well, and as it was about to reach Master Mahmut, I'd shout "Here it comes!" as he'd instructed me to do. Master Mahmut would leave his pickax to one side, pull the bucket toward himself, and without detaching it quickly fill it with what he'd dug up in the meantime. In those early days, I could still hear him say "Oof!" with each determined, furious stroke of his shovel and pickax. But as he receded into the earth at a rate of a meter per day, the grunts that announced his every exertion became gradually inaudible.

Once the bucket was full again, Master Mahmut would shout "Puuull!" often without so much as an upward glance. When Ali and I were both ready, we'd grab the handles of the windlass and start cranking. But sometimes that slacker Ali would dawdle with the cart, and since it was difficult to operate the windlass on my own, I would have to wait for him. Occasionally, however, Master Mahmut slowed down, and Ali and I would have a moment to sit, gasping for breath, and watch Master Mahmut shovel earth from the well.

During these idle moments, our only breaks from the relentless labor, we would have a chance to make small talk. But I knew instinctively that there was no point asking him about the people I had seen in town, let alone about the identity of the Red-Haired Woman with the mysterious, melancholy eyes and perfect lips. Did I assume he wouldn't know who they were? Or was I afraid that he might tell me something that would break my heart?

The fact that I had begun to think of the Red-Haired Woman from time to time was something I was as eager to hide from myself as from Ali. At night, as I was about to drift off with one eye on the stars and the other on Master Mahmut's tiny television, I pictured the way she had smiled at me. If not for that smile, I reflected, the look that said, *I know you,* and the tenderness in her expression, perhaps I wouldn't be thinking about her this much.

Around noon every three days, the landowner, Hayri Bey, would come by in his pickup truck and ask impatiently if everything was going according to plan. If we happened to be on our lunch break, Master Mahmut would tell him, "Join us," and invite him to share our meal of tomatoes, bread, fresh cheese, olives, grapes, and Coca-Cola. If Master Mahmut was still inside the well, three, four meters down, Hayri Bey would peer inside and watch him at work, standing with us two apprentices in respectful silence.

When he emerged, Master Mahmut would walk Hayri Bey to the other end of the plot where Ali dumped the earth we extracted, showing him pieces of rock, rolling in his hands clumps of soil of various shades, and speculating on how much farther the water was. We'd started off at a moderate pace, through light soil, but after three meters, we had hit a particularly hard layer, which had slowed us down on the fourth and fifth days. Master Mahmut was confident that once we broke past this hard vein, we would get to the more humid layer, to which the textile merchant replied, "Of course, God willing." He promised once more that as soon as we found water, he'd slaughter a lamb to roast in celebration and the master and his apprentices would receive a sizable tip. He even mentioned which shop in Istanbul he'd order the baklava from.

Once Hayri Bey was gone and after we'd had our lunch, we would slow down. There was a large walnut tree about a minute's walk from the site. I would lie down in its shade and start dozing off as the Red-Haired Woman appeared in my mind, vivid and unbidden, telling me with that look, *I know you!* I felt euphoric. Sometimes I would remember her while toiling in the noonday heat and feeling as if I was about to pass out. Thinking about her regenerated me and filled me with optimism.

When it got really hot, Ali and I drank large amounts of water, as well as pouring it over each other to keep cool. The water came from enormous plastic jerricans loaded onto Hayri Bey's pickup truck. When the pickup came, every two or three days, it also delivered the provisions we had ordered from town—tomatoes, green peppers, margarine, bread, olives. The driver collected payment for these from Master Mahmut, but he also brought things that Hayri Bey's wife had sent us: melons and watermelons, chocolates and sweets, and sometimes even pots of lovingly cooked meals, like stuffed peppers, tomato-flavored rice, and meat stew.

Master Mahmut was very particular about our evening meal. Every afternoon, before preparing to pour concrete into the well, he'd have me wash whatever ingredients were on hand—potatoes, eggplant, lentils, tomatoes, fresh peppers—before meticulously chopping everything up himself and throwing it with a knob of butter into the small pot we'd brought from Gebze. This was then placed on the gas stove over a low flame. It was my responsibility to watch this pot until sunset, making sure its simmering contents didn't stick.

The last two hours of each workday were devoted to pouring concrete into a wooden mold lining the depth he'd dug that day. Ali and I would mix the cement and sand with water in the handcart and then use a wooden contraption that looked like half a funnel, which Master Mahmut proudly claimed to have invented himself, to transfer the concrete directly into the well, without need for another bucket. As we tipped the mixture into the wooden slide, he would direct the flow from the depths of the well: "A little to the right, now ease up a bit!"

If we took too long to mix and pour the concrete into the well, Master Mahmut would shout at us that it had gone cold. In those moments, I would miss my father, who never raised his voice and never told me off. But then I would get angry at him, too, since it was his fault that we were poor and I had to work here. Master Mahmut took much more of an interest in my life than my father ever had: he told me stories and taught me lessons; he never forgot to ask if I was all right, if I was hungry, whether I was tired. Was this why it made me so angry to be dressed down by him? For had my father done the same, I would have taken his point, felt suitably contrite, and then forgotten the whole thing. But for some reason, Master Mahmut's scolding seemed to leave a scar, and I would nurse a rage against him even as I deferred to his instructions.

At the end of the day, Master Mahmut would step into the bucket and shout, "Enough!" Slowly, we'd crank the windlass, using it like an elevator to raise him up into the light. Once he emerged, he would lie down under the nearby olive tree, and a sudden silence would envelop the world; I would become more aware of our being entirely surrounded by nature, of our total isolation, of how far I was from Istanbul and its crowds, and then I would long for my mother and father, and for our life in Beşiktaş.

I would follow Master Mahmut's example and lie down in a patch of shade somewhere, watching Ali walk back home to his nearby town. Instead of following the meandering road, he would take shortcuts through empty tracts, fields of grass and nettles. We hadn't seen his house; what part of town was it in? Did he live anywhere near where we'd seen that ill-tempered woman in jeans standing outside her house?

As my thoughts idled along these lines, I would smell the pleasant aroma of Master Mahmut's cigarette, hear the buzzing of a bee and the soldiers in the distant garrison shouting "Yessir! Yessir!" at the evening muster, and I would think to myself how peculiar it was to be here to witness this world, how strange it was to be alive.

One day, as I got up to check on dinner, I found that Master Mahmut had fallen asleep, and just as I used to do when I was little and caught my father sleeping, I began to watch the way he lay there like an inanimate object, examining his long arms and legs and pretending that he was a colossus and I a tiny creature like Gulliver in the land of giants. Master Mahmut's hands and fingers were hard and knobby, not graceful like my father's. His arms were covered in cuts, moles, and black hairs, the true pallor of his skin visible only under the short sleeves of his shirt, where the sun didn't reach. As he breathed through his long nose, I watched in wonder—as I used to do when my father was asleep—as his nostrils slowly flared and contracted. Little clumps of earth clung to his thick mane of hair, which I could now see was graying, and curious harried ants clambered over his neck.

7

"Do you need to bathe?" Master Mahmut would ask me every evening at sunset.

The plastic jerricans the pickup truck brought every two or three days were equipped with taps, but these dispensed only enough water to wash our hands and faces. To bathe properly, we needed to collect the water in a large plastic barrel. As Master Mahmut bailed water from the barrel with a pitcher and poured it over my head, I would shiver—not because the water was still cold despite the sun, but because Master Mahmut could see my nakedness.

"You're still a child," he told me once. Was he implying that my muscles were underdeveloped, that I was a weakling? Or was it something else? His own body was sturdy and strong, and he had hair both on his chest and his back.

I had never seen my father or any other man naked. When it was my turn to take the tin pitcher and pour water over Master Mahmut's soapy head, I tried to avoid looking at him. Although I could see that his arms, legs, and back were covered with the bruises and scars he'd gotten from digging, I never said a thing. But when helping me to bathe, Master Mahmut, half out of concern and half to tease, would press his thick, coarse fingers into any bruises he spotted on my back or arms; and when I shuddered and groaned "Ow!" in response, he would laugh and tell me tenderly to "be more careful next time."

Tenderly or reproachfully, Master Mahmut warned me to be careful rather a lot: "Unless he has his wits about him, a welldigger's apprentice can risk maiming his master, and if he's careless, he could even end up killing him." "Now remember, your eyes and ears must always be alert to what's going on down inside the well," he'd say, describing how the bucket could come loose from its hook and fall, crushing the welldigger below. With a few quick words, he would likewise paint the scene of a welldigger overcome by a gas leak, and how he could cross over into the afterlife in the three minutes it might take a particularly distracted apprentice to notice.

I loved it when Master Mahmut looked me in the eye and told me these fearsome stories of instruction. Listening to his vivid accounts of careless apprentices, I could sense that in his mind, the underworld, the realm of the dead, and the farthest depths of the earth each corresponded to particular and recognizable parts of heaven and hell. According to Master Mahmut, the deeper we dug, the closer we got to the sphere of God and His angels—although the cool breeze that blew at midnight reminded us that the blue dome of the sky and the thousands of trembling stars that clung to it were to be found in the opposite direction.

In the peaceful silence that reigned at sunset, Master Mahmut would divide his attentions between the progress of dinner by intermittently unlidding the pot, and the image on the television, which required incessant adjustment. This television, too, he'd brought from Gebze, together with an old car battery to power it, but when the battery died on the second night, he loaded it onto the pickup and sent it off to Öngören to be recharged. It worked now, but that didn't spare Master Mahmut the eternal struggle for a clear signal. When his patience failed, he'd call me over, shove the metal aerial, which looked like an unsheathed cable, at me, and try to direct me—"A little to the right, but not too far"—into a position which would reveal a clear image.

After our protracted efforts, a picture would finally appear onscreen, though as we ate our meal and watched the news, it would soon go blurry again like a distant memory, coming and going of its own accord, in waves and shudders. At first we'd resume the effort to adjust it, but when that only made things worse, we gave up, making do with the news anchor's voice and the commercials.

Around that time, the sun would begin to set. We would hear the songs of strange rare birds that were nowhere to be seen during the day. A pinkish full moon would appear before nightfall. I could hear rustling around the tent and dogs barking in the distance, smell the dying fire and feel the shadows of cypress trees that weren't even there.

My father had never told me stories or fairy tales. But Master Mahmut did so every night, inspired by the blurry, fading image he'd seen on TV or some obstacle we'd overcome that day or simply an old memory. It was hard to tell which parts of his stories were real and which imagined, let alone where they began and ended. Still, I liked getting swept up in the telling and hearing what lessons Master Mahmut derived from it. Not that I could always *fully* understand what these stories meant. He once told me that when he was little, he was kidnapped by a giant and taken to the underworld. But it wasn't dark down there: it was bright. He was taken to a shimmering palace and invited to feast at a table littered with walnut shells and spider carapaces, fish heads and bones. They served him the world's most delicious dishes, but when Master Mahmut heard the sound of women weeping behind him, he couldn't eat a single bite. The women crying in the underground sultan's palace sounded just like that female presenter on TV.

Another time he told me about two mountains—one of cork, the other of marble—which had spent thousands of years staring at each other without any mutual comprehension, and he concluded this tale by telling me about the verse in the Holy Koran which says to build your homes on high ground. This was because earthquakes never struck there. We were lucky to be digging a well so far up. It was easier to find water on high ground.

Darkness would descend as Master Mahmut told these stories, and since there was nothing else to look at, we would both stare at the snowy image on TV as if the picture were clear and we could actually tell what was going on.

"Look, you can see it in there, too!" Master Mahmut would sometimes say, pointing at a spot on the screen. "That's a sign."

Among the ghostly pictures on the screen, I too might suddenly spot two mountains staring each other down. Before I could even think to myself that this might just be an illusion, Master Mahmut would change the subject, offering some practical advice: "Don't fill up the handcart too much tomorrow." I marveled at how a man who seemed like a bona fide engineer when it came to pouring cement, wiring a television to a car battery, and drawing the plans for a windlass could also speak of myths and fairy tales as if they'd really happened.

As I tidied up after dinner, sometimes Master Mahmut would say, "Let's go to town, we need to buy more nails" or "I've run out of cigarettes."

During our first few nights, moonlight shone off the asphalt road as we walked to Öngören in the cool darkness. I felt the presence of the sky, so close overhead, stronger than I'd ever felt it before, and thought of my father and my mother as the cicadas *click-clicked* pleasantly through the night. When there was no moon, I looked up in wonder at the tens of thousands of stars in the spangled sky.

In town, when I called my mother to tell her everything was fine, she started crying. I tried to comfort her, saying Master Mahmut had paid me (this was true). I told her I'd be back in a fortnight (though I wasn't so sure about that). Deep down I knew I was content to be here with Master Mahmut. Perhaps it was because I was able to make my own living this way, as the man of the house, now that my father was gone.

But on those nighttime visits to Öngören, I understood distinctly that the true cause of my gladness was the Red-Haired Woman. I wanted to see her again after that first time at the Station Square. Whenever I was in town with Master Mahmut, I tried to steer us toward that house. If the evening had gone by and we still hadn't passed the Station Square, I would find any excuse to leave Master Mahmut's side and go there myself, slowing my pace as I walked by.

It was a shabby, unplastered three-story building. The lights on the top two floors stayed on after the evening news. The curtains on the middle story were always shut. On the top floor, though, they stayed half drawn, and sometimes one window was left open.

I thought the Red-Haired Woman must live on either the top or the middle floor with her brother and the rest of her family. If it was the top floor, they were likely somewhat better off. What did her father do for a living? I hadn't seen him. Maybe he'd gone missing, too, like my own father.

As I toiled by day, slowly turning the handle of the windlass to lift up the heavy bucketfuls of earth, or as I lay dozing in the shade during our lunch break, I would find my thoughts turning to her, the picture of her filling my daydreams. I was a little embarrassed, but not to be dreaming of a woman I didn't even know while doing something that required my undivided attention; rather, I was mortified by my own naïveté and the childishness of these fantasies. For already I was imagining how we would get married, make love, and live happily ever after in a home of our own. I couldn't take my mind off the time I'd seen her in that doorway: her quick gestures, her little hands, her tall frame, the curve of her lips, and her tender, sorrowful expression—and, most of all, the teasing look that had crossed her face as she laughed. Such dreams blossomed all over my mind like wildflowers.

Sometimes I pictured us reading a book together, before at last kissing and making love. According to my father, the greatest happiness in life was to marry the girl you'd spent your youth reading books with in the passionate pursuit of a shared ideal. I'd heard him tell my mother as much while describing someone else's happiness.

8

ON THE WAY back to our tent after these evenings in town, I would feel as if we were walking toward the sky itself. There were no houses on the slope that led up to our plateau, so it would be pitch-black, and I would have the impression of getting closer to the stars ahead of us with every step we took. When they were veiled by the cypress trees in the little cemetery at the top of the hill, the night turned even darker. Once, a shooting star traversed a sliver of sky still visible between the cypresses, and we both turned to each other at the same time, as if to say, *Did you see that?*

We often saw shooting stars when we sat by the tent to talk. Master Mahmut believed that each star corresponded to a life. Almighty God had made summer nights starry to remind us of how many people and how many lives there were in the world. Whenever he saw a shooting star, Master Mahmut would grow mournful and say a prayer as if having witnessed someone's death. Observing that I wasn't particularly interested, he would resent my indifference and immediately start telling a new story. Did I have to accept everything he told me just so he wouldn't be angry at me? Many years later, when I grasped the immeasurable effect that Master Mahmut's stories had over the course of my life, I started reading anything I could find about their origins.

Most of Master Mahmut's stories were derived from the Koran. One, for instance, was about the devil who led people onto the sinful path of idolatry by tempting them to draw portraits so they could remember the dead by looking at them. But Master Mahmut's were modified versions of familiar tales, as if he'd heard them from a dervish, or at a coffeehouse, or even as if he'd lived them himself, as when he unexpectedly tied them into personal recollections that sounded completely credible.

He told me once about how he'd inspected a five-hundred-year-old well from the Byzantine era. Everyone thought the well was haunted by jinn or under some spell or curse. To show them that it harbored nothing more than an ordinary gas leak, Master Mahmut spread open the pages of a newspaper like the wings of a dove, which he set on fire and dropped into the well. As the blazing newspaper drifted slowly down the well, the flames faded until it reached the bottom, where they died entirely "because there was no air there." "You mean there was no oxygen," I corrected him. Unperturbed by my childish impertinence, he went on to explain how all the lizard- and scorpion-infested Byzantine wells of brick and hewn stone used Khorasani mortar just like the Ottomans did. And that furthermore all the master welldiggers in Istanbul before Atatürk and the founding of the republic were in fact Armenian.

He would reminisce fondly about the countless wells he'd dug in the poor neighborhoods behind Sarıyer, Büyükdere, and Tarabya, and all the apprentices he'd taught back in the 1970s, when business was so brisk he sometimes had more than one dig going at a time. In those years, it felt as if the whole Anatolian population was coming to settle in Istanbul, building ramshackle houses on the hills overlooking the Bosphorus, where there was neither water nor electricity. A few neighbors would pool their money to hire Master Mahmut, who in those days had his own swanky horse-drawn cart, painted with flowers and fruits; like a rich developer overseeing the projects in his portfolio, he might in a single day visit up to three separate neighborhoods to inspect a dig. At each site, he would enter the well himself, rushing off to the next only once he was confident the apprentice there had the job in hand.

"If you don't trust your apprentice, you can't be a welldigger," he'd say. "The master has to know that the apprentice will do his job properly, quickly, and accurately. You can't focus on your work down there if you're worried about what's going on up here. To survive, a welldigger must be able to trust his apprentice as he would his own son. Now tell me, who was *my* master?"

"Who?" I'd ask, despite knowing the answer.

"My father was my master," he would reply with the air of a teacher, ignoring how often he'd already told me the story. "If you want to be a good apprentice, you will have to be like a son to me."

According to Master Mahmut, it was every master's duty to love, protect, and educate his apprentice as a father would—for the apprentice would eventually inherit his master's job. In return, it was the apprentice's duty to learn from his master, to heed his instructions, and to treat him with due deference. If the relationship was soured by antipathy and defiance, it would injure both parties—just as with an actual father and son—and work on the well would have to be abandoned. Knowing that I was a good boy from a good family, Master Mahmut wasn't worried; he did not expect impudence or disobedience from me.

Born in the district of Suşehri near the city of Sivas, Master Mahmut had moved to Istanbul with his parents at the age of ten, spending the rest of his childhood in a makeshift house they'd built somewhere behind the neighborhood of Büyükdere. He liked pointing out that his family was poor. His father had worked many years as a gardener at one of the last few family mansions left in Büyükdere. Eventually, he learned how to dig a well when, by chance, he found himself assisting a master digger. When he realized how lucrative the work could be, he decided to change occupations, selling all of his livestock and taking his son Mahmut as an apprentice. Mahmut served his father all the way through high school, until it was time for his military service. When he returned from that in the 1970s, wells were being dug everywhere to supply water to orchards and poor neighborhoods. Soon enough the old man passed away, whereupon Mahmut bought himself a horse-drawn cart and took his father's place. He'd go on to dig more than one hundred and fifty wells over nearly twenty years. He was now forty-three, like my father, but he'd never been married.

Did he know that my father had left us penniless? I wondered about that every time Master Mahmut described his own boyhood in the grip of poverty. Sometimes it seemed that he was taunting me for being forced to work as a welldigger's apprentice, having started off in life as a "little gentleman" from a family that owned a pharmacy—in other words, for being genteel.

One evening a week after we'd started to dig, Master Mahmut told me the story of Joseph and his brothers. I listened closely to how their father, Jacob, had favored Joseph out of all his sons, only for the jealous brothers to trick Joseph and throw him down a dark well. The most memorable part was when Master Mahmut looked right at me and said, "True, Joseph was good and very clever, but a father mustn't have favorites among his sons." And then he added: "A father must be fair. A father who isn't fair will blind his son."

What was behind this talk of blindness? How had the topic even come up? Was it to emphasize how dark it had been inside the well where Joseph was confined? I have asked myself this question countless times over the years. Why did that story upset me so much and make me so angry at Master Mahmut?

9

THE NEXT DAY, Master Mahmut hit upon an unexpectedly hard layer of rock, and for the first time, we felt deflated. It was so hard, he was worried about breaking his pickax, so he had to proceed very cautiously, which slowed us down even more.

While we waited for the empty bucket to fill up, Ali would lie down on the grass to rest. But I never took my eyes off Master Mahmut chipping away down below. The heat was exhausting and the sun burned my neck.

The landowner, Hayri Bey, who came by at noon, was displeased to hear about the rock. He stood under the blazing sun, staring into the depths of the well as he smoked a cigarette. He returned to Istanbul, leaving us a watermelon, which we had for lunch with some white cheese and warm fresh bread.

Master Mahmut hadn't been able to dig far enough that day to warrant pouring more concrete into the well in the afternoon. So he kept stubbornly at his digging until sundown. He was tired and restless when I served him his dinner after Ali left; we didn't exchange a word.

"If only we'd started digging in the spot I showed you," Hayri Bey had said earlier that day. I thought this comment, questioning Master Mahmut's expertise and instincts, must explain why Master Mahmut seemed so despondent.

"Let's not go to town today," he said as we finished our dinner.

It was late, he was tired, and I understood his reluctance. But I was upset anyway. In the space of a week, I had reached the point where I could not do without walking to the Station Square every evening and looking up at the windows of that building hoping to see the Red-Haired Woman inside.

"You go ahead, though," said Master Mahmut. "You can get me a pack of Maltepe cigarettes. You're not afraid of the dark, are you?"

The sky above was clear and luminous. I looked at the stars and walked briskly toward the lights of the little town of Öngören. Before reaching the cemetery, I saw two stars falling simultaneously and felt a thrill, taking it as a sign that I was certain to meet her.

But when I got to the Station Square, the lights in their building were out. I went to the bespectacled tobacconist's and bought Master Mahmut's cigarettes. The sounds of a chase scene carried over from the outdoor Sun Cinema. I peeped at the screen through a gap in a wall, hoping to spy the Red-Haired Woman and her family in the audience, but they weren't there.

On the outskirts of town, at the start of the road that led to the army garrison, there stood a tent surrounded by theater posters. A sign on the tent said:

THE THEATER OF MORALITY TALES

One summer when I was little, a theater had been set up this way in a tent, not far from the amusement park in the empty lot behind the Ihlamur Palace. But that theater didn't do too well, and it soon shut down. This one must be the same sort of provisional affair, I mused, as I lingered in the street. At length, the cinema crowd dispersed, the last TV broadcast signed off, the streets emptied out, but still the windows facing the train station remained dark.

I scurried back, gnawed by guilt. My heart was beating fast as I climbed the hill toward the cemetery. I sensed an owl watching me silently from its perch on the cypress tree.

Maybe the Red-Haired Woman and her family had left Öngören. Or maybe they were still in town, and I'd panicked for no reason and cut my reconnaissance short for fear of Master Mahmut. Why was I so wary of him?

"What took you so long? I was worried," he said.

He'd had a nap and seemed in a better mood. He took the pack of cigarettes and lit one up straightaway. "Anything going on in town?"

"Nothing going on," I said. "There was a traveling theater."

"Those degenerates have been there since we got here," said Master Mahmut. "All they do is dance suggestively and tell dirty jokes for the soldiers. Those places are no different from brothels. Steer clear! Now, since you're the one who has just been to town and among people, why don't you tell a story tonight, little gentleman?"

I wasn't expecting that. Why had he called me "little gentleman" again? I tried to think of something that would upset him. If Master Mahmut meant to bring me to heel with his stories, then I must at least try to unsettle him with one of mine! I kept thinking of things like blindness and theaters. So I began to tell him the story of the Greek king Oedipus. I had never read the original, but at the Deniz Bookstore last summer, I'd come across a summary, and it had stayed with me.

This text, which I'd found in an anthology called *Dreams and Life*, had been lurking in some corner of my mind for the past year, like the genie in Aladdin's lamp. Now here I was telling that same story, not as I'd learned it—secondhand and abridged—but with all the intensity of a real memory:

As the son of Laius, king of the Greek city of Thebes, Oedipus was heir to the throne. So important was he that even while he was still in his mother's womb, an oracle was consulted about his future. But a terrible prophecy was pronounced . . . Here I paused a little and, just like Master Mahmut, fixed my eyes on the indistinct apparitions that populated the TV screen.

According to this awful prophecy, Prince Oedipus was destined to murder his father, marry his own mother, and take his father's place on the throne. Terrified by this prospect, Laius had his son taken away at birth, to be left in the forest to die.

The abandoned baby Oedipus was saved by a lady from the court of the neighboring kingdom who found him among the trees. Everything about the foundling indicated that he was of noble birth, so even in this other country, he was raised as a prince by the childless king and queen. But as soon as he grew up, he began to feel he did not belong there. Wondering why that might be, he too asked an oracle to divine his future and heard the same awful story again: God meant for Oedipus to kill his own father and sleep with his own mother. To escape this terrible fate, Oedipus immediately fled.

He arrived in Thebes, not knowing that it was his true homeland; and while crossing a bridge, he got into a pointless argument with an old man. This was his real father, Laius. (I lingered on this scene for a long time, describing how father and son could fail to recognize each other and start fighting, as if in some scene from a melodramatic Turkish movie.)

They grappled fiercely until eventually Oedipus prevailed, cutting his father down with a furious swipe of his sword. "Of course he had no idea that the man he'd just killed was his father," I said, looking right at Master Mahmut.

He was listening with his brows furrowed and a troubled look on his face, as if I were relaying bad news rather than just recounting an old fable.

No one had seen Oedipus kill his father. No one in Thebes accused him of the murder. (As I listened to myself, I wondered what it might be like to get away with a crime as serious as murdering your own father.) But then the city had other problems: a monster with the head of a woman, the body of a lion, and giant wings on its back was destroying crops and killing passersby unable to answer its riddle. So when he solved the impossible riddle set by the Sphinx, Oedipus was hailed as a hero for having rid the city of this nuisance, and for good measure was crowned the new king of Thebes. That's how he ended up married to the queen, his own mother, who didn't know that he was her son.

I told this last part in a hurried whisper, as if to make sure no one overheard. "Oedipus married his mother," I repeated. "They had four children. I found this story in a book," I added so that Master Mahmut wouldn't think I'd dreamed up these horrors myself.

"Years later, a plague came to the city where Oedipus lived happily with his wife and children," I continued, watching the red tip of Master Mahmut's cigarette. "The plague was decimating the city, and its terrified citizens sent a messenger to the gods, desperate to know their will. 'If you want to be rid of the plague,' said the gods, 'you must find and banish the murderer of the previous king. When that is done, the plague will be gone!' "

Unaware that the old man he'd fought and killed on the bridge was both his father and the previous king of Thebes, Oedipus immediately ordered the killer to be found. In fact, he himself worked harder than anyone to discover the murderer. The more he looked, the closer he came to the truth that he had killed his own father. Even worse was the realization that he had married his mother.

I paused at this point in the tale. Whenever he told religious stories, Master Mahmut always grew quiet at the most meaningful moment, and I would sense a vague warning in his manner: it could happen to you. I was trying to do the same now, though without even knowing what the moral of my story was. So as I reached the end of the tale, I almost felt sorry for Oedipus, and my tone sounded sympathetic:

"When he realized he'd been sleeping with his own mother, Oedipus gouged out his own eyes," I said. "Then, he left his city for a different world."

"So God's will came to pass, after all," said Master Mahmut. "Nobody can escape their fate."

I was surprised that Master Mahmut had drawn a moral about fate from this story. I wanted to forget all about fate.

"Yes, and once Oedipus had punished himself the plague ended and the city was saved."

"Why did you tell me this story?"

"I don't know," I said. I felt guilty.

"I don't like your story, little gentleman," said Master Mahmut. "What was that book you read?"

"It was a book about dreams."

I knew that Master Mahmut would never again say: "Why don't you tell a story tonight?"

10

DURING OUR EVENINGS in town, Master Mahmut and I always did things in a particular order. First we bought my master's cigarettes from the bespectacled tobacconist or from the grocer whose TV was always on. Then we visited the ironmonger, whose shop stayed open late, or the carpenter from Samsun. Master Mahmut had befriended him and sometimes sat down for a smoke on the chair outside his shop. I'd take the opportunity to slip away for a quick run by the Station Square. When the carpenter's shop was closed, Master Mahmut would say, "Come on, I'll get you a cup of tea," and we'd sit at one of the empty tables outside the double doors of the Rumelian Coffeehouse, on the street that led to the Station Square. You could see the square from there, but not the building where the Red-Haired Woman lived. Every now and then I'd make an excuse to get up and walk until I could see the windows of the building, and when I saw that the lights were out, I would come back to the table.

In that half hour we spent drinking tea outside the Rumelian Coffeehouse, Master Mahmut invariably offered a quick assessment of how far we'd dug that day and our progress generally. "That rock is very hard, but don't worry, I'll get the better of it," he said on the first night. "An apprentice must learn to trust his master!" he said on the second night, when he saw me getting impatient. "It would be a lot easier if we could use dynamite the way we used to do before the military coup," he said on the third night. "But the army has banned it."

He took me to the Sun Cinema one night, like a doting father; we watched the film sitting on the lower stretch of the cinema wall with all the children. When we got back to our tent, he said: "Call your mother tomorrow and tell her not to worry, I'll find water in a week."

But the rock wouldn't break.

One evening when Master Mahmut didn't accompany me to town, I went up to the theater tent to read the posters and the banners stretched across the entrance: THE REVENGE OF THE POET, ROSTAM AND SOHRAB, FARHAD THE MOUNTAIN-BREAKER. ADVENTURES NEVER SEEN ON TV. I was most curious about the parts that hadn't been on television.

Tickets cost about a fifth of the daily wages Master Mahmut paid me; there was no indication of a discount for kids and students. The biggest poster of all read EXTRA DISCOUNTS FOR SOLDIERS, SATURDAYS AND SUNDAYS, 13:30 AND 15:00.

I knew that I wanted to go to the Theater of Morality Tales exactly because Master Mahmut had criticized it. Whenever we went down to Öngören, whether he was with me or not, I made it a point to pass by there, finding any excuse to catch a glimpse of the warm yellow tent.

While Master Mahmut sat nursing his tea one evening, I walked over to the Station Square to take another look at the windows that seemed always to be dark. Later, as I wandered up and down Diners' Lane to pass the time, I saw the young man I thought was the Red-Haired Woman's brother emerging from the Liberation Restaurant. I started to follow him.

When he reached the Station Square and slipped into the building whose windows I always stared at, my heart raced. Which floor would light up? Was the Red-Haired Woman in? When the lights on the top floor came on, my excitement grew unbearable. But right at that moment, the Red-Haired Woman's younger brother emerged from the building again and started walking in my direction. This puzzled me; he couldn't have been turning the lights on upstairs and walking out the door at the same time.

He was coming straight at me. Perhaps he'd realized I'd been following him, or even that I was obsessed with his sister. Panicking, I ducked into the station building and sat on a bench in a corner. It was cool and quiet inside.

But rather than the train station, the Red-Haired Woman's brother made for the street where the Rumelian Coffeehouse was. If I followed him now, Master Mahmut, who was still drinking his tea, would see me, so instead I rushed up a parallel street and stood waiting behind a plane tree at the top. When the Red-Haired Woman's brother ambled past me, lost in thought, I tagged along. We walked down the carpenter's street, behind the Sun Cinema, and past the blacksmith's horse cart. I saw the late-night grocery, the barbershop windows, and the post office I called my mother from, and I realized that in just two weeks of wandering Öngören, I'd already walked down every street in town.

When I saw the Red-Haired Woman's brother walk into the beaming yellow theater tent just outside town, I ran straight back to Master Mahmut.

"What took you so long?"

"I thought I'd give my mother a call."

"You miss her, then?"

"Yes, I do."

"What did she say? Did you tell her that we'll find water as soon as we've dealt with this rock, and you'll be back home in a week at most?"

"I did."

I would call my mother from the post office that stayed open until nine every evening, reversing the charges. The girl on the switchboard would ask for my mother's name, and then she would say: "Mrs. Asuman Çelik? Cem Çelik is calling you from Öngören, do you accept the charges?"

"I accept!" my mother's eager voice would confirm.

The presence of the girl on the switchboard and the surcharge for calling collect meant that neither of us could ever act quite naturally. We would run through the usual small talk before falling silent.

The same tight-lipped distance that had crept into my relationship with my mother came between me and Master Mahmut on our way home that night. We gazed at the stars while walking up our hill and didn't talk at all. It was as if a crime had been committed, and since the countless stars and crickets around us had all witnessed it, we lowered our gaze and kept quiet. The cemetery owl greeted us from the black cypress.

Master Mahmut lit one last cigarette before retiring to the tent for the night. "Remember that fable you told last night about the prince?" he said by way of introduction. "I've been thinking about that today. I know a story like it about fate."

At first I didn't realize he was talking about the Oedipus myth. But I said immediately: "Please tell me, Master Mahmut."

"A long time ago, there was a prince just like yours," he began.

The prince was his father the king's favorite and firstborn. The king doted on this son and granted his every wish, throwing banquets and feasts in his honor. One day, during one of these feasts, the prince saw a man with a black beard and dark countenance standing by his father and recognized him as Azrael, the angel of death. The prince's and Azrael's gazes crossed, and they looked at each other in astonishment. After the feast, the worried prince told his father that Azrael had been among the guests, and that he was surely after him: the prince could tell from the angel's mien.

The king was afraid: "Go straight to Persia, don't tell anyone, but hide in the palace in Tabriz," he told his son. "The shah of Tabriz is our friend, these days; he won't let anyone get you."

So the prince was sent off to Persia immediately. Afterward, the king threw another feast and invited the dark-faced Azrael again, as if nothing had happened.

"My king, I see that your son isn't here tonight," said Azrael with a look of concern.

"My son is in the prime of his youth," said the king. "He will live a long life, God willing. Why do you ask about him?"

"Three days ago, God commanded me to go to the palace of the shah of Tabriz in Persia and take your son, the prince!" said Azrael. "That's why I was so surprised, and so pleased, when I saw him yesterday, right here in Istanbul. Your son saw the way I looked at him, and I think he knew what it meant."

Without further delay, Azrael left the palace.

11

AT NOON THE NEXT DAY, with the July sun scorching the backs of our necks, the rock Master Mahmut had been valiantly warring with finally cracked open ten meters down the well. We were ecstatic until we realized that things wouldn't necessarily speed up; Ali and I were taking far too long hauling up the heavy fragments. In the afternoon, Master Mahmut finally called us to pull him up to the surface. "This will go faster if I man the windlass and one of you goes down in there," he said. "Now, who's it going to be?"

Neither Ali nor I said anything.

"You do it, Ali," said Master Mahmut.

I was thrilled that Master Mahmut was sparing me. Ali stood with one foot in the bucket, and we slowly lowered him down on the windlass. Now it was the master and me working the windlass together. I fretted over whether my words and gestures were enough to convey just how grateful I was. I didn't like how eager I was to please him. But I also knew that if I did as he said, we would find water faster, and that would make my life easier. At Ali's signal we cranked the windlass in silence, listening to the sounds around us.

The steady chirping of crickets seemed to come from one direction, and below that trill was a bass line, an indeterminate hum, the din of Istanbul thirty kilometers away. I hadn't noticed it when we first arrived. It was overlaid with other sounds: the chatter of crows, swallows, and countless other birds I didn't know, squawking plaintively; the *chug-chug* of the endless freight train making its way from the city to Europe; and soldiers droning their marching tune, "Oh the prairies, the prairies," as they jogged, with full gear, in the heat.

Every so often, our gazes crossed. What did Master Mahmut really think of me? I yearned for him to care for me and watch over me even more than he already did. But whenever our eyes met, I always looked away.

Sometimes he would say, "Look, another airplane," and we'd lift our faces up to the sky. The planes took off from Yeşilköy, and after climbing for about two minutes, they changed course somewhere over our heads. Down in the well, Ali would shout, "Pullll!" and we'd slowly turn the creaking windlass, lifting fragments of rock streaked with iron and nickel, which Master Mahmut had taught us to recognize.

Every time the bucket came up, Master Mahmut warned Ali not to fill it up so much next time, to ignore the larger chunks for the time being, and always to make sure the load was securely fastened to the rope.

After tipping in a few bucketfuls, it was my job to empty the handcart. Soon, I'd made a little heap of those oddly textured metallic rocks. Their color, hardness, and density were so different from the earth we'd extracted in the first week that they seemed to come from another world altogether.

On Hayri Bey's next visit, Master Mahmut explained to him that though we were still hampered by this hard layer, he had no intention of starting over elsewhere. There was water here for sure.

Hayri Bey paid Master Mahmut by the meter. There would also be the lump sum due once water was found, as well as the customary gifts and tips. These terms had been cemented by tradition over hundreds of years of dealings between welldiggers and landowners. The digger did well to choose his spot carefully, for if he chose willfully or capriciously, he would only jeopardize the much-larger sum owed him on completion. In the case of a landowner who imperiously insisted, "Dig here," choosing some spot with no hope of yielding water, the welldigger could still depend on being paid by the meter. But a master welldigger could raise that rate if obliged to go against his own better judgment. He could thereby indemnify himself against the danger of finding no water at all. Or he might at least insist on a sliding scale, increasing the rate past the ten-meter mark.

Since the welldigger and the landowner had a common interest in finding water, it wasn't unheard of for them to decide jointly to abandon a particular dig and start afresh elsewhere. A landowner might become fixated on a difficult spot where the odds were long (where the terrain was too rocky, for instance, or too sandy, or the soil too dry and pale); but even if he was dubious about a site, the welldigger had a financial incentive to continue digging and indulge the landowner. Hitting a layer of rock that would slow him down, he might demand to be paid by the day rather than by the meter. But sometimes the owner decided that an already excavated site was a lost cause. In those instances, the welldigger, trusting his intuition, might need to appeal for a few days' forbearance. I could see that Master Mahmut was approaching that situation.

When I went down to town with Master Mahmut the next evening, I made my way to Diners' Lane and the Liberation Restaurant at eight-fifteen, a half hour earlier than I had seen the Red-Haired Woman's brother leave there four days before. A partly drawn lace curtain covered the window, through which I couldn't recognize anyone. So I opened the door and let my eyes roam around the near-empty room. Still, I saw no familiar faces amid the *rakı* fumes, no trace of that red hair.

The next day revealed a layer of soft earth beneath the hard layer we'd been battling; but before we could hit our stride, Master Mahmut came upon a new vein of rock. At the Rumelian Coffeehouse that evening, we were apprehensive and quiet. After about an hour of that, I stood up without offering any excuse and headed toward the square. A row of almond trees along the sidewalk hindered my view of the windows from that side, so I went into Diners' Lane instead. This time, looking through the gap in the lace curtains of the Liberation Restaurant, I saw the Red-Haired Woman, her brother, and her mother sitting with a group of friends at a table near the window.

Gripped by nervous excitement, and without being fully aware of my own actions, I stepped inside. They were laughing and teasing one another and didn't notice my entrance. There were *rakı* glasses and beer bottles all over their table. The Red-Haired Woman was smoking as she followed the conversation.

A waiter came up to me and asked: "Are you looking for someone?"

At that, everyone at the table turned and looked at me, their image reflected in the wide mirror on the wall beside them. The Red-Haired Woman and I shared a glance. She had that same tender expression on her face, though this time she seemed cheerful. She was observing me as I observed her. Perhaps she was mocking me. Her dainty hands flittered over the table.

I had left the waiter's question unanswered. "Soldiers aren't allowed in here after six," he said.

"I'm not a soldier."

"Under-eighteens aren't allowed either. If you're joining someone, go ahead, otherwise you're going to have to leave."

"Let him in, we know him!" said the Red-Haired Woman to the waiter. No one else said a word. She was looking at me as if she knew everything about me, as if she'd known me for years. Her eyes seemed so kind and so amiable that I was overwhelmed with joy. I returned her gaze passionately. But now she looked away.

I left without a word to the waiter and walked back toward the Rumelian Coffeehouse.

"What took you so long?" said Master Mahmut. "Where do you go every night when you leave me here?"

"This new rock is bothering me, too, Master Mahmut," I said. "What if we can't get past it?"

"Have faith in your master. Do as I say and rest easy. I will find that water."

My father's jokes and his sayings had always entertained me, made me think, and tested my wits. Yet I hadn't always believed everything he said. Master Mahmut's words, however, never failed to comfort and encourage me. For a time, I too believed that we would find that water.

12

THREE DAYS LATER, we still hadn't gotten beyond the new layer of rock, nor had I had a chance to see the Red-Haired Woman again. I kept reliving the moment when she had defended me against the waiter's attempt to throw me out of the Liberation Restaurant, remembering her affectionate expression, the pretty shape her lips took when she smiled her teasing smile. Her every move was graceful and irresistibly attractive. Master Mahmut and Ali took turns inside the well, slowly hacking away at the rock with the pickax. Progress was slow, and the heat agonizing. But hoisting up the rock fragments and carrying them to the handcart hardly seemed such a chore. All I needed was to think about the tenderness in the way the Red-Haired Woman had looked at me, the way she had declared that she recognized me, and I could carry on without complaint, confident that we'd find water soon.

One night when Master Mahmut didn't come to Öngören, I went all the way to the theater tent and queued up for a ticket. But a man I had never seen before who was manning the table that served as a box office said, "This isn't for you!" and turned me away.

At first I thought he might be referring to my age. But amid the general indifference that reigned in these small towns, it wasn't unusual for even small children to sneak into the worst sort of establishment without anyone batting an eye. Besides, I was almost seventeen now, and everyone always said that I looked older. Perhaps what the man had meant to say was that a well-bred little gentleman from the big city was above the cheap laughs and sordid scenes of this production. Could the Red-Haired Woman have anything to do with the kind of vulgarities and coarse humor being staged for the amusement of simple soldiers?

On my way back from town, I looked at the endless multitudes of stars and thought once more that I would be a writer. Master Mahmut was watching TV and waiting up for me. He asked me whether I'd gone to the theater tent again, and I told him I hadn't. I knew he didn't believe me. I could see it in his eyes and in the trace of disdain around the corners of his mouth.

I sometimes saw that same scornful expression as we were cranking the windlass together all day in the heat, and at those moments I would think contritely that I must have done something wrong or let him down without realizing it. Maybe he thought I wasn't pulling my weight at the crank, or maybe I hadn't taken enough care hooking the bucket securely. The longer the search for water continued, the more often I'd see that accusing, disdainful, maybe even slightly suspicious look frozen on Master Mahmut's face. It made me angry at myself but also at him.

My father would never have paid so much attention to me. I would never have been able to spend the whole day with him as I did with

Master Mahmut. But my father had never looked down on me. The only time I ever felt guilty on his account was when he was shut away in prison. So what was it about Master Mahmut that got under my skin? Why did I feel the constant need to be so obedient, so ingratiating? I would try to work up the courage to ask myself these questions when we were groaning at opposite ends of the windlass, but I couldn't even manage that. Instead I'd look away and stew in my own rage.

Listening to his stories became the most enjoyable part of the time I spent with him. As he looked at the snowy image on the television, he told me that night what he understood about the subterranean layers of the earth. Some of these were so deep and broad that an inexperienced welldigger could easily think they would never end. But you had to persevere. These layers were not so different from human blood vessels. Just as human veins carried the blood that fuels our bodies, so these enormous underground veins channeled the earth's lifeblood in the form of iron, zinc, and limestone. Nestled among these veins were streams, gullies, and underground lakes of all shapes and sizes.

Many of Master Mahmut's stories turned on how water could spring from a well when you least expected it. One time five years ago, for example, a man from Sivas had called him to a plot on the outskirts of Sarıyer, close to the Black Sea, but seeing bucket after bucket of sand come out of the hole, the man had lost faith in the whole endeavor and decided to call it off. Master Mahmut explained that sand could be deceiving, and that the different layers of the earth were sometimes tangled up like the organs of the body. Soon enough, he'd found water.

Master Mahmut would boast of being called to old, historic mosques. "You won't find a single ancient mosque in Istanbul that doesn't have a well," he once proudly proclaimed. He liked to pepper his anecdotes with trivia: the well in the Yahya Efendi Mosque, for example, was just inside the entrance, while the one at the Mahmutpaşa Mosque, thirty-five meters deep, was situated in the courtyard at the top of a slope.

Before descending into old wells, Master Mahmut would send down a lit candle placed in the bucket. If the flame continued to burn even at the bottom of the well, he knew there was no gas leaking down there, and he could safely enter the blessed place himself.

Master Mahmut also loved to describe the things that the people of Istanbul had been discarding or hiding in wells for hundreds of years; in his time, he'd discovered countless swords, spoons, bottles, bottle caps, lamps, as well as bombs, rifles, pistols, dolls, skulls, combs, horseshoes, and a whole host of other unimaginable things. He'd even found the odd silver coin. Clearly some of these things had been tossed into dried-out wells for safekeeping, only to be forgotten as years and then centuries passed. Wasn't that strange? If you cared about something, something valuable, but then left it inside a well and forgot about it, what did that mean?

13

On one of those stifling July afternoons, Hayri Bey drove by in his pickup truck and, deciding that the situation was desperate, made an announcement that broke all our hearts: if there was no progress after three more days, he would give up on this well and put a stop to the work. Master Mahmut was welcome to continue digging if he liked, but Hayri Bey would no longer pay our wages. Now, should Master Mahmut persist and find water in the end, Hayri Bey would, of course, reward him accordingly, as well as honor him in public for having made construction of the factory complex possible. But for now, he couldn't bear to see a skillful, industrious, and trustworthy welldigger like Master Mahmut squander his energies and talents on a hopeless patch of this unforgiving land.

"You're right, we won't find water here in three days. We'll find it in two," said Master Mahmut, seemingly unruffled. "Don't worry, boss."

Hayri Bey drove off amid the chirping of cicadas, and we didn't speak at all for a long time. After the *chug-chug-chug* of the twelve-thirty passenger train to Istanbul, I lay down under the walnut tree but couldn't sleep. Even thinking of the Red-Haired Woman and the theater couldn't console me.

Five hundred meters from the walnut tree, beyond the boundaries of the boss's land, stood a concrete casemate dating from World War II. We'd gone to look at it once, and Master Mahmut guessed it must have been part of a machine-gun turret built to defend against infantry charges. With childish curiosity, I tried to rip through the nettles and brambles blocking the entrance, but when I couldn't get through, I lay down in the grass to think. Unless we found water in the next three days, I wouldn't be getting my bonus. But I calculated that I'd already saved more than I needed. So if there was no water after three days, the best thing to do was to forget about the prize and go home.

That evening as we sat enjoying a gentle breeze at the Rumelian Coffeehouse in Öngören, Master Mahmut said, "How long has it been since we started digging?" He liked to ask me this question every few days, though he knew the answer perfectly well.

"Twenty-four days," I said carefully.

"Including today?"

"Yes, we're done for today, so I'm counting it, too."

"We've built thirteen meters of wall down there, fourteen at most," said Master Mahmut, and he looked at me for a moment as if I were the cause of all his disappointments.

I had started to notice this look on his face more frequently as we toiled at the windlass together. I felt a certain guilt, but also a mutinous desire to take off, and my own rebellious thoughts frightened me.

Before I knew what was happening my heart sped up. I stood completely still, as if turned to stone. There was the Red-Haired Woman and her family walking across the square.

If I started following them now, Master Mahmut might realize my fixation. But my legs sprang into action before I could think things through. I bolted from the table without a word of explanation. Taking care not to lose sight of them, I took a detour across the square so that Master Mahmut would think I was going to phone my mother from the post office.

She was taller than I remembered. Why was I following them? I didn't even know these people, but it felt good to go after them. I longed for her to look at me once more with that tender expression of recognition. It was as if this woman's kind, gently teasing gaze had revealed to me just how wondrous the world could be. And yet a part of me couldn't help but feel that all these thoughts were just fantasies.

In those moments, I thought: I am most completely myself when nobody's watching. I had only just begun to discover this truth. When there is no one to observe us, the other self we keep hidden inside can come out and do as it pleases. But when you have a father near enough to keep an eye on you, that second self remains buried within.

There was a man by the Red-Haired Woman's side who might have been her father. They were walking ahead of her brother and mother. From behind I got close enough to hear that there was a conversation, but I couldn't make out what they were saying.

When we got to the Sun Cinema, they stopped at the gap in the wall where passersby inevitably paused to steal a look at the film. There was a smaller gap, five or six steps away from them and closer to the screen, where no one else was standing. I positioned myself there, between them and the screen, but I was so focused on them that I couldn't concentrate for a moment on what was playing.

From up close, her face was not as pretty as I recalled. Perhaps the bluish glow from the screen was to blame. But the same playfully tender expression was there in her eyes and on her perfectly round lips, that look whose charms had sustained me through more than three weeks of backbreaking work.

Was she amused by what she saw on the screen? Or was it something else? Then, as I looked over my shoulder, I realized quite abruptly that the Red-Haired Woman was smiling not at the film but at me. She was looking at me with that same expression again.

I began to sweat profusely. I wanted to get closer and talk to her. She had to be at least ten years older than me.

"Come on, let's get going, we'll be late," said the man I took for the father.

I can't remember what I did exactly, but I think I must have stepped away from the wall and stood in their way.

"What's this? Are you following us?" said the brother.

"Who is this, Turgay?" the mother asked him.

"What do you even do all day?" said Turgay, the Red-Haired Woman's brother.

"Is he a soldier?" said their father.

"He's no soldier . . . he's a little gentleman," said the mother.

The Red-Haired Woman smiled at what her mother said, never losing that kindly, playful look she'd worn when I noticed her looking at me.

"I'm in high school in Istanbul," I said. "But right now I'm helping my master dig a well up there."

The Red-Haired Woman kept observing me, looking intently, meaningfully, into my eyes. "You and your master should come to our theater one of these evenings," she said, and off she walked with the others.

They were heading toward the theater tent. I didn't follow. But as I watched them continue until the turn in the road, I realized that they weren't a family but a theater troupe, and I began to dream and wonder.

On my way back to Master Mahmut, I saw the aging, tired horse that had pulled our cart three weeks ago, when I'd first seen them. He was chewing on some grass by the roadside, tethered to a pole, his eyes now filled with an even-greater sorrow.

14

JUST BEFORE OUR LUNCH BREAK the next day, we heard Ali whooping with joy from inside the well. We had gotten past the rocky layer, and he could see soft soil again. Master Mahmut pulled him up and clambered down there to see for himself. He emerged shortly to announce that we had in fact broken through, and that darker soil and water would certainly follow. It raised our spirits to see him stop work to have a smoke and pace by the well with a glint in his eye.

We pressed on until late that day, and when evening came, we were too tired to go down to town; waking up at the crack of dawn the next day, we picked up right where we'd left off. But soon we found that all we excavated was a dry and grayish-yellow dirt. It was so soft there was almost no need for the pickax. Master Mahmut shoveled it straight into the bucket, and since it was so light, Ali and I could hoist it up and wheel it off quickly. Before long I began to lose hope.

It wasn't even eleven when Master Mahmut came up and sent Ali down in his place.

"Work slowly, don't kick up too much dust," he told him. "Dust like that could suffocate you, and you wouldn't even be able to see the light above."

Though neither Ali nor I said a thing, it was obvious from how different this sandy soil was from what we'd found right under the rock that we were nowhere near any water. Earlier that morning, Ali had started piling this earth up separately. I added buckets and buckets to Ali's new pile.

After dinner, we headed down to Öngören. Sitting at the Rumelian Coffeehouse, I returned to the issue I'd been mulling over for two days, until finally it was decided: I wouldn't tell Master Mahmut that the Red-Haired Woman had invited him to the theater, too. I wanted to watch her performance alone. Besides, if he caught wind of my interest in her, he would try to interfere, and we might end up quarreling. I had never even once been as scared of my own father as I was of Master Mahmut now. I couldn't say how this fear had come to lodge inside my soul, but I did know that somehow the Red-Haired Woman only exacerbated it.

Before I'd even finished my tea, I got up, saying, "I'm going to call my mother." I rounded the corner, loping toward the theater tent as if in a dream.

The sight of the glossy yellow tent thrilled me, just as the circus tents visiting Dolmabahçe from Europe during my childhood used to do. I read the words on the posters again without registering what any of them said, until I spotted a new sign, whose words on rough brown paper in big, black letters came as a shock:

LAST TEN DAYS

I wandered the streets like a sleepwalker. I didn't see the man who sold tickets at the tent, I didn't see Turgay (who must, I thought, be the ticket seller's son), and I didn't see the Red-Haired Woman or her mother, either. There was plenty of time before the show was to begin, so I went to Diners' Lane, where, looking through one of the windows, I saw Turgay at a crowded table. I went inside.

The Red-Haired Woman wasn't there, but Turgay gestured me over as soon as he saw me. No one paid me any heed as I sat beside him.

"Help me get a ticket for the theater," I said. "Tell me how much it costs and I'll give you the money."

"Don't worry about money. Whenever you want to go, come and find me here before the show starts."

"But you don't come here every night."

"Have you been following us?" He raised an eyebrow and smiled archly. Picking up two ice cubes with a pair of tongs, he placed them in an empty glass, which he filled with Club Rakı. "Here you go!" he said, handing me the tall, slender drink. "If you down it all in one go, I'll sneak you into the tent through the back."

"Not tonight," I said, but even so I gulped all the *rakı* down at once like a streetwise tough. I didn't linger for much longer, and soon returned to Master Mahmut.

Back at the Rumelian Coffeehouse, I felt how difficult it would be to bring myself to disobey him. I realized I was bound to him and to the well by our duty to find that water, not to mention all the effort we'd put in so far. The only conceivable way I could defy him was to ask for my money and say I'd decided to go home. But that would mean admitting defeat regarding the water—like a coward losing his nerve in the face of adversity.

The *rakı* made my head swim. On the way home, as we climbed up the cemetery hill, I felt as if every star was a thought, a moment, a fact, a memory of mine. You could see them together, but it was impossible to conceive of them all at once. It was the same way the words in my head couldn't keep up with my dreams. My emotions moved too fast for words to do them justice.

Emotions, then, were more like pictures, like the gleaming sky before me. I could feel the whole of creation, but it was harder to think about it. That was why I wanted to be a writer. I would contemplate all the images and emotions I couldn't express and finally put them into words. What's more, I'd do a much better job of it than those friends of Mr. Deniz's who used to drop by the bookstore.

Master Mahmut marched full steam ahead, stopping only every now and then to yell, "Hurry up!" into the darkness behind him.

We took shortcuts through the fields, and every time my foot caught on something, I paused and stared, bewildered at the beauty of the sky. Already the evening chill could be felt among the tall grasses.

"Master Mahmut! Master Mahmut!" I called into the night. "What if the shards of iron and nickel we keep finding in the well are shooting stars that have fallen from the sky?"

15

NOT THREE, but five whole days passed before Hayri Bey returned in his pickup truck. He knew we still hadn't found any water but acted as if this didn't bother him. He'd brought his wife along, too, and their young son. He took them around his land, pointing out where the washing-and-dyeing workshops were to be built. He'd brought the blueprints with him, and he could indicate these locations in relation to where the warehouse, the offices, and the workers' cafeteria would be. Hayri Bey's son was wearing new soccer shoes and cradling a rubber ball as he listened to his father.

Father and son went to practice penalty kicks at one end of the land, using two rocks for goalposts. Their mother spread a blanket under my walnut tree and unpacked a basket of food she'd prepared. When she sent Ali around to call us all over for lunch, Master Mahmut was irked. He could see that this elaborate and unnecessary picnic was a stunted version of the celebrations that usually marked the discovery of water in a well. Hayri Bey had obviously long fantasized about the day water would be found. Master Mahmut finally joined us with great reluctance, sitting on the edge of the blanket and taking only a single bite of the boiled eggs, the onion and tomato salad, and the savory pastries.

After the meal, Hayri Bey's son lay down next to his mother and went to sleep. The mother—an overweight lady with strong arms and a permanent smile—smoked a cigarette and read the daily *Günaydın,* its edges rustling in the soft breeze.

I followed Master Mahmut and Hayri Bey to where we'd piled up all the earth we'd excavated. I could see from the landowner's demoralized expression that he knew there was no water to be found down that hole and that there wouldn't be anytime soon, either—perhaps ever.

"Hayri Bey, give us three more days, if you please . . . ," said Master Mahmut.

He sounded so meek. It was embarrassing to see Master Mahmut reduced to this, and I resented Hayri Bey for it. Hayri Bey returned to the walnut tree and came back after talking to his wife and son.

"Last time we were here, you asked us for three more days, Master Mahmut," he said. "I've given you more than three days. But still there is no water. The soil here is terrible. I'm pulling out of this well. We're neither the first nor the last people to give up on a well that's been dug in the wrong place. Find another spot to excavate; you'll know best where."

"The veins in the earth can switch over when you least expect it," said Master Mahmut. "I want to keep going right here."

"Then if you find water, let me know. I'll come straightaway. And I'll give you an even bigger bonus. But I'm a businessman. I can't keep pouring cement into a dry hole forever. From now on, I won't be paying you any more wages or buying your supplies. Ali won't be working here anymore, either. If you decide to start digging in a new spot, I'll send him back, of course."

"I will find water here," said Master Mahmut.

Master Mahmut and Hayri Bey stepped away to work out the final balance of fees and wages due. I watched the landowner pay Master Mahmut everything he owed him and saw that there was no disagreement between them as to the amount.

Hayri Bey's wife sent Ali over with the leftover boiled eggs, pastries, and tomatoes, as well as the watermelon they'd brought. She felt as bad for us as for her husband's business plans.

"We'll drop you home," they told Ali, and when he stepped into the pickup truck, Master Mahmut and I were left alone. We stood watching as they drove off with Ali waving at us from the back. I noticed once again how quiet the world was. The only sound was the incessant droning of the crickets, and even the thrum of Istanbul was inaudible.

We didn't do any work that afternoon. I lay down under the walnut tree, lost in lazy daydreams. I thought of the Red-Haired Woman, of becoming a playwright, of going home, of seeing my friends in Beşiktaş. I was studying an anthill near the brambles at the entrance to the concrete casemate when Master Mahmut came by.

"Son, let's give it another week here," he said. "I owe you a few days' wages . . . We'll be done by next Wednesday, God willing, and then we'll get the big prize, too."

"But Master Mahmut, what if the bad soil goes on forever and we never get to the water?"

"Trust your master, do as I say, and leave the rest to me," he said, looking into my eyes. He stroked my hair and grabbed my shoulder, pulling me into a reassuring hug. "You're going to be a great man, one day. I can feel it."

I could no longer muster the strength to contradict him. This in turn made me inwardly resentful and despondent. I remember thinking, *Only one week to go.* During this last week, I planned to find the Red-Haired Woman again and see the play in the tent theater.

16

FOR THREE DAYS, the color of the soil stayed the same. Since I struggled to turn the windlass on my own, Master Mahmut didn't fill the bucket to the brim, and that only slowed us down even more. The soil was so soft that he made quick work of it; I'd lower the empty bucket and he'd fill it up again with a few swipes of his shovel. "Pulllll!" he'd cry immediately.

Even so, it took me ages to hoist the half-filled bucket and empty it into the handcart. Growing impatient in the well, Master Mahmut would soon be complaining about my sluggishness, occasionally losing his temper. As I ran to tip the earth and dust out of the handcart, sometimes all my strength would desert me, and I'd have to rest on the ground for a while. By the time I got back to the well, Master Mahmut would be shouting even louder. Sometimes I'd take so long that he'd insist I pull him up, so he could see with his own eyes why I was so slow. But since hauling him up on the windlass was the hardest job of all, he'd emerge to find me completely spent and wouldn't have the heart to really tell me off. "You look like a wreck, son," he might say, going to lie down under the olive tree while he waited for me to recover. It was both disconcerting and touching to hear him show such fatherly concern. I would have barely gone to lie down under the walnut tree myself before I heard Master Mahmut's voice commanding and cajoling me to get up.

We now went down to Öngören together every evening. Each time, I'd get up from the table outside the Rumelian Coffeehouse and start wandering the streets in the hopes of running into the Red-Haired Woman or sneaking into the theater tent.

I had no luck on the first two nights, but on the third night, Turgay caught up with me near where the carpenter had his shop.

"You seem distracted, little welldigger!"

"Get me into the theater," I said. "I can pay for the ticket."

"Come to the restaurant."

We headed for the lace curtains of the Liberation Restaurant and went inside to join the actors' table. "Before attending the theater, one must learn the proper way to drink *rakı,*" said Turgay.

He looked five, maybe six, years older than me. While I gulped down the ice-cold potion he'd mirthfully set in front of me, Turgay whispered something to the people sitting next to him. What time was it? Was Master Mahmut waiting impatiently? Never mind him; if they let me in tonight, I was going.

"Come back this time the day after tomorrow," said Turgay. "And bring your master."

"Master Mahmut doesn't approve of drinking and theaters."

"We'll persuade him. You come back here on Sunday evening. My father will pick you up and take you to the theater. No need for money or tickets."

I didn't stay much longer, and soon I was again at Master Mahmut's side. On the way back to our tent, he reminisced about happier days, when he had discovered water. One time, the landowner who'd hired him celebrated the good news with a feast by the well, roasting four whole lambs and feeding a hundred people. Water could spring up from the earth at the most unexpected moments, catching you by surprise. God Himself would intervene to douse the faithful welldigger's face with water, the first spray always as powerful as the arc of a baby boy's urine. On first seeing the water, the welldigger would smile delightedly like a father beholding his newborn son. Once, a welldigger's success had caused such jubilation that those up on the ground accidentally dropped a stone into the well, injuring his shoulder. There was also the time a village elder was so beside himself with joy at the discovery of water that he visited the site every day just to hear the two apprentices describe one more time the moment the water had first sprung. Every time, he would reward each storyteller with two large old banknotes. But there were no elders like that left anymore. In the old days, no landowner would ever dream of telling a devoted, hardworking welldigger, "That's it from me, but you're welcome to keep digging with your own men and at your own expense if you want to!"—a man of means would have felt paternally honorbound to supply the welldigger on his land with food, cover all his expenses, reward him appropriately, and tip him handsomely, regardless of whether water was found. But there were no hard feelings with Hayri Bey; he was a decent man, and as soon as we found water, he would give us all that we were due and bury us under a mountain of gifts, just as those good men of old used to do.

17

THE NEXT DAY, the soil we dug turned even paler and lighter. With every bucket, I could see it was arid and as light as hay. The dusty sand contained frayed, membranous pieces of animal skin, smooth fragments like mother-of-pearl and fragile as the toy soldiers made of mica I played with as a child, million-year-old pebbles the color of my skin, translucent shells, strange pieces of rock as big as ostrich eggs, and stones so light they'd float like pumice if you threw them in water. It seemed the more we dug, the farther we got from water, so we toiled in grim silence.

But inwardly I was elated to know that I'd finally be going to the theater the next evening—nothing could spoil my mood. I worked even harder than Master Mahmut asked of me, so that by the end of the day I could barely stand. There was no reason to go down to Öngören that day anyway. After dinner, I lay down at the edge of the tent; I fell asleep looking at the stars.

Sometime after midnight I woke up with a start. Master Mahmut wasn't in the tent. I walked warily into the black night. It seemed the whole world was empty, and I was the last living thing left in the universe. The thought made me shiver, as did an impalpable wind. Yet everything also seemed imbued with an enchanted beauty. I felt the stars drawing closer above my head, and I sensed that I had a very happy life ahead of me. Could it have been the Red-Haired Woman herself who had asked Turgay to let me into the theater tomorrow evening? But where could Master Mahmut have gone at this hour?

A fresh gust of wind blew, and I retreated into the tent.

When I woke up the next day, Master Mahmut was back. I also saw a fresh pack of cigarettes in the tent. We worked until late that day, not getting anywhere. The bottom of the well was really far now and constantly churning up dust. When we were finished for the day, Master Mahmut and I poured water over each other's heads. By now I was used to seeing his naked torso. I noticed how many bruises and scratches marked his body, how thin and bony he was despite his broad frame, and how pale and wrinkled his skin was, and I thought that we would never find water.

I hoped Master Mahmut would decide not to come down to Öngören that evening so that I wouldn't have any trouble going to the theater. But he said, "Let me buy some cigarettes," and set off before I did. I was nervous as we sat at our usual spot at the Rumelian Coffeehouse. At eight-thirty, I quietly got up and went to Diners' Lane. I had fantasized about how glorious it would be to get to sit at the restaurant and talk to the Red-Haired Woman before the play, but neither she nor her brother was there. Someone else who was sitting at their usual table waved me over.

"Come to the back of the tent at five past nine," he said. "They're not around tonight."

At first I took this to mean "They're not at the theater tonight," and I felt devastated. I sat at the table as if I were joining my friends for dinner, filled an empty glass with ice and *rakı,* and drank it all in one go, quick as a thief.

Leaving the restaurant, I made my way to the theater tent through the backstreets, where Master Mahmut wouldn't see me. At five past nine, I was waiting behind the yellow tent when someone emerged and quickly pulled me inside.

The show had started, and there were somewhere between twenty-five and thirty people in the audience, give or take. I couldn't make out what the shadows in the darkened corners were. The high space in the center was lit brightly with naked lightbulbs, which gave the tent of the Theater of Morality Tales an otherworldly appearance. The inside of the tent cloth was dark blue, like the night sky, and painted with large yellow stars. Some of these came with tails, while others were small and remote. For years after, the memory of the starry sky above our plain would merge in my mind with the sky inside the Theater of Morality Tales.

The *rakı* had gone to my head, and I was drunk. But I could never have predicted the indelible effect on my life of some of the things I would see during the hour I spent in the tent that evening, much like the story of Oedipus, which I'd happened to read one day and have never forgotten since. In that moment, however, I wasn't interested so much in the story being enacted onstage as in watching the Red-Haired Woman. So I will try to describe what I saw that night through my clouded senses, filling in the gaps with what I learned years later from reading and research.

The Theater of Morality Tales was seeking to carry on the tradition of the itinerant theater companies which, from the mid-1970s up until the military coup of 1980, had toured the Anatolian peninsula, putting on politically charged left-wing shows for local communities. But instead of anticapitalist agitprop, its repertoire consisted mostly of old love stories, scenes from ancient epics and folktales, and parables from the Islamic and Sufi traditions. Some of these were completely lost on me at the time. When I entered the tent, they were performing two short sketches satirizing some much-loved television commercials. In the first, a little boy wearing shorts and sporting a mustache walked onstage holding a piggy bank and asked his hunchbacked granny what he should do with the money he'd saved up. When the granny—played, I think, by the Red-Haired Woman's mother—responded with a dirty joke, everyone laughed at this mockery of those advertisements that banks always ran.

I really couldn't say what the second sketch was about because by then the Red-Haired Woman had appeared in a miniskirt: I had never seen such long legs; her neck and shoulders were also bare, making for a magnificent and unsettling presence. She had drawn thick lines of kohl around her eyes and painted her full round lips red, a kind of lipstick that seemed to glisten under the lights. She picked up a box of laundry powder and spoke. A yellow-and-green parrot onstage answered back. It was only a stuffed parrot, but someone spoke its lines from the wings. The setting was maybe meant to be a grocery store, with the parrot playing pranks on customers while making pronouncements on life, love, and money. As everyone laughed, I thought for a moment that the Red-Haired Woman was looking at me, and my heart raced. Her smile was so kind; her delicate hands moved so nimbly. I was so in love with her, and that feeling, together with the *rakı*, prevented me from entirely following what was happening onstage.

Each sketch lasted a few minutes and was quickly followed by another. Years later, I consulted various books and films to trace the sources of each piece. One sketch, for instance, saw the man whom I took for the Red-Haired Woman's father come onstage with a nose the length of a carrot. Initially I thought this must be Pinocchio, but then the man launched into a long monologue which I would eventually figure out had been taken from *Cyrano de Bergerac*. The moral of this little sketch was "What matters most is not physical appearance, but the beauty of your soul."

After a scene from *Hamlet* featuring a skull, a book, and "To be or not to be," the actors all joined in singing an old folk song. The song said that love was an illusion, but money was true. Now, the Red-Haired Woman was trying deliberately to catch my eye, which made my head spin. Under the effects of love and *rakı*, I couldn't fully understand everything being said or what the sketches were about, but the things I did see etched themselves permanently in my memory, just as the Red-Haired Woman's eyes had.

There was one sketch I understood for sure, and that was because I'd learned the story of the prophet Abraham from my father, as well as our lesson on the Feast of the Sacrifice at school. The childless prophet was played by the man who'd first turned me away from the tent. Abraham pleaded with God to give him a son, and eventually his wish was granted (in the form of a doll). When his son—now played by a child actor—grew up, Abraham lay him down on the floor and put a knife to his throat, making throughout the scene a number of profound pronouncements about fathers and sons and obedience.

His words made a powerful impression on everyone. The ensuing hush that fell over the tent was broken by the return of the Red-Haired Woman. She was in a new costume, an angel now with cardboard wings and fresh makeup. It suited her perfectly. Flanked by a toy lamb, she was met with loud applause, in which I joined enthusiastically.

The last and most striking scene presented a tableau I would never forget. I knew so even as I watched, though again I did not understand the full story at the time.

Two armored knights in steel helmets and visors took center stage, brandishing swords and shields. As they clashed, a recording of clanging swords was played over the loudspeakers. The knights stopped briefly to exchange a few words, but soon resumed doing battle once more. I guessed that Turgay and the Red-Haired Woman's father must be hidden under each set of armor. They wrestled and lunged for each other's throat, became entangled on the floor, and finally broke apart.

I was hardly alone in being swept away by this exhilarating spectacle. Suddenly, the older warrior knocked the younger one down with a single blow, straddled him, and plunged the sword into his opponent's heart. It all happened so fast, and everyone was startled, forgetting momentarily that this was a play and the swords were only plastic.

The young knight cried out; he was not dead yet. There was something he had to say. The older warrior leaned in to hear, doffing his helmet with all the confidence of a righteous victor (he was indeed played by the man I took to be the Red-Haired Woman's father). But then he noticed a bracelet on the dying man's wrist, and he was horrified. Lifting the visor off the young man's face (it wasn't Turgay, actually, but some other actor), he shrank back in agony. His exaggerated gestures made clear that there had been a terrible mistake. His suffering seemed bottomless. Just moments ago we'd all been laughing at the same actors' spoof of television commercials. But now a respectful silence fell over everyone, because even the Red-Haired Woman was crying.

Sinking to the floor, the older knight sobbed as he cradled the dying young warrior. His tears seemed so genuine that we were all unexpectedly touched. The old warrior was weeping with remorse. And soon I was feeling remorseful as well.

I had never seen this emotion expressed so openly before, not at the cinema or in comic books. Until that moment, I had understood it as something that could be described only in words. But now I was feeling the torment of remorse merely by watching someone's experience of it onstage. It was like reliving a forgotten memory.

The Red-Haired Woman was anguished by the scene before her. She was no less full of remorse than the two warriors. Her tears fell thicker than before. Perhaps the two men were related, just as she and her fellow actors were. No other sound could be heard inside the tent. The Red-Haired Woman's weeping turned into a lament and then into an epic poem. In this poem, her concluding speech, the Red-Haired Woman spoke angrily of men, and what they'd put her through, and of life; I listened, trying to catch her eye, but it was too dark for her to spot me in the crowd. Because our eyes never met, it was almost as if I couldn't properly follow or remember the things she said. I felt an overwhelming urge to talk to her and be close to her. The show ended with her extended monologue in verse, after which the small crowd of spectators quickly dispersed.

18

On the way out of the theater tent, I took a few backward steps and I saw the Red-Haired Woman near the table that served as the box office.

She'd already exchanged her costume for her street clothes and was wearing a long sky-blue skirt.

My unpracticed passion, the action onstage, and the *rakı* I'd been drinking had conspired to leave me unable to grasp that this was the present. Instead I felt that I was somewhere in the past. Everything seemed fragmented, like a memory.

"Did you enjoy our play?" said the Red-Haired Woman, smiling at me. "Thank you for clapping."

"I loved it," I said, emboldened by her gentle smile.

Many years have now gone by, and jealousy urges me still to keep her name a secret, even from my readers. But I must provide a full and truthful account of what happened next. We introduced ourselves the way Americans did in the movies:

"Cem."

"Gülcihan."

"You were really good," I said. "I was watching you throughout the whole performance." I had to force myself to use the informal "you," since she was plainly older than she had seemed from afar.

"How is the well coming along?"

"Sometimes I think we will never find water," I said. I also wanted to add, *The only reason I'm still here is so I can see you!* but I thought she might find that off-putting.

"Your master came to our tent yesterday," said the Red-Haired Woman.

"Who?"

"Master Mahmut. He's convinced he'll find that water. He loved the theater, and he loved our show. He bought himself a ticket."

"I doubt Master Mahmut has ever been to the theater before," I said possessively. "I told him about Oedipus and Sophocles once, and he got angry at me. How did you persuade him?"

"He's right. Greek plays don't work in Turkey."

Did the Red-Haired Woman mean to make me jealous of Master Mahmut?

"He disapproves of that play because the son sleeps with the mother."

"It didn't bother him at all when the father killed his son at the end of our show . . . ," she said. "He really seemed to enjoy all the old myths and legends."

Had she approached Master Mahmut and spoken to him after the play? Somehow I couldn't picture him going down to Öngören after I went to sleep to see the show like some soldier out on a weekend pass.

"Master Mahmut is very hard with me," I said. "All he cares about is finding water. He didn't even want me going to the theater. He'd be furious if he knew I came here tonight."

"Don't worry, I'll talk to him," said the Red-Haired Woman.

I was so jealous I could scarcely speak. Had Master Mahmut and the Red-Haired Woman become friends?

"Is your master very domineering? Is he strict?"

"Well, yes, but he looks out for me like a father, and he talks to me and cares about me. But he also expects me to obey his orders and always do as he says."

"So do as he says!" said the Red-Haired Woman, smiling sweetly. "He's not forcing you to be his apprentice . . . Isn't your family well-off?"

Had Master Mahmut told the Red-Haired Woman that I was a little gentleman? Had they spoken about me?

"My father left us!" I said.

"Then he wasn't a father at all," she said. "Find yourself a new father. We all have many fathers in this country. The fatherland, Allah, the army, the Mafia . . . No one here should ever be fatherless."

The Red-Haired Woman now seemed to me clever as well as beautiful.

"My father was a Marxist," I said. (Why had I said "was," and not "is"?) "He was arrested and tortured. He went to prison for years, when I was little."

"What's your father's name?"

"Akın Çelik. But our pharmacy was called Hayat, like 'life,' not Çelik, like 'steel.' "

At this the Red-Haired Woman fell into a reverie. She seemed to withdraw and said nothing more for quite a while. Had I made a mistake? What did she care if my father was a Marxist? Perhaps she was just tired and pensive. So I told her about my father's late nights at the pharmacy, how I used to bring him dinner, and I described the shopping district in Beşiktas. She listened closely to everything I said. But I didn't like talking about my father in the same way that I didn't like bringing up Master Mahmut. We fell silent for a time.

"My husband and I live here," she said, pointing at the building I had passed countless times, and whose windows I'd so often scrutinized.

I was heartbroken and furious, as if I'd been cheated on. But even though I was drunk, I could still understand that for a woman as old as she was, traveling through Turkey with a ragtag theater troupe, it was essential to be married. How hadn't I thought of this before?

"What floor are you on?"

"You can't see our windows from the street. A former Maoist who invited us to Öngören lives here; we're staying in his first-floor rooms. Turgay's parents live on the floor above. Our windows face the back garden. Turgay told me he's seen you staring at the windows every time you walk by."

I was ashamed that my secret was out. But the Red-Haired Woman's smile was kind, her lips lovely and luscious as ever.

"Good night," I said. "It was a wonderful play."

"No, let's go for a walk. I'm curious to hear about your father."

A note to inquisitive souls reading this story in the future: unfortunately, in those days, when an attractive, red-haired woman, possibly in her thirties, wearing makeup (even if just for the stage) and a pretty sky-blue skirt, told a man, "Let's go for a walk" at ten-thirty at night, most men could infer only one thing. Of course I wasn't one of those men, only a high-school boy who couldn't hide his childish infatuation. Besides, this woman was married, and we were near Istanbul, and therefore Europe—far from the conservative Anatolian heartland. And by this point my head was full of the morality of leftist politics—my father's morality, in other words.

We walked for a stretch without a word, and I thought all the while about how we weren't talking. Dark corners seemed less so, but the sky over Öngören was starless. Someone had rested a bicycle against the Atatürk statue in the Station Square.

"Did he ever talk to you about politics?" asked the Red-Haired Woman.

"Who?"

"Did your father's militant friends ever come to the house?"

"Actually, my father was never home. And both he and my mother wanted to make sure I didn't get involved in politics."

"So your father didn't turn you into a leftist?"

"I'm going to be a writer . . ."

"You can write us a play, then," she said, smiling mysteriously. Now that her mood had lifted, she had become breathtakingly, dizzyingly beguiling. "I would love for someone to write a play or a book about my life, something along the lines of my monologue at the end of the show."

"I didn't really understand that monologue. Do you have it written down somewhere?"

"No, those speeches tend to be improvised, whichever way inspiration takes me. A glass of *rakı* helps."

"I've been thinking of writing plays," I said, with the self-important air of a pretentious schoolboy. "But first I should read some. I'll start with the classics: *Oedipus the King*."

That night in July, the Station Square felt as familiar as a memory. Nighttime had disguised Öngören's poverty and general disrepair, the pale-orange streetlamps having transformed the old station building and the square into a picture postcard. The fierce headlights of the military jeep prowling slowly around the square fell upon a nearby pack of wild dogs.

"They're looking for fugitives and troublemakers," said the Red-Haired Woman. "I don't know why, but the soldiers in this town seem to be particularly shameless."

"But don't you put on special weekend matinees for them?"

"I suppose we have to make money somehow . . . ," she said, looking straight into my eyes. "We're a folk theater, we can't rely on a government salary like state companies."

She leaned in to pick a stalk of hay off my collar. Her body, her long legs, and her breasts felt very close to my body.

We walked back in silence. The Red-Haired Woman's black eyes seemed to turn green as we passed under the almond trees. I was anxious. In the distance, I could see the building whose windows I'd spied on so often in the past month.

"My husband says you handle your *rakı* pretty well for your age," she said. "Did your father drink, too?"

I answered with a nod yes. My mind was busy trying to work out when and where I might have sat down for a drink with her husband. I couldn't remember, but I couldn't bring myself to ask, either; my heart was breaking and I just wanted to forget all about them. I was already suffering like a child at the thought that I would never see her again once the well was finished. The pain was worse than the knowledge that my secret fixation on their windows (which, as it turned out, weren't even theirs) had been discovered.

We stopped under one of the almond trees about a hundred meters from their house. Even now I can't recall whether she or I stopped first. She seemed so intelligent, so tender. She smiled at me with kindness and affection, and the same certain, optimistic look she'd given me from the stage. I felt again that remorse I'd felt at the theater watching the warring, weeping father and his son.

"Turgay is away in Istanbul tonight," she said. "Perhaps you could have some of his *rakı,* if you like it as much as your father does."

"I'd like that," I said. "And I'll get to meet your husband, too."

"Turgay *is* my husband," she said. "You had a drink with him the other day and you told him you wanted to see the play, remember?"

She said nothing more for a while, letting the revelation sink in. "Sometimes Turgay feels embarrassed that his wife is seven years older than he is, so he forgets to mention that we're married," she said. "He may be young, but he's very bright, and a good husband."

We started walking again.

"I was trying to remember where it was that I had a drink with your husband."

"Turgay told me you shared a Club Rakı at the restaurant that night. There's half a bottle left at home. Our old Maoist friend has some local cognac, too. He'll be coming back soon, and then we'll be off. I'll miss you, little gentleman!"

"What do you mean?"

"You know how it works, our time here is up."

"I'll miss you, too."

We stood outside their building, our bodies close. I found her astonishingly beautiful.

She took out her keys and unlocked the main door, saying, "We have ice and snacks for your *rakı*."

"No need for snacks," I said, as if I were in a rush and couldn't stay long.

The front door opened, and we walked through a narrow, pitch-black hallway. I could hear her fumbling with her key ring, looking for the other key in the dark. Then she flicked her lighter on, and as the flame's menacing shadows surrounded us, she found the key and the keyhole, opened the door, and walked into the apartment.

She turned to me as she switched the lights on. "Don't be scared," she said, smiling. "I'm old enough to be your mother."

19

THAT NIGHT, I slept with a woman for the first time in my life. It was momentous, and it was miraculous. My perception of life, of women, and of myself all changed instantaneously. The Red-Haired Woman showed me who I was, and what happiness meant.

She was thirty-three, it turned out, so she had lived almost exactly twice as much as I had, but it could have been ten times as much. I didn't think too hard, that day, about the age difference—a point that I was aware would be cause for much interest and admiration among my friends at school and around the neighborhood. But even as I was living those moments, I already knew that I would never share a full account of them with anyone. Even now, I will not delve too much into the details, which, even had I disclosed them then, my friends would have only dismissed as "lies." Suffice it to say that the Red-Haired Woman's body was better than anything I had imagined, and this, together with her uninhibited, fearless, perhaps even slightly brazen behavior that night, had turned the whole night into an extraordinary experience.

I had finished all of Turgay's *rakı* and also drunk a last-minute glass of the cognac that belonged to the former Maoist (now a signmaker who worked out of his home), so by the time I left Öngören, well after midnight, I couldn't walk straight and felt as if I were in a dream, watching every moment unfold from outside myself. Even my happiness seemed to be registered by an outside observer.

Once I started climbing the cemetery hill, however, I was gripped with fear of Master Mahmut. I felt I had to protect this blissful thing within me from his anger. He might even begrudge me such happiness. Once I'd passed the cemetery (where even the owl was asleep by now), I took a shortcut through someone else's land, tripping over a mound of earth and landing gently on the grass, from where I noticed the heavens twinkling above me.

I could see, now, how wonderful the whole universe was. What was the rush? Why was I so scared of Master Mahmut? If what the Red-Haired Woman had told me was true, he himself had gone to see the show in the yellow tent, which still made me inexplicably jealous. I couldn't believe they'd spoken after the show, and I wanted to forget it had ever happened. At the same time, I knew it didn't matter: sleeping with someone like the Red-Haired Woman had lifted my self-confidence to the point that I felt there was nothing I couldn't do. There would never be any water in the well, but I would get my money anyway, go back home, enroll in cram school, ace the entrance exams, and go on to become a writer, living a life as resplendent as any of the stars I could see before me. It was clear that I was destined for something; I knew that now. Perhaps I would even write a novel about the Red-Haired Woman.

A star was falling. I felt with every bit of me that the world before my eyes coincided perfectly with the world inside my head, and I focused intently on the summer sky. If only I could decipher the language of the stars, their disposition would surely reveal all the secrets of my life. All things wonderful, all of them astral. That night I truly understood that I would become a writer. All you had to do was to look and see, to understand what you saw, and put it into words. I was full of gratitude to the Red-Haired Woman. Everything in the universe and in my mind had aligned for a single purpose.

Another star fell. Maybe I was the only one who'd seen it. I thought: I exist. It was a good feeling. I can count the stars, and I can count the *chirp-chirp-chirping* of the cicadas. I am here: 1, 2, 3, 5, 7, 11, 13, 17, 19, 23, 29, 31 . . .

The grass tickled the back of my neck, and I remembered the Red-Haired Woman's touch on my skin. We had made love on the couch in the living room, with some of the lights still on. I continued to picture her body, those ample breasts, the way the light hit her copper-hued skin, and as I remembered all the kisses that fell from her pretty lips, and the way she ran her hands all over my body, I wanted to make love to her all over again. But her husband, Turgay, would be back from Istanbul tomorrow, so of course that was impossible.

Turgay had been kind enough to befriend me during my lonely nights in Öngören. In return, I betrayed my friend by sleeping with his beautiful wife the night he was away. In my drunkenness, I racked my brain for ways to excuse my crime and prove to myself that I wasn't a horrible, two-faced traitor: it was true that by the time I learned that Turgay was her husband, things had already gone too far. It wasn't as if Turgay was my longtime friend, anyway—I'd only met him three or four times, I reasoned. Besides, these rootless theater migrants who danced so suggestively and told vulgar tales to entertain soldiers did not exactly subscribe to wholesome family values. Who knows, maybe Turgay himself cheated on his wife with other women. Maybe they entertained each other with tales from their extramarital adventures. Maybe tomorrow the Red-Haired Woman would tell Turgay about her night with me. Maybe she wouldn't even do that much and forget all about me instead.

My mood soured, and I was overcome once again by the remorse I'd felt while watching the show in the tent. I still couldn't work out how those scenes had stirred that feeling in me. At the same time, I couldn't abide the thought that Master Mahmut had watched the same play. Had the Red-Haired Woman and Master Mahmut ever met again, apart from the time he came to the theater?

My footsteps on the dry grass approached our miserable little tent. The sky was so wide, the universe limitless, yet I still had to squeeze into that constricting place.

Master Mahmut was sleeping. I was quietly getting into bed when I heard him say: "Where were you?"

"I fell asleep."

"You left me at the coffeehouse. Did you go to the theater?"

"No."

"It's four in the morning. How are you going to cope with the heat tomorrow if you haven't even slept?"

"I was bored, they gave me *rakı*," I said. "It was hot. I lay down to look at the stars on my way back and I must have drifted off. I've slept plenty, Master Mahmut."

"Don't lie to me, kid! Welldigging is no joke. You know we're close to the water now."

I didn't respond. Master Mahmut stepped outside. I thought I would quickly forget this unpleasantness and fall asleep gazing at the stars through the tent flap, but I couldn't get him out of my mind.

Why had he asked me if I'd gone to the theater? Was he jealous of me? Surely a sophisticated theater actress like the Red-Haired Woman would never give a hick like Master Mahmut the time of day. Though with her, there was no telling. That's perhaps why I had fallen for her so fast.

I got out of the tent and went to look for Master Mahmut. Unbelievably, he seemed to be walking toward Öngören now, in the middle of the night. My insides churned with ungovernable rage and suspicion. In the everlasting night, under the glow of the stars, I could discern with difficulty the dark shadow that was Master Mahmut.

But then he left the road and headed for my walnut tree. I saw him sitting under it as he lit a cigarette. I lay on the grass for a long time waiting for him to finish his smoke. All I could see was the bright orange tip of his cigarette.

When I was sure he wasn't going to Öngören after all, I returned to the tent before him and went to sleep. But the memory of having watched him from afar that night would stay with me for years. Sometimes in my dreams there was a third eye, and I would simultaneously watch Master Mahmut and observe my younger self watching him.

20

THE NEXT MORNING, I woke up, as usual, with the sun's first rays piercing through the narrow gap in the tent like long, golden sabers. I couldn't have slept for more than three hours, but I felt thoroughly rested, invigorated by my experience with the Red-Haired Woman the night before.

"Have you had enough sleep? Are you alert?" said Master Mahmut as he sipped his tea.

"I'm fine, Master, never been better."

We didn't mention how late I'd come back the night before. Master Mahmut descended into the well, as he'd been doing for the past five days, becoming a small, dark blur at the bottom, shoveling earth into an even-smaller bucket, shouting "Pullll!" at regular intervals.

He was twenty-five meters belowground, but through that tube of concrete, the distance seemed magnified. Sometimes, when the glare of the sun blinded me and I anxiously realized that I could no longer make him out at the bottom, I would lean over to take a closer look, dreading the thought that I might accidentally fall in.

Lifting each bucket to the top was even harder than before. The rope wouldn't stay plumb now, and the swaying bucket would crash against the walls as if buffeted by a mysterious wind. We could not figure out the cause of this swaying. As I had to operate the windlass on my own, I didn't always notice the bucket's swinging arcs until Master Mahmut, fearing that it might fall on his head, bellowed up at me from below.

The tinier Master Mahmut grew, farther and farther from the top of the well, the more frequent and the more unduly severe his bellowing seemed. He yelled at me for being too slow to lower the bucket; for taking too long to empty it; and sometimes simply because the dust raised by the bone-dry earth made him lose his temper. My master's shouts reverberated in the concrete well, eerie echoes of the guilt within me.

I would take refuge in daydreams about the Red-Haired Woman's gentle smile, her beautiful body, her eagerness in making love. It felt so good to think about her. Should I run to Öngören and visit her on my lunch break?

I was grateful to be up here on the surface of the earth, but in the heat, my job was actually much harder than Master Mahmut's. With Ali now gone for a while, I had almost gotten used to turning the windlass on my own, but even so, sometimes my strength ran out.

After hoisting the loaded bucket up from the well, I always struggled to set it down properly on the wooden shelf. Ali and I used to take great pains with this. You had to raise the load just a little clear of the shelf while slackening the rope, as when dropping the bucket into the well, but gently pull it toward the shelf instead—a tricky maneuver for one man.

The bucket often tilted slightly in the process, causing clumps of sand, mussels, and fossilized snail shells to roll out and fall down the well.

Moments later came the sound of Master Mahmut's furious snarls from the bottom of the well. How many times did he have to explain how dangerous a force even little shells and pebbles gathered when they fell from a great height? They could seriously injure a man and even kill him if they happened to land on his head. That was why he never filled the bucket up to its brim—a precaution which slowed us down.

Hauling the handcart away to unload the dry, dusty sand and stones and mussels from the bottom was an equally arduous task. On the way back, I could always hear Master Mahmut's indiscriminate, scolding drone. I couldn't make the words out, but his complaints sounded like the furious utterances of some old shaman or some creature of the underworld, a cross between a giant and a jinni.

With the depth of the well now equal to the height of a ten-story building, it had become impossible to see how far down the bucket had reached. So toward the end of its descent, I would lock the crank in place, calling out to Master Mahmut, and pause until I heard him say, "A little further." He seemed so small, so helpless, down at the bottom!

We'd been working for about an hour that day when I felt a spell of dizziness. I thought I was going to fall into the well. On my way back from emptying the handcart, I stopped and lay down on the ground. I couldn't have been asleep for more than a minute.

But when I got back to the well, Master Mahmut was already muttering. Sending the empty bucket down did not silence his complaining this time.

"What is it, Master?" I shouted into the well.

"Pull me up!"

"What?"

"I said, pull me up."

When the bucket got suddenly heavy, I knew he must have stepped into it.

Pulling him up was the hardest part. As I pushed the handle of the windlass with all my remaining strength, my head spinning, I fantasized that Master Mahmut would give up on this well, pay me, and set me free. I would then run straight to the Red-Haired Woman to confess that I was in love with her and ask her to leave Turgay and marry me instead. What would my mother think? The Red-Haired Woman would no doubt be amused at that: "I'm old enough to be your mother!" Maybe I would nap for ten minutes under the walnut tree before my lunch break. I'd read somewhere that when you were really tired, a ten-minute nap could restore you as effectively as hours of sleep. I could visit the Red-Haired Woman after that.

As soon as Master Mahmut's head appeared at the top of the well, I pulled myself together and tried to hide my exhaustion.

"You're flagging today, kid," he said. "Look, I will find this water, and until then, you will do exactly as I say. Don't slow us down."

"Understood, Master."

"I'm not joking."

"Of course, Master."

"Where there is civilization, where there are towns and villages, there have to be wells. There can be no civilization without the well, and no well without the welldigger. And there can be no welldigger's apprentice who doesn't bow to his master's will. As soon as the water comes, we'll be rich. Got it?"

"I'm with you even if we don't get rich, Master."

Like a preacher, Master Mahmut then delivered a long sermon on the necessity of vigilance. I wondered: Had all this been on his mind even as he'd watched the Red-Haired Woman at the theater? I listened to Master Mahmut's words in a daydream, feeling no need to respond. The image of the Red-Haired Woman came to me again. I felt embarrassed.

"Take that sweaty shirt off and put on a fresh one," said Master Mahmut. "You're going inside the well. The work is easier down there."

"All right, Master."

21

AT THE BOTTOM of the well all I had to do was pick up the spade and fill the bucket with that stinking soil full of mussels, snail shells, and fish bones. The work was much less grueling than what had to be done aboveground. The hard part was being down there, twenty-five meters inside the earth.

As I approached the bottom of the darkening well, one foot inside the empty bucket and both hands wrapped tight around the rope, I saw that the surface of the concrete wall was already marred with cracks, spiderwebs, and mysterious stains. I watched a nervous lizard run up toward the light. Perhaps the underworld was trying to warn us against plunging a concrete tube into its heart. At any moment, there might be an earthquake, and I could be buried here, deep in the ground, forever. Strange, muffled noises came from below.

"Comiiiing!" Master Mahmut shouted into the well whenever the empty bucket was descending.

Every time I looked up, the sight of the opening so terrifyingly small and far away made me want to escape immediately. But Master Mahmut was impatient, so I hurriedly shoveled earth into the bucket and yelled, "Pullll!"

He was much stronger than I was, and it didn't take him long at all to hoist the bucket on the windlass, lifting it carefully onto the shelf before tipping its contents into the handcart, and return it empty to me.

I watched without moving a muscle, my face turned upward the whole time. As long as I could see Master up there, I didn't feel alone underground. Every time he moved aside to empty the bucket, a small disk of sky was revealed. How perfectly blue it was! It was remote, like the world at the wrong end of a telescope, but it was beautiful. Until Master Mahmut reappeared, I stood immobile, staring up at the sky at the end of that concrete telescope.

When I finally caught sight of him again, no bigger than an ant, I felt better. When the bucket arrived, I pulled it down and cried out, "Got it!"

But every time Master Mahmut's infinitesimal form moved out of sight again I was gripped by fear. What if he should trip? What if something happened to him while I was down here? He might even take his time returning to the well with the handcart just to teach me a lesson. Would he want to punish me if he knew about my night with the Red-Haired Woman?

It took about a dozen strokes of the spade to fill the bucket, and when I got carried away, digging deeper into the earth with the pickax, I'd find myself blinded by the dust and darkness so that everything seemed even blacker than before. Anyone could see this sandy soil was too soft and pale. There was obviously no water here. All this anxiety, and all this time—it was all for nothing!

The moment I was out of this well, I would make straight for

Öngören and the Red-Haired Woman. Who cares what Turgay might say. She loves me. I'd tell him everything. He might beat me up; he might even try to kill me. What would the Red-Haired Woman do at the sight of me standing before her in the middle of the day?

With these thoughts I could forget my fear long enough to send up three bucketfuls of earth (yes, I was counting) before I began to panic again. Master Mahmut was taking longer and longer to return to the well, and I kept hearing noises underground.

"Master! Master Mahmut!" I yelled. The blue sky was the size of a coin. Where was Master Mahmut? I started shouting as loud as I could.

Finally, he appeared at the top.

"Master Mahmut, bring me up now!" I called out to him.

But he didn't reply. He just returned to the windlass and hoisted the loaded bucket up. Had he not heard me? My eyes remained fixed on the top of the well.

Master Mahmut was so far away. I shouted as loud as I could. But as in a dream, my voice never reached him. As soon as he had emptied the earth, he gripped the crank and lowered the empty bucket.

I shouted again, but still he couldn't hear me.

A long time passed. I pictured Master Mahmut pushing the handcart to the spot where we emptied it; soon he'd be tilting it over to get the sand out; he must be on his way back, I calculated; surely he should be here by now. But Master Mahmut didn't come. Probably off having a cigarette somewhere.

When he appeared again, I shouted again as loud as I could. But he seemed not to hear. I made my decision: putting one foot into the empty bucket, I held the rope tight and cried, "Pulll!"

I was shuddering as Master Mahmut slowly raised me up to the ground, but I was happy.

"What happened?" he said as I gratefully stepped onto the wooden plank at the top.

"I can't go down there again, Master Mahmut."

"That's for me to say."

"Of course, Master," I said.

"Good boy. If you'd been like this since the day we started, maybe we'd have found that water by now."

"But, Master, back then I didn't know what I was doing. Is it really my fault the water hasn't come?"

He raised an eyebrow, arranging his features into a look of suspicion. I could see he didn't like what I had said. "Master, I will never forget you for as long as I live. Working with you has taught me so much about life. But please, let's give up on this well now. Here, let me kiss your hand."

He did not extend his hand. "You will never speak again of giving up without finding water first. Understood?"

"Understood."

"Now lower your master into the well. There's more than an hour to go until lunchtime. We'll make it a long break today. You'll have time to lie down under the walnut tree and take a nice, long nap."

"Thank you, Master."

"Come on, grab that handle and ease me down."

I turned the crank and Master Mahmut slowly descended into the well, fast disappearing from sight.

I emptied each load of earth smartly, listened closely for Master Mahmut's voice, and then heaved at the windlass with all my strength. Sweat rolled down my back, and I nipped into the tent every so often for a sip of water. I slowed down only once to look at a fossilized fish head that had come up with the sand. That delay set Master Mahmut muttering again. In the toughest moments, when I felt I couldn't go on, a fantasy of the Red-Haired Woman, her breasts, her coppery skin, sustained me.

An inquisitive butterfly with white and yellow spots made its joyful, unhurried way through the grass, by our tent, past the windlass, and onward over the well.

What could this mean? As the eleven-thirty passenger train headed toward Europe on the Istanbul–Edirne line trundled by, I remember taking this as a sign that everything would turn out fine. The train headed in the opposite direction, from Edirne to Istanbul, due to pass by in an hour's time, would be our signal to break for lunch.

I'll run to Öngören on my lunch break, I thought. I wanted to ask the Red-Haired Woman about Master Mahmut. I locked the windlass in place to stop the rope from unspooling. As I gripped the handle of the bucket and began to pull it over to the shelf, I heard Master Mahmut bellowing at me once more. My hand was moving skillfully of its own accord, tilting the load gently to rest it on the wooden shelf, when suddenly the bucket came off the hook and fell down the well.

I froze for a split second.

Then I shouted: "Master, Master!"

Only seconds ago, he'd been shouting at me, but in that moment, he had gone quiet.

Then a deep wail of pain came from down below, followed by a resounding silence. I would never forget that wail.

I drew back. There was no more sound from the well, and I couldn't bring myself to lean over and look down. Maybe it hadn't been a scream after all, and Master Mahmut had just been swearing.

The whole world now was as quiet as the well itself. My knees were shaking. I couldn't decide what to do.

A large wasp circled the windlass, looked inside the well, and plunged in.

I ran to the tent. I changed out of my sweat-soaked shirt and trousers. When I realized that my naked body was trembling, I cried a little but soon stopped. Even if I were to tremble in front of the Red-Haired Woman, I would not be embarrassed. She would understand,

and she would help. Maybe even Turgay would help. Maybe they'd call for someone from the army garrison or the municipality; maybe the firemen would come.

I was running to Öngören taking shortcuts through the fields. The crickets among the dry grass stopped chirping as I passed. I followed the road in parts before cutting through the fields again. All along the downward slope past the cemetery, a strange instinct had me looking over my shoulder, and far away in the direction of Istanbul, I saw black rain clouds.

If Master Mahmut was injured and bleeding, he needed help fast. But I had no idea whom to call.

When I reached town, I made straight for their house. Some woman I didn't recognize opened the door of the ground-floor apartment that faced the back. I think this was the signmaker and former Maoist's wife.

"They've left," she said before I even had the chance to pose a question. The door to the place where I'd slept with my lover for the very first time was shut in my face.

I crossed the square. The Rumelian Coffeehouse was empty, and the post office was full of soldiers making phone calls. On the pavement I saw villagers I'd never seen around at night converging on the town market from nearby settlements.

The tent of the Theater of Morality Tales was gone. At first I could see no trace of what until yesterday had stood in that spot, but then I noticed some discarded ticket stubs and the wooden stakes that had held the tent in place. It was true: they were gone.

I strode quickly out of Öngören without knowing clearly what I was doing. It was as if my reflexes had taken over, and it was someone else who was running, pausing, and trying to find meaning in the clouds gathering in the sky. Sweat poured off my forehead, my neck, and every other part of my body. At night, the trees in the cemetery would ripple in the cool breeze, but now it was hellishly hot and close on the slope that went past the graves. I saw sheep chewing contentedly on the grass between the headstones.

By the time I reached the plateau, I had stopped running and slowed down to a walk. I saw very clearly that whatever I did in the next thirty minutes would affect the rest of my life, but I couldn't decide what it was that I should do. I couldn't dwell too much on whether Master Mahmut had fainted, whether he was injured or dead. Perhaps the intense heat was getting to me. The sun was directly overhead, burning the back of my neck and the tip of my nose.

On the grassy shortcut through the last turn in the road, I first heard the rustling and then saw the shell of an agitated tortoise trying to get out of my way. If it had stepped to the left or to the right, away from the narrow path that Master Mahmut and I had trodden on our trips back and forth from town, it could have hidden in the taller grasses by the side. But it couldn't figure this out and tried instead to outrun me, as if its fate were inescapably tied to the very path I was walking on. Could I be doing the same, trudging fruitlessly down the wrong path while trying to escape my own fate?

When I was a child, there were kids in Beşiktaş who used to flip tortoises over and leave them to dry out and die in the heat. The tortoise retreated into its shell when it saw me; I gently picked it up and released it into the taller grass.

As I approached the well, I tried to breathe more slowly. I wished above all else that I might hear Master Mahmut again, shouting or groaning. I kept telling myself that this was just another of the countless ordinary things that had happened over the past month. The bucket hadn't fallen, and Master Mahmut was fine. I would raise a bottle of water to my lips and, as I drank, I would hear Master Mahmut's furious scolding from below.

But there wasn't a single sound from the well. Nothing but the cicadas made a sound. The silence filled my soul with remorse. I saw two lizards chasing each other on the windlass. I took another step toward the well. But I lost my nerve and stepped back before I could get any closer. It was as if I would go blind if I were to look.

I couldn't go down into the well on my own anyway. There had to be another person to lower me down. That was why I'd rushed off to Öngören and the Red-Haired Woman. But I'd come back without telling anyone there what had happened. I didn't know why I had done that. Perhaps I had assumed I wouldn't find anyone to help anyway, and Master Mahmut would be happier if I ran straight back to his side.

Or perhaps I'd decided that Master Mahmut was dead, and there was no taking back my crime. "O God, please have mercy on me!" I begged. What should I do?

Back in the tent, I started crying again. Everything in the place I'd shared with Master Mahmut for the past month was now unbearably painful to look at. The teapot, the old newspaper I'd read a thousand times, Master Mahmut's plastic slippers with the blue bands across the instep, the belt for the trousers he wore when he went to town, his alarm clock . . .

My hands began of their own accord to gather my things. It took less than three minutes to stuff everything, including the rubber shoes I'd never worn, into my old valise.

If I stayed here, they would at the very least arrest me for causing someone's death by my "negligence." My case would drag on for years, I could forget about cram school and university, my whole life would be thrown off course, I'd go to juvenile prison, and my mother would die of heartache.

I pleaded with God to let Master Mahmut live. As I approached the mouth of the well again I hoped that I might hear him talking or whimpering. But there was no sound whatsoever.

With only fifteen minutes to go before the twelve-thirty train to

Istanbul, I left the tent with my father's old valise in hand and hastily made my way down to Öngören in the heat, without looking back. I knew that if I turned around, I would start crying again. The dark rain clouds had almost reached the town, and everything had taken on an ominous purple hue.

The station was crowded with villagers who had come for the market. The train was late, and as I waited, amid the baskets, sacks, crates, farmers, and soldiers, I planned how I was going to pick a window seat on the left-hand side of the carriage so I could see, until the tracks turned away, the place where Master Mahmut and I had dug the well. All month I'd been thinking of how I would do this on the day of my journey back to Istanbul. But I had always imagined it would be the day we'd found water, and I'd be carrying the gifts and the bonus Hayri Bey had promised.

I tried to cast an eye on everyone who walked into the station until the train arrived, but it was too crowded. The Red-Haired Woman and her troupe might be returning to Istanbul on the same train, for all I could see. As the train finally pulled into the station, I took one last look at the square and at the town of Öngören before quickly stepping on board. By the time I'd settled into the carriage, I'd forgotten about all the times I'd had to swallow my pride and obey Master Mahmut and felt nothing but an immeasurable guilt.

· PART II ·

22

When I looked out of the carriage window, my eyes wet with tears, I could just about make out the well and our patch of land up on the plateau. Everything I saw—the cemetery on the way to town, the cypress trees—formed a picture I knew even then that I'd never forget as long as I lived. The land where we had dug the well seemed on the verge of disappearing into the blackened heavens. Lightning struck off in the distance. By the time the sound of thunder reached us, the train had already twisted away, and that familiar landscape—the well, our plateau—had fallen out of sight. A feeling of freedom swept through me. Relief and guilt mingled in time with the *click-clacking* of the train along the tracks.

For a long time, I would have nothing to do with anyone. I withdrew, distancing myself from the world. The world was beautiful, and I wanted my inner world to be beautiful, too. If I ignored the guilt, the darkness inside me, I thought I would eventually forget it was there. So I began to pretend that everything was fine. If you act as if nothing has happened, and if nothing more comes of it, you will indeed find that nothing has happened after all.

The train to Istanbul wound its way past factories, warehouses, and fields. It crossed streams, slipped by mosques, and chugged by coffeehouses and workshops. A group of boys was playing soccer in an empty schoolyard, and when it began to rain, they grabbed the shirts and bags they had arranged as goalposts and quickly dispersed.

Puddles, streams, and rapids soon formed over the hard soil wherever I could see from the carriage window. It could have been the great flood, but a man standing at the bottom of a well wouldn't have known the difference. Was Master Mahmut still there? Was he calling for me?

I got off the train at Istanbul's Sirkeci Station. I walked in the rain and bought a ticket for the car ferry to Harem, on the Asian side. The ferry was waiting for more passengers and took forever to push off, with drivers, families, crying children, bowls of sweet yogurt, the amplified noise of truck engines . . . I had forgotten how comforting it was to be surrounded by people. I felt like a savage who had returned to civilization. Water dripped from my hair down my neck and back as I sat motionless, watching Istanbul drift by slowly through the raindrops on the windowpane. Peering into the distance, I tried to make out Dolmabahçe Palace and the neighborhood of Beşiktaş behind it, and the tall residential block that faced the cram school.

I bought a packet of tissues from a kiosk after disembarking and dried myself a bit before taking the bus. It was hours since I had last eaten, but I took no notice of the pastries and kebab sandwiches for sale. I said to myself, *This must be what it feels like to be a murderer.*

That was the other voice inside me again, the voice I silently summoned to talk about matters I didn't care to discuss with anybody else. But don't think that I was losing my mind. At three o'clock, I caught a bus to Gebze. I was feverishly excited to see my mother. Basking in the warmth of the summer sun shining through the window on the right-hand side, I eventually fell asleep and dreamed I was in a sunny, balmy paradise, cleansed of crime and punishment.

I must have been dreading what my mother might say: *What's wrong with you? You're looking at me like a murderer.* When she said nothing of the sort, I realized just how worried I had been about how she would greet me, and as soon as I embraced her, I felt much better. My mother smelled like herself. She cried a little at first, then started chattering away lightheartedly, saying that, all things considered, life in Gebze wasn't so bad, and that she was going to make me meatballs and french fries. Her only cause to fret had been how much she'd missed me and worried about me. She started crying again. We hugged even harder.

"My goodness, how much you've grown in a month, your hands are so big, and look how tall you are," said my mother. "You're a man now. Shall I add some tomatoes to your salad?"

I would go for long walks on the hills surrounding Gebze and gaze on Istanbul in the distance. At times I would notice a faraway plot of land resembling our plateau, and I would become agitated, as if I were about to bump into Master Mahmut.

I never told my mother that I had been inside the well even though I'd promised her over and over again that I wouldn't go in. She could see that I was alive and well, so perhaps this detail was no longer relevant.

We never mentioned my father. I could tell that he never called her. But why didn't he call me? My last glimpse of Master Mahmut descending into the well often surfaced in my mind like a painting. I was sure that he was still doggedly digging, like a persistent fruitworm burrowing its way through a gargantuan orange.

We went to the shops in Gebze, and my mother bought a new television and an alarm clock. I banked all the money I'd saved working with Master Mahmut. I spent three days at home, resting and recovering. My dreams were of Master Mahmut, and I was being chased by villains. But no one came looking for me in Gebze; nobody was after me. On the fourth day, I went down to Istanbul, enrolled in a cram school in Beşiktaş, and started dutifully attending classes.

When I was alone, I couldn't get Master Mahmut and the well out of my mind. So I made a point of rekindling friendships with old neighborhood and school friends in Beşiktaş, and we all went to the cinema together. We even tried some of the bars downtown, but unlike my friends, I wasn't well accustomed to the art of cigarettes and *rakı*. They mocked me for draining my glass in one gulp like a beginner and getting drunk immediately. That didn't bother me, though I did resent their cracks that my beard and mustache weren't full enough, implying I wasn't yet a man.

"If the beard were all, the goat might preach," I replied. "Even a vixen has whiskers."

They liked that one! I had collected lots of aphorisms from the books I used to stay up reading until I couldn't see straight on nights I slept at the Deniz Bookstore.

But could someone heartless enough to leave his master to die at the bottom of a well ever aspire to be a writer? Had the bucket fallen entirely by accident? I often told myself that nothing bad had happened at the well. I'd simply been unable to cope with all the exertion, the scolding, and the lack of sleep. All I had done was to leave everything behind, take my money, and go home, as any normal person would have done—though I wasn't even sure if I liked that term "normal person" any longer.

Among my older friends were a few now attending Istanbul University. They'd grown beards and mustaches and participated in political protests, clashing with the police in the backstreets of the neighborhood, stories they were proud to tell as we drank and made merry. I knew they respected my father. But I realized one night how I inwardly resented them.

"Cem, have you ever even held a girl's hand?" they teased me.

A few of them had spoken openly of love letters they'd written to this girl or that, and how they longed for a response. So I blurted out how my aunt's husband had found me a construction job (construction sounded more impressive than welldigging) near Edirne and how I'd had a love affair with a woman there, in the town of Öngören. "Has anyone here heard of Öngören?" I asked around the table.

They hadn't expected something like this from me and were all briefly dumbstruck. One said he'd gone with his parents to visit his older brother doing his military service in Öngören, but he'd found the place small and dull.

"I fell in love with an amazing woman, a theater actress twice my age. I didn't even know who she was. I just saw her on the street. She took me to her apartment."

They looked at me in disbelief. I told them it was my first time with a woman.

"How was it?" the letter writers were now asking. "Was it good?"

"What was her name?"

"Why didn't you get married?" said another, taking a drag on his cigarette.

The one who'd visited his brother at the garrison said dismissively: "You can find all sorts there: traveling theaters with belly dancers performing for the soldiers, nightclub singers, and anything else you can think of."

That night, I understood that if I was to be unburdened of my pain and guilt, I'd have to stay away from these childhood friends. I was also gradually coming to realize that what had happened at the well would always bar me from the joys of an ordinary life. I kept telling myself, *The best thing to do is to act as if nothing happened.*

23

BUT WAS IT POSSIBLE to pretend nothing had happened? Inside my head there was a well where, pickax in hand, Master Mahmut was still hacking away at the earth. That must mean he was still alive, or the police had yet to investigate his murder.

I imagined that someone—perhaps Ali—would find the corpse, after which the district attorney would get on the case; he would alert Gebze first (that could take days or weeks in Turkey), my distraught mother would weep herself unconscious, and once the Gebze police had advised their counterparts in Istanbul (which in turn could take months more), they would come any day to pick me up at the cram school or the bookstore. Perhaps I should find my father and tell him everything, I thought. But he never called me, from which I inferred that even if he had, he wouldn't have been much help. Besides, telling him would mean acknowledging that this was serious. Each day that passed without the police coming to take me away seemed a sign that I was innocent and no different from everybody else, but it also felt like my last taste of the simple, ordinary life that everyone else expected routinely. Whenever a customer at the Deniz Bookstore was particularly brusque, I would become convinced that he was a plain-clothes officer and find myself on the verge of confessing. Other times I comforted myself, thinking Master Mahmut must have survived and hatefully forgotten all about me.

I was quick and efficient and worked hard at the bookshop. Mr. Deniz, who loved my innovative ideas for window displays, promotional deals, and which books to stock, told me that I could sleep on the couch upstairs even in winter. I was to consider that little room a second home and place to study. My mother was dejected to have me far from her and Gebze again, but she was also sure that if I continued to attend Kabataş High School and the cram school in Beşiktaş, I was guaranteed a good result on the university entrance exams.

I didn't want to disappoint her, and I knew how pivotal this exam was for my life, so I became a real swot throughout high school, leaving no formula I might possibly need unmemorized. In my most intent immersions in the work, a vision of the Red-Haired Woman would dawn in my mind out of nowhere like a sultry sun, and I would take a little break to fantasize about the color of her skin, her belly, her breasts, her eyes.

When the time came to register for the entrance exams and pick my subjects, my mother naturally wanted me to list medicine first. She was terrified that my literary aspirations were a road to poverty or, even worse, to the kind of political activity that had gotten my father in such trouble.

Luckily for her, my dreams of becoming a writer had withered quickly since I'd abandoned Master Mahmut at the bottom of the well. I knew my mother would settle for my becoming an engineer, if not a doctor. So I wrote down "engineering geology" on the form. My mother had noticed that the apprenticeship with the welldigger had left some sort of mark on me. I wondered in passing whether she realized somehow that the newfound "maturity" she observed was, in fact, a black stain on my soul.

At the end of the summer of 1987, I scored fifth highest on the entrance exam and was admitted to the faculty of engineering geology at the Maçka campus of Istanbul Technical University. The 110-year-old building that composed the campus had originally been an armory and barracks for some of the new army units created in the last years of the Ottoman Empire, and in 1908, when the Young Turks who eventually deposed Abdul Hamid II marched from Thessalonica to Istanbul, the soldiers who remained loyal to the sultan were stationed here. Actual battles were fought in what were now our classrooms. I read about these things in history books and told my classmates about them. I was fascinated by the old building, its high ceilings, its interminable flights of stairs, and its cavernous echoing corridors.

And it was only ten minutes up the hill from Beşiktaş and the Deniz Bookstore, where I was promoted to manager. Although the boss remained reluctant to admit that I wouldn't be a writer after all, he was warming to the idea of geology and allowed that engineers could be good novelists anyway. At the dorm, I was plowing through a new book almost every night.

In retrospect, part of pretending that nothing bad had happened involved willfully forgetting all about Sophocles's play, with its associations of my bedtime chats with Master Mahmut. I'd been able to stay clear of it through three years at university, until one day at the Deniz Bookstore, I chanced on that old anthology about dreams. This was the very book in which I'd first read Oedipus's story in synopsis. I now discovered that the summary was in fact by Sigmund Freud and had less to do with Sophocles than with a theory of Freud's that every man harbors the desire to kill his own father.

A few months later I came across a secondhand copy of Sophocles's work in a translation published in 1941 by the Ministry of Education. I was startled to see the title *Oedipus the King* across its yellowing cover. Turkish editions of the play were almost impossible to find. I devoured it, as if expecting to find therein some secret truth about my own life.

Unlike Freud's summary, the actual play didn't start at Oedipus's birth, but years later, when Prince Oedipus had, by mistake, already killed his own father, taken the throne, and fathered four children by his own mother. The play glossed over how a son was sleeping with his mother, a woman at least sixteen years older than he was. I tried but couldn't imagine what it would have been like, just as I couldn't fathom that Oedipus's children were also his siblings, in the same way his wife was simultaneously his mother. But at the start of the play, neither Oedipus, nor any of the other characters, nor even the audience, has any inkling of the scandal to be revealed. Maybe it is this ignorance that has caused the plague, and in order to save the city, they have to find out who murdered the old king. King Oedipus himself leads the search like a detective, unaware that he is the culprit. Step by step, he discovers the bitter truth until finally, racked by guilt, he carves out his own eyes.

I hadn't told Master Mahmut the story in this order that evening by the well three years ago. But as I read the play now, I somehow felt as if I had. I also noticed that I was feeling less guilty about having caused his death. After three years, I had stopped worrying that the police would burst into class one day and take me to jail. Maybe Master Mahmut wasn't even dead but had been rescued from the depths of the well as in one of those old religious allegories.

Master Mahmut used to tell me those stories and parables from the

Koran to teach me a lesson. This would upset me. In turn, I had told him the story of Prince Oedipus only to upset him, but then somehow I had ended up retracing the actions of the protagonist whose story I'd chosen. That was why Master Mahmut wound up stuck at the bottom of a well: it was all owing to a story, a myth.

Having set out trying to disprove a story and a prophecy, Oedipus ended up killing his own father. Had he laughed off the oracle's predictions, perhaps he would never have left his home and his country, encountering his father the king on the way and inadvertently killing him. The same was true of Oedipus's father. Had he taken no precautions to thwart Oedipus's terrible destiny, none of the subsequent calamities would have occurred. So it was that I had come to understand that if I wanted to live a "normal," ordinary life like everyone else, I had to do the opposite of what Oedipus did and act as if nothing bad had happened. Oedipus, who wanted so much to be good, became a killer because he was so desperate not to be one; he found out that he had killed his own father because he needed so much to know who the murderer was. Sophocles's whole play was built not around the evil acts themselves but around the probing of his inquiring protagonist.

But never mind the question of whether I counted as a killer; I wasn't even sure that a murder had taken place. I had no intention of being a murderer, or of being murdered by my own son. Master Mahmut could certainly have emerged from the well and returned to normal life. Wouldn't the police be banging on my door otherwise? I had better forget any of it had even happened; only then would I, too, be able to live like everyone else.

24

FOR A LONG TIME I told myself, *Nothing did happen, anyway.* I strolled down the corridors of the university, which smelled of damp dust and cheap cleaner; I went to the cinema with my classmates who used the ongoing political unrest and their clashes with the police as excuses to skip metallurgy classes; I glanced indifferently at serials on the dormitory TV; and I comforted myself to think that I had finally contrived to be like everyone else. Soccer matches on TV, the art films beginning to circulate on newfangled videotapes, ships crossing the Bosphorus: I casually watched them all. I checked out the new home appliances displayed in shop windows, I mixed with the crowds in Beyoğlu, and on Sunday evenings I thought glumly that another weekend was over.

There weren't many female students matriculated at Istanbul Technical University's faculty of engineering, housed in the former armory.

What few were there were courted by the entire male student body. I knew of very few women my age in the whole university. So my interest was piqued when, one weekend in Gebze, my mother mentioned that my aunt's husband had a relative whose daughter had been admitted to study pharmacy; she was going to stay in the dormitories but found the city and its crowds intimidating, so my aunt's husband would appreciate it if I showed her the ropes.

Ayşe's hair was light brown, but something about her was nevertheless reminiscent of the Red-Haired Woman, particularly the curve of her upper lip and her dainty chin. I knew on the day we met that I would fall in love with her, wanting so much to fall in love with someone, and I sensed that she would reciprocate my feelings. On Saturday afternoons we went to the cinema or saw Chekhov and Shakespeare plays at the Municipal Theater or took the bus to Emirgan for a cup of tea. Going out with a girl who could be deemed suitable and reasonably attractive—"dating" her, as some of my friends called it—made life seem so glorious that I believed I had finally moved on from Master Mahmut and the well.

In order to carry on with this life, I applied for a postgraduate degree in engineering geology, and being among the top students in my class, I was accepted. During our second year together, we progressed to holding hands and even kissing in cinemas, parks, and deserted streets, but from the earliest days of our relationship, I had already surmised that Ayşe, who came from a conservative family, would not sleep with me until we were married.

A friend in Beşiktaş, a bit of a lothario who regularly patronized brothels and believed wholeheartedly that any girl could eventually be seduced, arranged for me to spend an afternoon with Ayşe in a small private apartment, but the whole thing was a disaster. I tried to get her to join me in a glass of *rakı,* as if it were something we did every day, and after about two hours of steadfastly rebuffing my advances, she finally left the apartment in tears. For a long time thereafter, she wouldn't even come to the phone when I called her dormitory. I thus entered a phase of fantasies about seeking out the Red-Haired Woman, during which I masturbated to the memory of our night together.

But eventually I made up with Ayşe; we got back together and decided to get engaged. I savored those Saturday afternoons after the engagement party (for which my mother and her seamstress made a dress together) when Ayşe would come to collect me at the Deniz Bookstore, and I had the pleasure of hearing the boss and the young clerks comment on how pretty the "girl from Gördes" was. I liked to talk to her about books I was reading, the history of geology, and my mostly commonplace views on politics and soccer. When I went to the towns of Kozlu and Soma on summer jobs, I wrote her impassioned letters about the plight of the coal miners there, and it thrilled me to learn that Ayşe kept those letters and read them again from time to time. I kept her letters, too.

But even in the midst of this serenity, a minor development could unexpectedly unveil the darkness still in my soul. During a summer of drought and water shortages in Istanbul, when the minister for agriculture seemed on the verge of proposing rain dances, I found myself sinking into a protracted silence at my fiancée's suggestion that wells should immediately be dug in every garden. (I had never told her about my month as a welldigger's apprentice, years ago.) When I read in the newspaper that the refrigerator factory the prime minister had inaugurated near Öngören was the biggest of its kind in the Balkans and the Middle East, I recalled Master Mahmut and the religious parables he used to tell me. Once, I thought I'd pick up a new translation of *The Brothers Karamazov* as a birthday gift for my fiancée, but when I saw that the introduction was by Freud, a text on Dostoyevsky and patricide, and touching upon *Oedipus the King* and *Hamlet,* I decided, after reading the unsettling essay on the spot, to buy her a copy of *The Idiot* instead—at least its protagonist is naïve and innocent.

Some nights I saw Master Mahmut in my dreams. He was still digging away, somewhere up in space on a colossal bluish sphere spinning slowly among the stars. That must mean he wasn't dead and that I need not feel so guilty. But it still hurt if I looked too closely at the planet he stood on.

I wanted to tell my fiancée that Master Mahmut was the reason I'd decided to study geology, but I always held back. The compulsion to confess was strongest whenever I bonded with Ayşe over books. But instead I would tell her about the secrets and singularities of the geological sciences: for instance, how the mystery of seashells, fish heads, and mussels being in the cracks, crevasses, and hollows atop the highest mountains was solved in the eleventh century by a Chinese polymath named Shen Kuo. One hundred and fifty years after Sophocles, Theophrastus wrote a book called *On Stones,* and the theories he'd outlined about minerals remained undisputed for thousands of years. I may have failed to become a novelist, but I wouldn't have minded writing a book as widely trusted as that! I imagined penning a volume entitled *The Geology of Turkey,* covering everything from the height of the Taurus mountain range to the secrets of the loamy, fine-grained soils of Thrace, where we'd dug our well, to the tectonic formations in the south of the country and the distribution of national oil and gas deposits.

25

I KNEW THAT MY FATHER was somewhere in Istanbul. I resented him for not calling me, but I didn't try to call him, either. I would finally see him again after marrying Ayşe, just before leaving for my military service. We arranged to meet at a restaurant in a new hotel in Taksim Square one night after the wedding. I was taken aback by how happy I was to see him. "You found a girl just like your mother," he told me in private. He quickly established a rapport with Ayşe, and they even started ganging up on me over dinner, teasing me for being an engineering nerd who seemed to memorize numbers automatically.

My father had aged, but he looked good. I sensed his embarrassment about being well-off now and about the new life he'd made for himself. It left me feeling self-conscious about my fascination with stories of patricide. But it was by growing up without him all these years, toiling on my own, that I had become "myself."

Back when I still had him by my side, I had struggled to be myself, even though he had never meddled in my life and had always encouraged me. It was standing up to Master Mahmut, despite having spent only a month with him, that made me the person I now was. Was it right to think that way? I wasn't sure, but I knew my own feelings. I still craved my father's approval and wanted to believe I was leading the honorable life he would have expected of me, but I was also furious at him.

"You're very lucky, she's a wonderful girl," he said, looking at Ayşe as we parted. "I couldn't have left you in better hands."

As I headed home with my wife, walking from Taksim to Pangaltı under the tall chestnut trees, I was relieved to be done with my father. We lived in a cheap one-room apartment on a slope that went from Feriköy down to Dolapdere. As newlyweds, we made love most days for hours at a time; we laughed and talked a lot; I was happy. Sometimes I thought of Master Mahmut and wondered what had become of him. But I knew that probing an old crime, as Oedipus had done, could afford me nothing but further remorse.

After my military service, I found a job as a government clerk at the Istanbul bureau of the National Mineral Exploration Program. My university friends used to joke that in Turkey an engineering geology postgraduate's only way to make a living was to work in construction or else open a kebab shop. So I should be grateful to have even this low-paying position.

A number of Turkish construction firms had meanwhile begun building dams and bridges abroad in Arab nations, the Ukraine, and Romania and were looking for geologists and engineers to send on inspections. Eventually I found a more lucrative job which involved a posting in Libya, meaning we'd have to live there for at least six months a year. By this time, however, Ayşe and I had begun to grow concerned about still not having had a baby. Deciding it would be better to be near the doctors we already knew and trusted, we returned to Istanbul.

In 1997, I joined a company with projects closer to home, in Kazakhstan and Azerbaijan. I would spend the next fifteen years flying out from Istanbul to neighboring countries and began at last to earn a better living.

We moved to a nicer apartment in Pangaltı. On weekends when I wasn't away on business, we would go to shopping malls to watch films and have a bite to eat. In the evenings, we would have our dinner with state dignitaries and military men making their blustery declarations on TV. In between we might consider whether we should consult the eccentric professor reported to have developed a miraculous new fertility formula, or that brilliant doctor just come back to Istanbul from America. There would ensue long talks about not letting childlessness poison our harmonious marriage and destroy our zest for life.

Occasionally, I still went down to Beşiktaş to visit the Deniz Bookstore. Having finally accepted that I was not to be a writer, Mr. Deniz was now offering me a stake in the business. All in all, my life was just like everyone else's—perhaps even slightly better than average. Every now and then it would occur to me how successfully I was managing to pretend nothing had happened. I still thought about Master Mahmut and my crime, most often on airplane journeys. Sometimes I even wondered whether my true motive for taking all these trips to Benghazi, Astana, and Baku was for the chance to remember. As I looked out the window of the plane, I would think of him and brood over the children I didn't have.

Shortly after takeoff from the Atatürk Airport in Yeşilköy, the planes would all turn their noses westward like the flocks of migratory birds that overflew the city every year, and when I looked out I would invariably see the town of Öngören below. It wasn't too far from the Black

Sea and the Sea of Marmara, from the beaches and the new summer resorts along the coast, and from the oil and gasoline silos that looked so huge even from the air. But cut off from the trees and the lush vegetation near the sea, and isolated from the rich golden-reddish fields nearby, it was as ever surrounded by pale arid tracts and conjoined to the old military garrison.

The view would disappear in an instant as the plane turned again, rolling gently on its axis or passing through a cloud formation, but even then, I could sense the lay of the land beneath.

We were getting older, we still had no children, and meanwhile the farmlands between Öngören and Istanbul were filling up with industrial plants, warehouses, and factories, all of them dull and black as coal from the air. Some companies had emblazoned their names on the roofs of their factories and depots in huge bright letters, for the apparent benefit of airline passengers. These structures were surrounded by smaller workshops, obscure firms that dealt in manufacturing supplies, and shabby, nondescript buildings. As the plane gained altitude, the illegal residential neighborhoods sprawling around these establishments would also become visible. The little towns and villages near Istanbul were expanding as disconcertingly fast as the city itself. With every trip I took, I could see its tentacles reaching farther into the remotest recesses, and hundreds of thousands of vehicles advancing unerringly over ever-widening roads like so many patient ants, and I reflected that the pace of technological progress must long have rendered Master Mahmut's skills obsolete.

After the mid-1980s, the ancient traditional methods of welldigging with spade and pickax, of slow excavation by the bucketful on a wooden windlass, of lining the walls meter by meter with concrete, had all become extinct in Istanbul. During a summer holiday Ayşe and I spent with my mother in Gebze, I witnessed some of the first efforts at drilling artesian wells on various plots surrounding the land my aunt's husband owned. The early drills, still operated manually, like screwdrivers, would later be superseded by more powerful mechanized ones, noisy machines resembling oil derricks, hauled in on the backs of mud-spattered, big-wheeled pickups. They could bore fifty meters in a single day, laying pipes that would then pump water up from the depths of the earth in no time and at negligible cost, all on the very same land Master Mahmut and two apprentices would previously have toiled on for weeks.

From the early 1990s, these technical advances led for a time to an abundant supply of water in the greener neighborhoods of Istanbul, but soon the underground lakes and aquifers closest to the surface were depleted. By the early 2000s, the only groundwater left in many parts of the city was more than seventy meters below the surface, and it would have been practically impossible to get to it simply by digging with two apprentices in people's gardens, a meter a day, as Master Mahmut used to do. Istanbul and the soil it stood on had been denatured and defiled.

26

TWENTY YEARS after my Öngören days, a classmate from Istanbul Technical University invited me to meet with an oil firm in Tehran. A few minutes after takeoff, as the plane began to tilt away from the west and toward the southeast, I noticed that Öngören and Istanbul had grown toward each other to the point of having effectively merged. They now composed a single sea of streets, houses, rooftops, mosques, and factories. The future generations of Öngören would describe themselves as living in Istanbul.

How important is it for people to know what their city is called and remind themselves of where they live? More than twenty-five years after Ayatollah Khomeini's revolution, Iran had become an inward-looking nation. My friend Murat was confident that it could present plenty of lucrative business opportunities for a Turkish company, an optimism I understood without sharing.

Murat said he would bid for construction contracts in oil-rich Iran, and that we could sell them drilling equipment, taking advantage of the war of words they were waging with the West. Perhaps he was right, but I suspected that if we followed other Turkish companies in breaking the West's embargo on Iran, we'd soon be contending with the CIA and their ilk. Murat, who came from a conservative family in the city of Malatya, who still reveled in duplicity and minor chicanery as he had at school, was unperturbed by such complications. He was also nowhere nearly as unnerved as I was by the fact that women in Tehran had to cover their heads to go out in public.

It was a time when Western newspapers debated the merits of bombing Iran, and Istanbul's secular, nationalist newspapers asked, "Will Turkey become like Iran?" I cut our political discussion short, concluding very quickly that we could not have dealings with Tehran.

Yet I was mesmerized by how much alike Iranians and Turks were. So I delayed my return to Istanbul, intrigued by the shopping arcades, the bookstores (translations of Nietzsche everywhere!), and much else I saw as I rambled along the pavements of Tehran. The men's hand gestures, their facial expressions, body language, the way they lingered in doorways to let one another pass, how they stood around doing nothing in particular and whiled away the hours smoking cigarettes in coffeehouses, reminded me uncannily of Turkish habits. The traffic, moreover, was just as bad as in Istanbul. In Turkey, we'd forgotten all about Iran as soon as we'd turned toward the West. I browsed the bookstores on Enqelab Street, the road renamed after the Islamic Revolution, and marveled at the variety on display.

I discovered the existence of an angry class of modern, secular Iranians forced to lead their lives indoors. Murat took me to house parties where men and women mingled and drank freely. The women at these parties did not cover their heads. The alcohol was home-brewed. In Turkey, secularism had existed for some time, even if it had had to be propped up by the army, and was perceived as a value to be preserved at all costs; but in Iran, secularism seemed not to exist at all, which made it an even more fundamental need.

I went to another gathering one evening in a house full of children that resounded with the conversations and raucous laughter of extended families, women, and businessmen. Everyone was very gracious and kind when they found out I was Turkish. They loved Istanbul and often went there for some shopping and sightseeing. They asked me to say things in Turkish and smiled instinctively when I did, as if I'd done something amusing. One of the families at the party invited us to their summerhouse on the Caspian Sea. Murat, who'd had a lot more to drink than I had, accepted the invitation without a second thought.

As I looked out the window at the lights of Tehran under the dark, deep-blue sky, I had a nagging suspicion that my old friend's determination to strengthen ties between Iran and Turkey went beyond personal enrichment, that he was, perhaps, on a secret mission. I couldn't work out whether he was a spy working to pry Turkey away from NATO and the West, or to rescue Iran from its isolation. Maybe he was only in it to profit from breaking the embargo, but I couldn't be sure.

The fruit-flavored alcohol they were serving made my head swim. I was missing Ayşe and Istanbul, when I found myself unexpectedly thinking about my evening walks to Öngören with Master Mahmut. An uncanny yearning, a furious feeling that I had somehow been orphaned, overcame me, and my mind was thrown into disarray.

I was sure it had something to do with the picture on the wall in front of me, a vaguely familiar image, though I couldn't place or understand it. Part of me seemed to know the subject matter, while another part was anxious to forget it. The image, obviously taken from an old book and reproduced to decorate this calendar, was of a man crying as he cradled his son. It seemed based on a story like the one I'd seen enacted years ago in the yellow theater tent at Öngören. You could see the anguished father grieving, his son's blood all over them both . . .

Our hostess, a perceptive old lady, came up to me as I stood transfixed by the calendar. I asked her what the image represented. She said it was the scene from the *Shahnameh* in which Rostam weeps over his son Sohrab, whom he has just killed. Her proud expression seemed to say, *How could you not know?* I mused that Iranians were not like us Turks who had become so Westernized that we'd forgotten our old poets and myths. They would never forget—especially not their poets.

"If you're interested in this kind of thing, we'll take you to the Golestan Palace tomorrow," said my hostess, now feeling evident satisfaction. "That's where this picture comes from, and you'll find many other illuminated manuscripts and old books there."

She never did take me to the Golestan Palace, but I went there with Murat during my last afternoon in Tehran. The extensive garden, lush with trees, was dotted with a number of minor mansions. We entered the palace gallery, the Negar Khaneh, which reminded me of the Ihlamur Palace near my father's Life Pharmacy. It was a dimly lit building devoted to ancient Persian art, and apart from us, no one was there. The scowling guards eyed us suspiciously, as if to say, *Why did you even come here?*

We soon found more versions of the same man, either trying to save his wounded son or weeping over his dead body. The father was Rostam, hero of the *Shahnameh*, Iran's national epic. Despite being a bibliophile, like most Turks I was unfamiliar with the *Shahnameh* and the tale of Rostam and Sohrab. Even so, when I looked at this image, what I saw resembled an idea of fatherhood that I carried deep in me.

There were no books or postcards in the museum shop; I couldn't find any prints of the picture I'd seen or any other images of Rostam and Sohrab. I felt frustrated and uneasy, as if a fearful memory I refused to acknowledge consciously might suddenly well up and make me miserable. The image was like some wicked thought that keeps intruding on your mind no matter how much you yearn to be rid of it.

"Will you please tell me what's so special about that picture?" said Murat.

I wouldn't explain, but he finally promised to retrieve the illustration from the wall calendar in the house where we'd had dinner and send it to me in Istanbul.

As the plane descended on the trip home, I tried to spot Öngören from the window, but all I could see through the clouds was a vast continuous stretch of Istanbul. So it was then, after twenty years, that I began to feel an overpowering urge to return to Öngören and the place where I had last seen Master Mahmut.

27

BUT I RESISTED the temptation to go back. I spent subsequent weekends in Istanbul idling with my wife in front of the TV or at the cinema in Beyoğlu, trying to forget my worries. But could I call them that? I had no real concerns in life, apart from my inability to produce an heir. After countless days and months spent listening to doctors who judged the problem to be with Ayşe, not me, and gaining nothing by following their advice anyway, I decided that if we acted like it didn't matter, then it wouldn't matter.

It wasn't easy to find a translation of Ferdowsi's thousand-year-old epic in Istanbul. Most Ottoman intellectuals would have had a passing acquaintance with the *Shahnameh* or at least known some of its stories. But after two hundred years of striving to Westernize, no one in Turkey was interested any longer in this profusion of tales. A Turkish translation in free verse had been circulating since the 1940s and was published by the Ministry of Education ten years later, in four volumes. It was this edition of the poem, sporting the white livery of the World Classics series, the covers yellowed with age, that I finally tracked down and devoured.

The mixture of history and myth appealed to me, as did the way the book started off as an eerie fable before turning into a kind of morality tale about family and ethics. I was impressed that Ferdowsi had devoted his entire life to this national history, a full fifteen hundred pages in translation. The learned book-loving poet had read the histories, legends, and sagas of other nations; sought out books in Arabic, Avestan, and Pahlavi scripts; combined myths with heroic chronicles, religious parables with history and memory; and composed his own monumental epic.

The *Shahnameh* was a compendium of forgotten stories, the lives of kings, sultans, and heroes of the past. I felt as if I were simultaneously the hero and the author of some of these accounts. Ferdowsi had suffered the death of a child, and this imbued the passages about the father's loss of his son with a particularly moving depth and honesty. I imagined myself telling Master Mahmut these stories in the dark midnight hours, and I remembered the Red-Haired Woman. Had I been a writer, I too would have liked to create something comparable to this eternal, all-encompassing masterpiece, which seemed to capture every detail of any subject, a book at once thrilling and distressing in its unerring depiction of humanity, one that overwhelmed me with surprise and wonder at every turn. My book, *The Geology of Turkey,* would also be epic and encyclopedic in scope. Through the judicious use of anecdote, I would describe the worlds beneath the oceans, the mountain ranges, and the layers and veins of subterranean rock.

The *Shahnameh* begins with creation myths and tales of giants, monsters, jinn, and demons, but its landscape becomes more recognizable once the narrative shifts to the adventures of mortal kings and brave warriors and stories of how people just like us wrestled with family, life—and the state. As I read, I kept remembering my father and reluctantly became more and more convinced that I'd probably killed Master Mahmut after all. This feeling intensified as I turned from Sohrab's story to Afrasiab's, until I was in such distress I considered not finishing the book. But I also believed that if I kept exploring this boundless sea of stories, I might eventually solve the riddle of my own life and finally land on peaceful shores.

There was one story that I read so often after my wife went to sleep that I knew I would remember it forever, like a nursery rhyme, a recurring nightmare, or some other indelible experience:

Once upon a time, there was a man named Rostam, one of Persia's matchless heroes, an indefatigable warrior. Everyone knew and loved him. Rostam lost his way while he was out hunting one day, and when he went to sleep that night, he also lost his horse, Rakhsh. When he went looking for Rakhsh, he stumbled into the enemy territory of Turan. But as his good reputation preceded him, he was recognized and treated well. The shah of Turan showed his unexpected guest generous hospitality; he organized a banquet in his honor, and they drank together.

After dinner, Rostam had retreated to his room when someone knocked on the door. It was Tahmina, daughter of the shah of Turan; she'd spotted the handsome Rostam at the feast and had now come to declare her love. She wanted to bear the clever, famous hero's child. The shah's daughter, tall and slender, had shapely eyebrows, delicate lips, and luscious hair (in my mind, a beautiful shade of red). Rostam couldn't bear to reject this intelligent, sensitive, charming beauty who'd gone to the trouble of coming all the way up to his room. And so they made love. In the morning, Rostam left a bracelet for the unborn child he knew they had conceived and returned to his own country.

Tahmina named her bastard son Sohrab. When he grew to discover that his father was the renowned Rostam, Sohrab declared: "I will go to Iran, I will depose the cruel Shah Kay-Kavus and put my father in his place. Then I will return to Turan and depose Shah Afrasiab, who is as cruel as Kay-Kavus, and take his place on the throne. And so my father Rostam and I will bring together Iran and Turan, joining East and West, to rule justly over the whole of creation."

That was honest, kindhearted Sohrab's plan. But he had underestimated the slyness and cunning of his enemies. Afrasiab, the shah of Turan, knew of Sohrab's intentions but supported him anyway in his war against Persia. He also planted spies in the army to make sure that Sohrab wouldn't recognize his father, Rostam, when they finally came face-to-face. Behind their respective lines, father and son initially watched as the two armies clashed. Finally, a series of dirty tricks and ruses conspired with the vagaries of fate to bring the legendary warrior Rostam and his son Sohrab together on the battlefield. Of course they failed to recognize each other through their armor, just as Oedipus had failed to recognize his father. It was also Rostam's habit to take pains to conceal his identity in battle, lest his renown motivate an opponent, whoever he might be, to give the fight his all. As for the unworldly Sohrab, he was so eager to see his father on the Persian throne that he didn't even consider whom he was fighting. And so these two mighty, valorous warriors, father and son, drew swords and faced off, as the two armies looked on.

Ferdowsi describes at length how father and son grapple, their fight lasting for days, until finally the father slays the son. More than the inherent violence and pathos of the story, what unnerved me so was the feeling of reading something that had actually happened to me. It was at once unsettling and also a feeling I craved. As I leafed through those old volumes, immersing myself in the stories, I felt as if I were in the theater tent in Öngören. Whenever I read about Rostam and Sohrab, I felt as if I were reliving my own memories.

28

STEPPING BACK and examining the matter rationally, I could see what was so familiar about Sohrab and Rostam's tale and its resemblance to the story of Oedipus. There were in fact surprising parallels between Oedipus's life and Sohrab's. But there was one fundamental difference, too: Oedipus murdered his father, while Sohrab was murdered by his father. One is a story of patricide, the other a story of filicide.

Yet this key distinction only accentuated the similarities. As in Oedipus's story, the reader is repeatedly reminded that Sohrab does not know and has never met his father. One concludes that Sohrab is blameless, for he is not aware that the man he has set out to kill is his own father. But that fatal moment is continually delayed.

Just as Oedipus's murder investigation takes a long while to bear fruit, so the *Shahnameh*'s protracted battle between father and son seems to go on forever. On the first day, Rostam and Sohrab fight with short spears, and when these break against their armor, they draw scimitars and resume the battle. Both armies can see the sparks that shower father and son every time their swords clash.

When the swords also shatter, they switch to maces. Their weapons and their shields buckle under the weight of the blows exchanged, and both their exhausted horses slow down. The sketch in the theater tent at Öngören had presented the final moments of this battle.

On the first day, Sohrab is able to wound his father in the shoulder with a blow of the mace, and on the second day, the fight reaches a swifter end. When I got to the part where young Sohrab grabs his father's belt and throws him to the ground, I flinched. Sitting atop him, Sohrab draws a turquoise dagger and is just about to cut his father's throat when Rostam, fighting for his life, tricks the young warrior.

"You cannot slay me now; you must overcome me a second time," says Rostam to his son Sohrab. "Only then will you have earned the right to kill me. That is our tradition. If you respect it, you will be seen as a truly worthy warrior!"

Sohrab heeds the voice inside him telling him to spare his aging opponent this time. But that night, his comrades advise him that he has made a mistake and should not underestimate his enemies. The strong, youthful warrior does not, however, pay his friends much mind.

Then, not long into the third day of battle, Rostam suddenly overpowers his son and throws him to the ground. Before I even had the chance to grasp what had happened, Rostam swiftly thrust his sword into Sohrab's chest and sliced him open, killing his son. I was stunned, just as I had been years ago in the theater tent at Öngören.

Oedipus killed his father—whom he also didn't recognize—with equally surprising speed, and in a fit of mindless rage. In those moments, perhaps neither Oedipus nor Rostam was thinking clearly. It was as if God had driven these fathers and sons temporarily insane so that they would have no qualms slaying each other, thus fulfilling His divine will.

Since each acted in a fit of rage, could Oedipus, who had killed his father, and Rostam, who had killed his son, both be considered innocent? The ancient Greeks watching Sophocles's play would have believed Oedipus's chief crime to be not that he killed his father but that he tried to thwart the fate that God intended for him—just as Master Mahmut had suggested all those years ago. Similarly, Rostam's real sin was not killing his own child but siring a son during a night of passion and then failing to fulfill his paternal duties.

Oedipus punished himself by putting out his own eyes in remorse. Ancient Greek audiences would have been satisfied by this outcome, as due punishment for refusing one's God-given destiny. Likewise, logic dictates that Rostam should have had to pay some kind of price for killing his son. But there was no punishment at the end of this tale from the East—only the reader's sorrow. Wasn't anyone going to make the Eastern father pay?

Sometimes I would wake up in the middle of the night and think about these things as my wife lay sleeping beside me. The neon lights from the street would shine through the half-drawn curtains and onto Ayşe's elegant forehead and expressive lips, and I would think how happy we were even though we didn't have children. I would get out of bed and stare out the window that gave onto the street, and I'd wonder why I kept having the same thoughts over and over again. Outside, it would be snowing or raining in the Istanbul night, the gutters of our old building would sigh, and a flustered police car would drive down the road, flashing its stuttering blue light. These were the years when factions that favored Turkey's entry into the European Union clashed in the street with nationalists and Islamists. All sides deployed the national flag as both an ensign and a weapon, and so enormous Turkish flags billowed over military garrisons and all across Istanbul.

Some nights, the sound of an airplane passing would remind me of Master Mahmut. The whole city would be asleep, and I would have the impression that the plane cruising overhead was sending me a private message. Had I been on that early-morning flight, I would have looked out the window for Master's well, though I probably couldn't have spotted it. Istanbul had by now grown to the point of swallowing up Öngören; Master Mahmut and his well were lost somewhere in that metropolitan morass. I thought once again that if I wanted to know whether I was guilty or not, and at last banish my malaise, I would have to return to Öngören. But still I resisted, making do instead with rereading the *Shahnameh* and *Oedipus the King* and comparing Rostam and Sohrab's tragedy with Oedipus's and other tales.

29

AROUND THIS TIME, I started to develop what would be a lifelong compulsion to compare fathers and sons I met under ordinary circumstances with Oedipus and Rostam. The café manager loudly scolding his assistant as I walked distractedly home from work one evening was a far cry from Rostam, but I could see in his furious underling's green eyes the fleeting desire to grab a kebab knife and gut his boss. On the way to Ayşe's best friend's house for her son's birthday party, I considered whether her husband, a strict, intolerant father, might be comparable to foolish Rostam.

There was a period when I favored the kinds of newspapers that focused on scandals and murders and carried stories that reminded me of Oedipus and Rostam. In those days, two kinds of murder stories were particularly popular with readers in Istanbul and often featured in these tabloids. In the first kind, a father would bed his beautiful young daughter-in-law while his son was away on military service or in prison, after which the son, discovering the truth upon his return, would murder his father. The second kind, which occurred frequently with innumerable variations, was triggered by a sexually frustrated son forcing himself upon his mother in a fit of temporary insanity. When the father tried to stop or punish him, the son would end up killing the father. Such sons the public abhorred, refusing even to utter their names; people didn't hate them so much because they'd murdered their own fathers as because they had violated their own mothers. In prison, some of these patricides would end up getting killed by gang bosses, thugs, or contract killers, someone trying to make a name for himself by eliminating such a degenerate. Nobody objected to these assassinations—not the state, not the prison administrators, certainly not the public.

More than twenty years after digging that well with Master Mahmut, I began to explain my interest in Oedipus and Sohrab to my wife, Ayşe. I never mentioned Master Mahmut, but she began to share my fascination with Sophocles's play and with Ferdowsi's epic as a kind of speculative exercise about the son we didn't have. In private, we would categorize people as Rostam types or Oedipal types. Fathers who inspired fear in their sons despite loving and wanting the best for them reminded us of Rostam, though of course Rostam had abandoned his son. Perhaps sons who resented their fathers and rejected their authority were like Oedipus, but then the question arose: Where were all the abandoned Sohrabs? Sometimes we debated what we needed to do to ensure that a hypothetical son of ours didn't develop an Oedipus or a Sohrab complex. Whenever we called on our friends, we'd be eager to discuss their children as soon as we got home. We had simplistic theories about oppressive fathers and rebellious sons and, conversely, of submissive sons and permissive fathers. By recasting the sorrow of our childlessness into something more profound, we thus strengthened our conjugal bond.

Our household economics were equally opportunistic. Since my company had close ties to the municipal authorities and the national ruling party, we knew in advance what areas had been slated for urban redevelopment: the construction of residential high-rises, new roads, and so on. We bought land accordingly, as well as taking advantage of government subsidies for residential projects. I never thought there was anything unethical about this practice. But I did wonder sometimes what my father would say if he knew that his son's business interests involved rubbing elbows with the ruling party leaders, attending their ostentatious cultural events and fund-raisers, and listening to the pompous speeches they gave at the ceremonies. For years, I had nursed an abiding anger at my father for walking out on us. But now I didn't mind so much anymore, because I knew that he wouldn't approve of what I was doing.

It seems we would all like a strong, decisive father telling us what to do and what not to do. Is it because it is so difficult to distinguish what we should and shouldn't do, what is moral and right from what is sinful and wrong? Or is it because we constantly need to be reassured that we are innocent and have not sinned? Is the need for a father always there, or do we feel it only when we are confused, or anguished, when our world is falling apart?

30

IN MY FORTIES, I began to suffer from a mild insomnia, just as my father had. I would lie awake in the middle of the night until finally, thinking I might as well do something useful, I would move to the studio to pore over whatever files, construction brochures, and contracts I'd brought home from the office. But that material would depress me, and I would only end up even wider awake than before. Eventually, I discovered that reading the *Shahnameh* or *Oedipus the King* purged my thoughts of money and figures and helped me sleep better—like hearing an old fairy tale. Though they were both stories about terrible guilt, my own guilt seemed to subside when I read them again.

Reading the same thing over and over like a prayer was soothing, but in time I became aware that my mind did not respond equally to every scene. Both books were central to the cultures in which they'd originated—Greece or the West on the one hand, and Persia or the

East on the other—but however many times I reread them, I could relate to only so many of the troubles their protagonists suffered or the major ethical and existential questions that were posed. Take Oedipus's sexual relationship with his mother, Jocasta: I couldn't picture it at all but only define it in my mind as a "great crime" before hastily moving on. You might say I was unable to think about it in visual terms.

Another example was the tantalizing search for the father one had never known, the common quest in which Oedipus and Sohrab bore a brotherly resemblance. I'd never dwelled too much on how either had grown up separated from his true father. Perhaps I was afraid that if I did, I might become aware of my own want. When my father left me (as Rostam left Sohrab) and went to prison, later to make a new life for himself, I sought out father figures to replace him and guide me. And I still thought often of Master Mahmut: somewhere in the back of my mind, an ever-shrinking man was digging a well right through the core of the earth, and sometimes he entered my dreams in other guises and told me stories.

One gloomy autumn evening, I went to meet Mrs. Fikriye, chief librarian of the Topkapı Palace Manuscript Library, to whom I was referred by Dr. Haşim, a mutual friend from the Deniz Bookstore, who taught literature at a university. He had informed her of my interest in Rostam and Sohrab, and Mrs. Fikriye had told him, "He should come by so I can show him our beautiful illustrated *Shahnamehs*." (There were still plenty of good people left in Istanbul.) As we sat talking in Sultan Abdulmajid's residence on the palace's vast grounds, she reminded me that the hopeless search for a father could have consequences I hadn't foreseen.

Though the museum's directors never exhibited it, the Topkapı Palace Library held one of the world's finest collections of Persian illuminated manuscripts, its inventory from the fifteenth and sixteenth centuries rivaling that of the gallery of the Golestan Palace in Tehran.

The seeds for this collection were sown in 1514 when Sultan Selim I, having defeated Shah Ismail in the Battle of Chaldiran, south of Lake Van, proceeded to loot Tabriz, returning to Istanbul with a bundle of books and manuscripts. Shah Ismail's treasures had included a number of illuminated *Shahnameh*s, decorated volumes of exceptional beauty, which he had seized from the old Turkmens and the Uzbek Shaybanids he, in his turn, had conquered. In the two centuries to follow, the Safawids and the Ottomans would go to war again and again, and Tabriz would switch hands ten times. But after every battle, when the Safawids sent their peace envoys to the Ottomans, they were sure to include an offering of the illustrated *Shahnameh*s, whose beauty they were so proud of, and soon these manuscripts began to accumulate in the Topkapı Palace treasury.

Mrs. Fikriye generously allowed me to look through the most exquisite of the library's four- or five-hundred-year-old *Shahnameh*s, and together we pored over the miniatures depicting Rostam just after he'd killed Sohrab, wailing with grief over his son's bloody, lifeless form. The primary emotion evoked by these pictures was intense remorse, identical to what I'd been made to feel watching the scene in the theater tent at Öngören. It was the father's remorse for killing his son—the unbearable guilt and shame that conquers us the very moment we realize we have destroyed something beautiful and infinitely precious. In the best of these illustrations, one could practically read in the father's eyes his desperate wish to wind back the last few minutes of his life.

Mrs. Fikriye showed me many miniatures that day. "Thank you for coming," she said as the sky darkened outside. "It can get lonely in here. No one bothers with these old stories anymore. I'm glad you're so interested in Rostam and Sohrab. Why is their story so special to you?"

"The way the father kills his son and then regrets it really gets to me," I said. "I once saw something like it years ago in a theater tent outside Istanbul, and it has never left me."

"Are you on bad terms with your father?" inquired Mrs. Fikriye. When I didn't reply, she changed tack: "In Turkey, we've let the *Shahnameh* fall by the wayside. I suppose this is no longer a world in which to read and savor old epics of warring heroes. But even though Ferdowsi's book has been forgotten, the tales in the *Shahnameh* haven't. They are very much alive and recur in manifold guises."

"How?"

"The other night, we were watching an old movie on Channel Seven," said the chief librarian. "It was an adaptation of the love story of Ardashir and the slave girl Gulnar from the *Shahnameh,* starring İbrahim Tatlıses. My assistant Tuğba and I watch these old Yeşilçam films to remind ourselves of how beautiful Istanbul used to be, but also to identify storylines from the *Shahnameh* and other books. Istanbul has changed so much, hasn't it, Mr. Cem? But the eye can still pick out the old streets and squares. It's the same with the stories from the *Shahnameh.* We were watching another film one day, and though it was set entirely in the present, we could still detect each and every plot point borrowed from 'Farhad and Shirin.' I always say that even if these books are forgotten, their stories are retold so often that they live on somehow. And when we watch these old Yeşilçam melodramas, we remember those tales. Perhaps the people who keep turning to the *Shahnameh* for inspiration to write screenplays for Turkish and Iranian films are a bit like you. It's the same in Pakistan, India, and Central Asia; in all these place they also love these stories and make films of them just like our own Yeşilçam productions."

I explained to Mrs. Fikriye that I was a geologist, not a screenwriter, and that my interest in these ancient tales was the result of a trip I'd taken to Iran. Had she heard that the current Iranian government was trying to recover a miniature of Rostam mourning his son Sohrab? They'd offered rich rewards to anyone who could bring this illustration back to Iran from New York's Metropolitan Museum of Art and were using certain wily art dealers as middlemen.

"I see Dr. Haşim has been bringing you up to speed on the gossip in Islamic book collector circles," said Mrs. Fikriye. "That famous book you are referring to used to be right here in Topkapı. It was stolen and smuggled to the West when the Ottoman sultans decided to move out of the palace, leaving everything behind. First, it fell into the hands of the Rothschilds, then it was sold to the Americans. Like some of its tragic heroes, this book has spent its entire existence in foreign exile. That's why it is always invoked as a nationalist political symbol."

"How do you mean?"

"Have you ever stopped to consider that the people of Turan and Rumelia who frequently appear in the *Shahnameh,* always described in such sneering, resentful terms, are actually Turks?"

"But the *Shahnameh* was composed in the year one thousand," I said with a smile. "The Turks hadn't even left Asia yet."

"Ah, Mr. Cem, you may be better informed and more inquisitive than many so-called academics, but you're still an amateur," said Mrs. Fikriye, gently putting me in my place as she resumed her guided tour.

I wasn't hurt that she'd called me an amateur, but it did remind me how emotive my investigations were. All these illustrations were also populated by women watching their husbands wrestling with their sons and weeping at the sight of their offspring's bloodied corpses cradled in the arms of the men who'd sired and then killed them. As I kept coming across these women, I would sometimes imagine painting their hair red—as in a coloring book.

I thanked Mrs. Fikriye profusely for inviting me to her offices and for the benefit of her expertise, not to mention the hours of her time she was giving up solely to share her knowledge with me. We talked until nightfall on that autumn evening. There were no tourists around; the museum was closed to visitors. Later, as I walked under the Topkapı's porticoes and through its courtyards carpeted with the yellowed leaves of chestnut and plane trees, it occurred to me that what I felt was perhaps equal to alleviating the guilt I couldn't seem to dislodge from my soul, perhaps even turning it into an engineer's literary diversion: a sense of history!

Mrs. Fikriye, who otherwise had no interest in contemporary political intrigues, had nonetheless connected the fate of the most magnificent *Shahnameh* manuscript of all to nationalist politics. This in turn had reminded me of another trait common to Oedipus and Sohrab, one I'd previously overlooked: political exile and estrangement from the motherland . . . My father had always been very emotional on this subject. Some of his militant friends had fled to Germany straight after the military coup, knowing what would befall them if they didn't. Others, like my father himself, had stayed behind, perhaps lacking the means to go or feeling they'd done nothing so awful to warrant leaving. Others still simply thought they wouldn't get caught. But in the end they had all been captured and tortured by the police.

Their search for lost fathers had cast both Oedipus and Sohrab far from the cities and the lands to which they belonged, into places where, vulnerable to exploitation by their countries' foes, they ended up traitors. In both stories, loyalty to family, to king, to father, and to dynasty is placed above loyalty to nation, and the protagonists' treasonous predicaments are never emphasized. Still, in seeking out their respective fathers, Prince Oedipus and Sohrab both ultimately collaborate with the enemies of their own people.

31

Once Ayşe turned thirty-eight and I forty, my wife began resigning herself to the idea that our dream of having children would never come true, and I soon followed her lead. You might say that, faced with the callousness of Turkish doctors and an endless and exhausting series of attempts at Istanbul's American and German hospitals, we simply gave up.

The greatest blessing was that our fatigue and disappointment drew us closer together. We became even better friends, distancing ourselves from other families and more inclined toward intellectual pursuits. Ayşe was fed up with being pitied—and occasionally even subject to calculated cruelty—by the child-rearing housewives she was friends with. She stopped seeing them and started looking for a job. Soon I proposed that she run the company I had decided to start to exploit smaller construction opportunities passed up by my current employers. She would learn fast how to manage engineers and deal with foremen. I'd be the one in charge behind the scenes, anyway. We named the firm Sohrab. This would be our child now.

We started taking trips together like a young couple on a honeymoon. Every time our plane took off, I leaned across my wife's lap and looked out of the window (Ayşe found this very endearing) to find Öngören. In the first year of our travels, I spied from the plane that our plateau in Öngören was now covered with buildings and factories, and the sight made me feel oddly peaceful.

At the start of summer, we moved to an expensive four-room apartment in Gümüşsuyu with a view of the sea. While traveling, we always stayed in the best hotels and saw all the sights, and between museum trips, we squeezed in the occasional consultation at a fertility clinic in London or Vienna. These visits invariably raised our hopes, and the heartbreak was worse with every failure.

At Mrs. Fikriye's suggestion, we sought out museums with Persian manuscripts in their libraries, like the Chester Beatty in Dublin, which a diplomat friend got us into, and the British Museum library the following year, to feast our eyes on illustrated copies of the *Shahnameh.* These sketches and miniatures were very rarely exhibited, and most museumgoers never got to see them. The capable and exceedingly attentive young curatorial assistants, the white gloves they sometimes wore, and the smell of wood and dust that permeated the storerooms with their lemon-colored lighting reminded us of how ancient, how alive, and how fragile these images were

What we learned from these painstakingly detailed miniatures was how ephemeral all those ancient lives had been, how quickly they'd all been forgotten, and how vain we were to think that we could grasp the meaning of life and history by learning a handful of facts. We emerged from the shadowy halls of these museum libraries onto the streets of European capitals feeling we'd been made wiser by virtue of having admired the art.

Like all educated Turks of my father's generation, what I really hoped to find on these trips wandering the shops, the cinemas, and the museums of the Western world was an idea, an object, a painting—anything at all—that might transform and illuminate my own life. One such artifact was Ilya Repin's famous oil painting *Ivan the Terrible and His Son,* which Ayşe and I had stared at awestruck in Moscow's Tretyakov Gallery. The painting shows a father, like Rostam, cradling the bleeding form of the son he's just killed. It looked like the work of a Persian painter who'd been inspired by the foremost exemplars of Rostam and Sohrab scenes but who had also been exposed to Renaissance perspective and chiaroscuro techniques. The way the father—and king—having killed his son in a moment of blind fury, now clasped the bloodied body, horror and remorse etched on his face; the way the son—and prince—lay supine in his father's arms: these were all familiar features. This murderous father was the merciless czar Ivan IV, founder of the Russian state, subject of Eisenstein's film *Ivan the Terrible,* and a favorite of Stalin's. The brutality and remorse emanating from the painting, its stark simplicity, and its single-mindedness were uncannily reminiscent of the ruthless authority of the state.

I felt that same intimately familiar and intimidating fear of authority as I looked up at Moscow's dark starless sky that evening. Ivan the Terrible seemed both regretful of what he'd done and also full of boundless love and tenderness toward his son. I was reminded of a horrifying aphorism my father had taught me, expressing the ambivalence of officials toward gifted artists and writers who criticize their regimes:

"Poets must first be hanged, then mourned at the gallows."

There was a time when any new Ottoman sultan's first act upon ascending the throne was to execute all the other princes (whose deaths he would subsequently mourn, for they were his brothers, after all). This bloodshed he would justify according to the logic that, where the state is concerned, one has to "be cruel to be kind." I yearned to discuss all this with my father, but while I still missed him, I was reluctant to seek him out and perhaps discover he disapproved of me.

Our travels to the museums of Europe were intended to blot out the pain of childlessness and also, as we kept breezily telling ourselves, to find "a picture of Oedipus." But apart from one or two academic depictions of Sophocles's play, we couldn't find much at all. Ingres's *Oedipus and the Sphinx,* displayed at the Louvre, made a minimal impression. The only thing I can remember about it is wondering whether the outline of Thebes, a pale hill in the background through the mouth of the cave in the foreground, was even a remotely realistic representation of the city.

Another version, Gustave Moreau's *Oedipus and the Sphinx,* at the museum bearing his name in Paris, was painted fifty years after the Ingres. It, too, focuses on Oedipus's triumph over the "riddle" of the Sphinx, rather than on his crimes and sins. There was a copy of this painting at the Metropolitan Museum in New York, and forty steps farther, in the gallery of Islamic art, we were confounded by the sight of Rostam killing his son Sohrab. The Metropolitan's dimly lit Islamic wing was typically empty, and we felt as if we were investigating someplace long abandoned. While Moreau's painting could be appreciated even by those who did not know the story behind it, this illustration from the *Shahnameh* was moving to us only because we knew what it was about. The aesthetic enjoyment it evoked was, so to speak, of a much narrower kind.

Even more intriguing was the fact that Europe, with its far broader and richer tradition of depicting human subjects, had failed to produce more images of Oedipus; there were no paintings of the pivotal scenes, such as when Oedipus murders his father or when he sleeps with his mother. European painters may have been able to describe these moments in words and comprehend their significance. But they were incapable of visualizing the acts described and rendering them on the canvas. And so they confined themselves to the scene in which Oedipus solves the riddle of the Sphinx. By contrast, in Muslim lands, where portraiture had never thrived and indeed was often banned, artists had fervently created thousands of depictions of the exact moment when Rostam kills his son Sohrab.

Only Pier Paolo Pasolini, the Italian novelist, painter, and filmmaker, had ever broken the unwritten rule with his film *Oedipus Rex*. I watched his disquieting adaptation when it was screened as part of a weeklong Pasolini retrospective sponsored by the Italian consulate in Istanbul. The young actor playing Oedipus embraces, kisses, and sleeps with his mother, played by the older but still captivating Silvana Mangano. When mother and son made love, the audience of Istanbul cinephiles and intellectuals filling Casa d'Italia's wood-paneled auditorium that night sank into a deafening silence.

Pasolini had shot the film in Morocco against a backdrop of local landscapes, reddish soil, and an ancient, ghostly red fort.

"I wouldn't mind watching this red film again," I said. "Do you think we might find a DVD or cassette copy somewhere?"

"That beautiful Silvana Mangano . . . even her hair was red," said my wife.

32

READERS SHOULDN'T IMAGINE us as a couple of effete intellectuals who did nothing but watch art films and look at old manuscripts and paintings all day. Ayşe went out with me every morning, taking her place at the helm of our company, Sohrab, whose rapid growth astonished us both. I'd stop by its bustling offices in Nişantaşı every evening after leaving my day job. We would work with our engineers until late at night and dine out somewhere before finally going home.

Toward the end of 2011, a year to the day after the Pasolini retrospective opened, I handed in my resignation, planning to devote my time exclusively to Sohrab. I still spent my days supervising construction sites all over Istanbul, except now I was doing it for my own firm, and while our driver from Samsun crept through the city's traffic jams, I kept doing business on my mobile phone. Most of the suppliers, site managers, and estate agents I spoke to during those inching rides were likewise stuck in traffic somewhere else in the city. Sometimes they would interrupt our discussion of building codes or profit margins to argue with the driver or to stop people on the street and ask them what that area was called. I would be dismayed to realize that my interlocutor was probably gridlocked in some rising neighborhood no one had ever heard of before but which was already overflowing with people. Everyone was building, buying whatever they could afford to buy, and the city was growing at a baffling pace.

Whenever I noticed poor people, young people, street vendors, or parking attendants jostling in the street, I would recognize that I was now a wealthy middle-aged man, and—more important—one well accustomed to this condition. I would ask myself, *Are there any joys in my life other than my wife's companionship and my layman's enthusiasm for some ancient tales?* I would think about my father, I would call my wife, and I would try to convince myself that I was at peace in the urban throng. Childlessness had trained me in melancholy and humility. Sometimes I stopped to think that if I'd had a child, he or she would have been twenty by now.

Initially we spent all the money we were making on designer clothes, decorative figurines, Ottoman treasures, antiques, handwritten royal edicts, exquisite carpets, and Italian furniture; but this conspicuous consumption, far from fulfilling either of us, merely left us feeling shallow and insincere. A part of me was still strongly disposed to resent the very friends to whom we would have wanted to display our finery, precisely because their existence encouraged us to do so. This was probably owing to the influence of my father's left-wing views. So even as our fortune grew, we continued to get by with our ordinary Renault Megane.

We started investing most of our money in land for new construction projects and old buildings in promising neighborhoods. As we bought up empty plots on the outskirts of the city, I felt like a sultan trying to forget his lack of an heir by annexing new provinces to his empire. Like Istanbul itself, Sohrab was growing at an astonishing rate.

We'd equipped our car with one of those satellite navigation devices that announced what street you were on at any given moment. We would follow the route traced on its screen all the way to new neighborhoods we'd never seen before, and up hills from which you could see the Princes' Islands on the horizon, and marvel at the city's sprawl. But instead of endlessly complaining, as so many others did, that the old city was being wiped out, we welcomed these new neighborhoods as business opportunities. Every day at the office, Ayşe perused the public auction notices in the government's *Official Gazette* and combed through the daily *Hürriyet*'s and other websites' real-estate pages.

One day, Ayşe called my attention to an auction she thought we should bid in. Before I'd even had the chance to look at the notice, she'd already located the lot on Google Maps and zoomed in. When I saw the word "Öngören" on the screen, my heart leaped. But like a seasoned assassin, I remained impassive. I maneuvered the cursor around the screen and stole up on the most important town in my life.

The word "Öngören" had been affixed to the Station Square. Some of the surrounding streets seemed vaguely familiar, but Google's map had marked them as they were officially known rather than with names like "Diners' Lane," by which the locals had known them nearly thirty years ago. So there were very few names I could recognize. I found the station first, then the cemetery, and by these I tried to work out where our plateau would be on the map, but there was no way to tell by the street names, for the whole area was now covered with roads.

"Murat says they're going to build a new highway through here and there is a spot with nice views that might be perfect for a new residential. Shall we go take a look on Sunday morning on the way to your mother's?"

Murat was that same university friend who'd invited me to Tehran. He'd dropped all his other business ventures to join the construction gold rush, and thanks to his friends in the conservative ruling party, his turnover dwarfed ours, though he was kind enough to tip us off when an area was likely to appreciate.

"I feel there's some sort of curse on this Öngören," I told Ayşe, "like a place in one of those fairy tales they used to tell us as children. Let's leave it for now. Besides, what kind of view could you sell to people who've always had that glimmering night sky to look at?"

33

There was a drought in Istanbul that summer after an unusually dry spring. With the reservoirs low, the city's decrepit plumbing could pump only half as much water as usual. In some neighborhoods, mothers and fathers would wake up in the middle of the night to listen to the pipes, just as they used to do as children, so that when the water was turned back on they could be ready to shower and to refill the tub with a reserve of fresh water. Water rationing became a subject of fierce political debate and occasional violence throughout the city.

The end of summer brought days of lightning and heavy, roaring rainfall, flooding some areas of Istanbul. One night in the wake of those stormy days my father invited us for dinner. His new wife had sent Ayşe an e-mail. "Is he in such a bad state that he can't write to us himself?" I wondered.

He was renting an apartment in a new residential development behind Sarıyer, on a hill overlooking the Black Sea. It took us two hours to drive there. The Black Sea was a smudge in the distance, and even though the tiny place was new, it already looked dilapidated, teeming with my father's forty-year-old possessions, which I remembered from my childhood. Rainwater had stained the ceilings. Once we'd dragged ourselves through the initial pleasantries, strained jokes, and exchange of endearments, I was struck by my father's weariness and his deprivation.

As a child, I had idolized him, always desperate to enjoy a little more of his time, to talk to him, to have him pick me up in his arms and tease me. But now that man had grown feeble; he'd slowed down, hunched over, and worst of all accepted the defeat handed him by life. The former womanizer who'd always dressed so impeccably no longer seemed to care about the clothes he wore or about his health, joking half-heartedly about the sorry state of each: "Leftists care about principles, not appearances."

Nevertheless, he kept flirting with his beaming, bucktoothed, busty wife, firing off double entendres that hinted at their robust sex life. Ayşe joined in their banter, and soon the conversation drawing on our collective experience turned to love, marriage, and youth. Since I couldn't bring myself to discuss such personal matters in front of my father, I took my glass of *rakı* and retreated to the bookshelf in the corner, where I glanced at the spines of the old leftist tomes he'd owned since I was a child. I did, however, continue to listen to the conversation at the dinner table, and when my father's wife mentioned the terrible water shortage that summer, I thought of Master Mahmut.

"I bet you could still dig a well the old way, up here in Sarıyer," I piped up. "You'd just need a wooden mold and a slide to pour the concrete through."

"What do you know about it?" said my father.

"In 1986, the summer after you left us, I needed to pay for cram school so I spent a month as apprentice to an old master welldigger," I said. "I've never even told Ayşe about it."

"Why not? Were you ashamed of your stint in the proletariat?" said my father.

I was glad to have finally told him about my time of toil—though my father had no objections to our being well-off. My mistake was not letting it go at that; instead, I let myself get carried away, telling my father about Oedipus and Sohrab and Rostam, all the reading I'd done, the museums we'd visited in Europe, all just to show him how well versed I was in cultural and social history.

"The real authority on these matters is Wittfogel," said my father dismissively. "I've got his book here somewhere. Not that anyone reads him anymore, they've forgotten all about him . . . What would he say if he knew there was a French translation of one of his books tucked away on an Istanbul leftist's bookshelf?"

He had formulated the same kind of question I'd often asked myself about him ("What would my father say if he knew?"), and so my curiosity was piqued. I scanned the dusty volumes on the rickety bookshelf.

As I drank another glass of *rakı*, my father sat quiet at the end of the table. Our wives had started talking between themselves.

"Dad . . . ," I said. "Those militant groups from your time . . . do you remember the National Revolutionary Maoists . . . what were they like?"

"I knew a lot of guys from that group," said my father. "And plenty of girls, too," he added lasciviously, like a drunken schoolboy.

"What *kind* of girls?" asked my father's wife, as if to boast of her husband's youthful dalliances.

I'd had a sneaking suspicion for all these years, however artfully I'd managed to keep it hidden even from myself: it was perfectly possible that during his militant heyday my father had been acquainted with the troupe that staged the Theater of Morality Tales and might even have seen the Red-Haired Woman perform one of its political plays. I wondered: What would he have thought of the first woman I'd ever slept with?

By now, however, he'd started to sober up, his face again composed in that same careful expression of detachment he customarily assumed whenever he wanted to conceal the details of his personal life and militant activities from me. He seized upon a lull to ask me gravely how my mother was doing. I told him I'd bought her a house in Gebze—she didn't want to move to Istanbul—and Ayşe and I drove up to see her every other Sunday. That was enough: "I'm glad your mother is well!" he said, closing the subject.

I'd had too much drink, so Ayşe drove on the way home. "Why didn't you tell me you'd worked as a welldigger's apprentice?" she asked like a mother gently reprimanding her son. It was past midnight, and as the car wound its way through the Belgrad Forest and its dams, I dozed off in the front passenger seat to the sound of cicadas croaking in a cool thyme-scented breeze.

A copy of Wittfogel's now-outmoded treatise *Oriental Despotism* rested on my lap. But when we got home, I switched the computer on instead. I found Öngören on Google Maps and quietly zoomed in from the sky. I saw billboards advertising a patisserie and a bank on the Station Square and a service station on the highway to Istanbul. I tried to remember each of these spots and to picture all the places I'd passed while following the Red-Haired Woman around.

If she had been truthful about her age when we met in Öngören, she would be sixty by now. My father's new wife was more or less the same vintage, and so I could easily imagine him living with the Red-Haired Woman in that little apartment overlooking the Black Sea.

I'd forbidden myself from trying to find out where she was or what she was doing, and I hadn't happened upon a single trace of her in the almost thirty years since our meeting. Of course, I did wonder about her from time to time, particularly during TV commercials for detergents, credit cards, and retirement plans featuring women of her generation—including some who no doubt had come up performing in the same folk theaters as she had, playing the part of the contented mother (or, in later years, the happy grandmother). Some evenings I would watch soap operas set in Ottoman palaces hundreds of years ago, and I'd peer at the screen through senses dulled by *rakı,* trying to work out whether the tall, full-lipped courtesan teaching the sultan's latest young consort how to handle harem politics and keep her man interested was actually Her or whether I had simply forgotten the face of the first woman I'd slept with. Sometimes a voice-over actress dubbing a foreign TV series into Turkish might sound like her, and I would try to recall how she'd delivered her furious final monologue years ago in the yellow tent and the sound of that voice I'd latched on to as we strolled through the Station Square that night.

Our company was flourishing, but I was overworked, and when stress woke me one night, I stared in wonder at an e-mail from the veteran engineer who now handled Sohrab's real-estate investments and was forwarding an advertisement for a property in Öngören. On offer was an old warehouse and workshop near where Master Mahmut and I had dug our well. Thirty years on, the derelict buildings themselves were mostly useless; what was really being advertised was the land they sat on and the development opportunities presented. Without consulting Ayşe, who was still sleeping, I wrote our employee to express our interest.

34

KARL A. WITTFOGEL'S *Oriental Despotism* had certainly had its moment, but neither Ayşe nor I could understand at first why my father had referred to it. It contained nothing about Oedipus or Sohrab or anything else I'd been talking about. It was obvious that he had never read it but merely leafed through it because it was considered a classic leftist text on Eastern societies.

First published in 1957, at the height of the Cold War, the book contains long discussions of droughts and floods. Wittfogel devotes much attention to the network of canals, dams, roads, and aqueducts needed to support agriculture in the challenging terrain of certain Asian nations, like China, as well as to the vast bureaucracies required to build that kind of infrastructure. He argues that such organizational structures can be established only under strictly authoritarian regimes, whose rulers brook no resistance or rebellion. Thus, Wittfogel continues, rather than fill the harems and the ranks of officialdom with the independent-minded, such rulers prefer to govern by surrounding themselves with slaves and sycophants.

"When a king treats his wives and ministers that way, it's not hard to imagine him killing off his own son," said Ayşe. "That's no surprise. We know exactly what these people are like. But it doesn't explain the court painters. Why should they have so relished depicting that awful moment?"

"Because they had a chance to paint a weeping king," I said. "Besides, those scenes are only in appearance all about remorse and sorrow . . . The real purpose was to emphasize the sultan's absolute power. After all, he's the one commissioning the art in the first place—not the foolish, pathetic Sohrabs of this world."

"So Sohrab was just foolish, but was Oedipus any smarter?" said Ayşe.

The lure of Wittfogel may have quickly faded, but this book suggested by my father did point to a connection between the nature of a civilization and its approach to notions of patricide and filicide. For that alone I was glad to have consulted this encyclopedic historical and anthropological treatise on waterways and "hydraulic societies" in Asia.

By winter, I'd decided to buy that parcel of land in Öngören. Istanbul's surplus population was sweeping into the area in wave upon wave. Furthermore, a while back, Murat had told us that the roads and ramps to the third bridge over the Bosphorus, soon to be built across the Black Sea side, would pass through and thus breathe new life into these neighborhoods. I needed to stop finding excuses in folktales, bad omens, and old memories and start putting Sohrab first.

We'd dedicated all our energies to the firm, but whenever I considered our lack of children, I lost heart: Who would inherit all this once I was gone? Anyway, even if I'd had a son, he would probably have done just as I had, choosing a completely different path instead of following in his father's footsteps. But at least he would still have been my son! He might even have become a writer. The stories of Oedipus and Sohrab seemed altogether trivial in comparison.

My father's wife called Ayşe's mobile one night to tell us he'd been unwell. We got into the car immediately, but the drive there took exactly three hours and fifteen minutes from our office to their house. I was taken aback, and even somewhat irritated, when I saw no light in their windows, and when my father's wife opened the door in tears, my first thought was that they must have had an argument. But as soon as I stepped inside, I realized that my father had died. Someone switched the lights on, and I felt remorseful as I gazed at what I hadn't wanted to see: my father stretched out on the same couch on which he'd sat regaling us with his stories on our last visit.

When had he passed away? If it happened while we were stuck in traffic, it somehow had to have been my fault. But perhaps he was already dead when we got the phone call. I couldn't look at him, but, like some detective, I kept asking his weeping widow that same question over and over. She couldn't answer.

Once we had decided that we would spend the night with her at the house, I started drinking the Club Rakı I had found in the fridge. We called a doctor who confirmed what we already suspected, that my father had died of heart failure. As I read the certificate, I myself was on the verge of tears and, again later, when the three of us carried him into the bedroom and laid him on a fresh set of sheets. Maybe I did cry, but his wife's sobs were so loud that they drowned out any sound I might have made.

It was well after midnight when my wife went to sleep on the couch and my father's wife on the spare bed while I lay down in bed beside him. Everything about my poor father—his hair, his cheeks, his arms, the creases in his shirt, and even his smell—was exactly as I remembered it from childhood.

My eyes roamed over the skin on his neck. One day when I was seven, my parents took me to the beach on Heybeli Island. They wanted to teach me how to swim: my mother would lower me belly-first into the water, and I would flail and splash about trying to reach my father standing three steps away. Every time I came close, he would take another step back so that I'd have to swim just a bit farther. But in my desperation to grasp him, I'd yell, "Daddy, don't go!" I'd scream so much and become so agitated that he couldn't help smiling as he raised his sturdy arms to lift me out of the water like a kitten, nestling my head against his chest or in the crook of his neck, the very spot I was looking at now, which even at the seaside retained his unique scent of biscuits and floral soap. Every single time, he'd furrow his brows and say:

"There's nothing to be afraid of, Son. I'm here, all right?"

"All right," I'd gasp, basking in the joy and comfort of his arms.

35

WE BURIED MY FATHER in Feriköy Cemetery. There were three types of mourner at the funeral: in the front rows, close and distant relatives—including us and his weeping widow—toward the back; assorted contractors, engineers, and businessmen there mostly for my sake; and finally, standing around in twos and threes, his old militant friends, smoking as we awaited the call to prayer.

I would love to tell you more about the funeral, but I suppose it isn't strictly relevant, so I won't go into detail. As the crowd in Feriköy Cemetery dispersed, a stocky man with an endearing face came up to me and embraced me with all his strength. "You might not know who I am, but I've known you for years, Mr. Cem," he said.

When he realized I didn't recognize him, he apologized and stuck his business card in my breast pocket.

I didn't look at it again until I went back to work two weeks later. I tried to remember the names and faces of all the people I'd met during my summer in Öngören, when I was sixteen, trying to place this Mr. Sırrı Siyahoğlu, who'd said he'd known me back then, and whose card indicated he was now offering "printing services for business cards, invitations, and advertisements." My mind kept calling up the face of Ali, my fellow apprentice. After the Red-Haired Woman and Master Mahmut, he was the one whose fate I was most interested in.

But I still couldn't remember Mr. Sırrı, so I sent him an e-mail at the address on the business card he'd printed for himself. I thought that if we met, I could ask him what had become of that old Öngören crowd while also sounding him out on the area's real-estate prospects. And what better way of acting as if nothing had happened than to return to the scene of the crime years later in the guise of a contractor?

Our meeting ten days later at the Palace Pudding Shop in Nişantaşı was as brief as it was disconcerting. We didn't bother with small talk; that might have been my fault. I spent every moment of our encounter feeling that I had only to ask and I would find out everything I'd always wanted to know, while sensing simultaneously that I might be too afraid to do so.

Mr. Sırrı was even more thickset and overweight than he'd seemed at the funeral. I still couldn't place him among the faces I recalled from that month in Öngören. But before I could fret too much about that, he admitted that while he'd always known who I was, we'd never met face-to-face until my father's funeral.

He'd known my father personally and had always thought very highly of him. So he was glad of the chance to pay his respects. He could tell who I was on first sight, since I looked a lot like my father: just as handsome and wearing the same kind, honest expression. My father had been a paragon of patriotism and self-sacrifice. He'd given up everything for his country, and he'd done it all out of the goodness of his heart. He'd been tortured for his beliefs, but they'd never broken him; he'd languished in prison, but unlike some others, he hadn't changed his tune. It was unfortunate that his own friends had slandered him and caused him such distress.

"What kind of slander, Mr. Sırrı?"

"It's ancient history now, militant gossip, Mr. Cem, and I don't want to waste your valuable time with such deplorable nonsense. There is just one favor I'd like to ask of you. Your company Sohrab is after my humble patch of land, but your estate agents and your engineers are trying to cheat me. Your father was the kind of man who would not tolerate injustice, and I thought you should know what's been going on."

He'd been offered less than the going rate for his land because others had come forward claiming to own a share. But actually the place belonged to him alone.

"Mr. Sırrı, can you tell me the exact location of your property, and where it's registered?"

"I've made a photocopy of the title deed. As you'll see, it says there are other stakeholders, but don't let that fool you."

While I examined the deed and tried to work out where his land was situated, I said with feigned indifference: "I spent some time in Öngören myself, years ago. I'm familiar with the area."

"I know, Mr. Cem. You visited my friends' theater tent in the summer of 1986. Mr. Turgay and his wife were my guests for about a month around that time; they stayed in my apartment while Mr. Turgay's parents stayed on the floor above, facing the Station Square."

Mr. Sırrı was the signmaker in whose apartment I'd made love with the Red-Haired Woman! The woman who'd answered his doorbell later and told me the theater troupe had left, she was surely his wife. How could I not have seen it before?

"You were digging a well with Master Mahmut on that plateau outside town," he said. "My little plot is just down the road from your well. When Master Mahmut finally hit water, all the industrialists came running to try and get their hands on some land. I wasn't making much from painting signs . . . But my wife and I managed to scrape a bit together and bought ourselves a little parcel a couple of years later. Now this land is my family's only asset."

I had just discovered what some part, perhaps every part, of me had known all along but never really believed: not only had Master Mahmut survived, he'd gone on digging until he found water. I tried to digest what I'd learned, staring at the customers that populated the pudding shop without really seeing them—students getting a quick snack, housewives shopping, and men in business suits—but my mind was irretrievably in the past.

Why had I spent almost thirty years believing that I might have accidentally killed Master Mahmut?

It was probably because I'd read *Oedipus the King* and relied on its truths. At least that's what I wanted to think. From Master Mahmut I'd learned to believe in the force of old stories. And like Oedipus, I couldn't resist investigating my ancient crime.

"Mr. Sırrı, may I ask, how did you know Master Mahmut?"

When Master Mahmut found water after my return to Istanbul, Hayri Bey rewarded him with gifts and further jobs. He was treated with great reverence because his shoulder had been maimed when a bucket fell on him during a dig. Hayri Bey commissioned Master Mahmut to dig two more wells, linking them with underground tunnels and storage tanks. Other factories and wash-and-dye plants began to enlist his services to design their own water storage systems, as well as to oversee excavations and the pouring of cement. With welldigging having become a dying art, Master Mahmut had ended up settling in Öngören with his crippled shoulder, remaining there until the day of his death.

"When did Master Mahmut die?"

"It's been more than five years," said Mr. Sırrı. "They buried him in the cemetery on the slope. His funeral was attended by his apprentices from Öngören, fellow welldiggers, and many businessmen."

"Master Mahmut was like a father to me," I said, wide-eyed.

I could tell from the way Mr. Sırrı was looking at me that he knew I'd wronged Master Mahmut in some way and that Master Mahmut had died holding a grudge. But since he needed my help, Mr. Sırrı was reluctant to overstate the matter. Did he realize that I'd panicked and abandoned my master at the bottom of a well thirty years ago because I thought I'd killed him?

How had Master Mahmut made it out of the well? I was desperate to find out, and to ask everything there was to know about the Red-Haired Woman, but I held my tongue.

"Master Mahmut always spoke of you as his most cultured apprentice," said Mr. Sırrı, fumbling for something nice to say.

I suspected that this wasn't all Master Mahmut had said about me, that he must have added something like "It's the bookish ones you have to worry about." I couldn't blame him. It was my fault his shoulder had been crushed.

Mr. Sırrı was oblivious to the fact that his house had been the scene of my first sexual encounter. Resisting the direct questions I actually wanted to ask, I was able, in a roundabout way, to learn the following: Mr. Sırrı and his wife had moved out of that ugly block with big windows overlooking the Station Square. The building had been demolished, and a shopping mall built in its place. Nowadays all the local youths hung out there. He would be happy to show me around Öngören if I cared to see his property in person, and he'd have me over for dinner whether I liked it or not. He'd long left the movement, but he hadn't severed all ties with his old friends. He still bought a copy of *National Revolution* every now and then, but not as faithfully as he used to, since its positions had grown rather extreme. "They'd do better to write about fraud and injustice in the construction industry instead of harping on American imperialism," he said.

Was there a threat hidden in these words?

"Don't worry, Mr. Sırrı, I'll talk to my people, they'll make sure you're treated honorably. But now there's something I'd like to ask you. These rumors you mentioned about my father . . ."

My father's case wasn't unique. Turkey was then a backward country. Even well-meaning Marxist militants, especially those from the eastern regions, could still possess a "feudal" mentality. They disapproved of men and women mixing, of overt flirtation, and certainly of love affairs within the group. Such banned behavior was sure to result in jealousies and rows within the movement. So the organization frowned on my father's romance.

"The girl was beautiful, but she'd already caught the eye of someone in the very top ranks of the National Revolutionaries," said Mr. Sırrı.

This caused the situation to get out of hand, until eventually my father left that group and joined another. The more senior militant went on to marry the girl, but eventually he was shot dead by the gendarmes, and the girl, unable to break with the group, wound up marrying his younger brother. My father's passion for that spirited girl had been thwarted, but perhaps it was just as well, for it had allowed him to do the smart thing and marry a girl outside the movement, and together, they'd had me. He hoped I wouldn't be too troubled by these old stories, now that my father had passed away.

"It's all in the past, Mr. Sırrı, there's nothing to be upset about. They're just old stories."

"Actually, Mr. Cem, these are all people you know."

"Which people?"

"The younger brother the girl ended up with was Mr. Turgay. Your father's sweetheart was that actress who lived in my apartment."

"What?"

"That woman with the red hair, Gülcihan. Well, her hair used to be brown back then, but she was your late father's young lover."

"Oh, really? And what might they all be up to these days?"

"We've all drifted apart, Mr. Cem . . . They pitched their tent and put on shows for the soldiers for two more summers, but after that they never came back. I left the movement, too, like all those militants who give up and move on to other cities once they start having children . . . Her son is an accountant, he does my bookkeeping. But there are a few old-timers like me left in Öngören; we'd be happy to have you."

I didn't ask him anything more about the Red-Haired Woman that day. Mr. Sırrı had tried to soften the blow by improvising a little, bringing his account forward by six or seven years to a time before my parents had met. But I remembered that when I was nine, my father had disappeared for two years. During that absence my mother seemed to lose all regard for him and was far angrier at him than usual. Politics had certainly figured in his disappearance, but there seemed to be another, more furtive element to it as well. I inferred as much from the whispers I overheard at the time and from the nature of my mother's fury, which seemed directed less toward the state and more toward my father's friends from the movement.

On leaving the pudding shop with Mr. Sırrı, I felt myself in a stupor, worn out from all the things I'd learned from the old sign painter and the effort of masking my shock. I walked the streets of the city for miles like a fatherless, childless phantom.

36

THAT EVENING I told Ayşe how, while looking into some land we might want to buy, I'd met someone who'd told me all about things in old Öngören. More than guilty or regretful, I felt betrayed and belittled. What would my father have said were he still alive? What would he have thought knowing that we had both slept with the same woman within seven or eight years of each other? I tried not to dwell on that. I wanted to confide in my wife. But I didn't want her to see how affected I was by what I'd found out. I was afraid of the Red-Haired Woman.

I had a gnawing urge to know more, but I dreaded what I might learn. For all the effort I'd put into being a decent human being, I was still oppressed by the same bottomless remorse. The terror of being blamed for something even when we've done nothing wrong is a fear that manifests itself only in dreams. I felt it all too often.

Sohrab's construction portfolio continued to expand, to the point where we could no longer deal with everything by ourselves. We put Ayşe's cousin in charge of buying and selling real estate. We even started talking like Murat: "We've bought all this land behind Beykoz, and do you know, I don't think we've ever even been there!" When we confessed to friends that we had no idea what lay beyond Şile, even though Sohrab had purchased "a ton of acres over there," we glowed with the oblivious pride of parents—for Sohrab was our son. He was growing up much faster than most children, outperforming his peers, and winning accolades for his business acumen.

Sometimes I would naïvely ask myself what the purpose of my life was and grow disheartened. Could the reason be that we had no children, nobody to inherit all this once I was gone? The more demoralized I felt, the more I took refuge in Ayşe's companionship. She had intuited that our bond was nourished by my need to be close to a strong, intelligent woman. She knew I would never cheat on her. She did not believe I could sustain any kind of emotional life, keep a secret, or pursue a clandestine fling without her knowledge. At work, if we went more than an hour without speaking, one of us would call the other's mobile and ask "Where are you?" In fact, our intimacy bred such a sense of self-satisfied superiority that it ultimately caused us to make a mistake costing Sohrab dearly.

It was the beginning of 2013, and other construction companies were growing just as we were, exploiting changes in the building code to erect multiple-story blocks, and conducting national advertising campaigns on TV and in newspapers to sell their apartments. We succumbed to temptation and followed suit, signing on with one of the slick advertising agencies behind these efforts.

Leading contractors would often appear in their own ads to attest to the quality of the homes they'd built. This had been a popular ploy ever since the first residential high-rises began to appear: here was the venerable builder himself in suit and tie standing by his work, obviously not the kind of man to cut corners and sell you a home destined to collapse with the smallest earthquake!

The advertising agency pointed out how young, sophisticated, and modern we were compared with those old men in most of the commercials; if we were to appear together in a campaign for Sohrab, it would immediately set us apart from our provincial rivals. We initially demurred at the idea, but the yoking together of the words "modern" and "Sohrab" dazzled us, and soon we were starring in our own ads.

Even while still filming, we already had misgivings. We were made to enact the affected, ostentatious, Westernized lifestyle of a wealthy couple—a kind of life we didn't even lead. Our images first appeared in newspapers and on billboards, and once they started running on TV, they became famous, causing us no end of embarrassment with friends and family, just as we'd feared. Sohrab quickly sold all of its relatively expensive and still-unfinished apartments in residential developments spread over three different corners of Istanbul (Kavacık, Kartal, and Öngören), while the clothes we'd worn and the manner we'd assumed in the commercials became the object of mockery among everyone who knew us. Our more well meaning friends, though no less amused at first, tried to warn us: "Is such exposure really wise?" In the Ottoman Empire, as in Russia, Iran, or China today, the rich would always hide their wealth for fear of the ruthless state.

So we stayed indoors and kept the television switched off as we waited for this media nightmare to blow over. Sohrab, our son, seemed to have temporarily transfigured into a jailer.

Meanwhile, we'd begun receiving letters—including some hate

mail. We never got more than a dozen of these a week, and I discarded most of them immediately. But there was one which I held on to:

Mr. Cem,

I wish I could respect you; you're my father.
Sohrab has crossed the line in Öngören.
As your son, I wanted to warn you.
Write to me at this address and I'll explain everything.
Don't be afraid of your son.

Enver

An e-mail address was given at the bottom. I figured it must be someone from Öngören trying to squeeze money out of us with threats and gossip, like Sırrı Siyahoğlu. Admittedly, I liked the respect he'd shown calling me his father. But I wondered what he could have meant by "crossing the line," so I consulted our lawyer, Mr. Necati.

"Everyone knows that you were a welldigger's apprentice in Öngören about thirty years ago, back when it was still nothing more than a little godforsaken military outpost," he explained. "But after those splashy commercials, what was once gossip has become the stuff of legend. The people of Öngören are flattered to see that a young man who used to dig wells among them is now a rich contractor showing off his modern lifestyle on TV with his wife. But that same pride also promotes unreasonable expectations about what their land is worth, and so at the first round of negotiations, their affection turns into loathing. The hatred is fed partly by your television persona, which makes you seem a snob and perhaps even a bit of a heathen, but it's also stirred by the thought that something bad happened between you and their beloved Master Mahmut all those years ago. As the man who brought water to

Öngören, he is virtually a local saint. It's this perception you'll have to rectify somehow. If you would just take a moment to explain in person to the people of Öngören how you spent a whole summer there thirty years ago searching for water at Master Mahmut's side, they'd realize you're one of them, and Sohrab would be spared further grief."

37

BUT I WAS STILL HESITANT to go to Öngören. Perhaps I'd spent so many years brooding over the stories of Oedipus and Sohrab that my soul was permanently beset with foreboding.

Five weeks later, Mr. Necati asked to have a word with me in private.

"Mr. Cem, there is a man claiming to be your son."

"Who is that?"

"Enver. The one who wrote to you."

"He's an actual person?"

"Apparently. He's twenty-six. He says you slept with his mother in Öngören in 1986."

Low leaden clouds hung over Istanbul. We were sitting in my office in Sohrab's headquarters, which took up the top three floors of the business center–cum–shopping mall at the end of Valikonağı Avenue in Nişantaşı.

"You would have been sixteen at the time he claims it happened," said Necati as he registered my silence. "It was almost thirty years ago. Back in the day, a judge wouldn't even have considered a suit in which so much time has passed. Until recently there were strict statutes of limitations on paternity claims. Ordinarily they had to be filed within a year from the child's birth . . . but at the very latest within a year after the child's eighteenth birthday . . . It's been eight years since this child turned eighteen."

"What if he's telling the truth?"

"We've looked into it and it appears that the mother was married to an actor when the child was conceived. In order to protect the institution of the family as well as preserving the authority and honor of fatherhood, Turkish law stipulates that a child born of a married woman must be registered as her husband's son, whatever anyone else might claim. How could it be any other way? Just imagine what would happen if a woman were to say, 'I slept with another man and this child is his son, not my husband's'; if her husband and in-laws didn't kill her, she'd end up in prison for adultery."

"But the law has changed?"

"It's medical science that's changed, Mr. Cem. In the past, a particularly conscientious judge would have had to haul the supposed father and son into court and stand them side by side to look for similarities. 'Do you know this child's mother?' he'd ask the older man. 'Are there any photographs or witnesses?' he'd ask the young claimant. But now all they need to match fathers to their sons is a couple of blood samples for a DNA test. Time was, this would have been considered an assault on the very foundations of society."

"But how does it hurt society for a child to find out who his real father is?"

"You'd be amazed at the stories of my lawyer friends who handle such cases, Mr. Cem. There are men who like to carry on with girls from poorer backgrounds, and if they happen to get them pregnant, they use their superior knowledge of the law to lead the girl on with promises of marriage 'next year' only to marry her off finally to some underling, as the old Ottoman generals used to do . . . I've also heard of cases of an extended family living under a single roof; a nephew seduces his uncle's young wife, or a relation visiting from the village impregnates the neighbor's wife, or his brother's wife, or even his own sister . . . It all gets swept under the carpet to save face, prevent unnecessary bloodshed, and spare the institution of the family. But people don't forget this kind of thing too easily . . . So, Mr. Cem, is it true that you slept with this boy's mother, Ms. Gülcihan, in 1986, when you were sixteen years old?"

"Only one time," I said. "It's hard to believe that would have been enough to produce a child."

"The lawyer they've found is relentless; he won't give an inch. He's one of these young, dedicated guys. He spent his own childhood thinking his father was someone else, so he never takes on this kind of case unless he believes his client is right."

"How can anyone be sure who's right?" I said. "Is Ms. Gülcihan still alive?"

"She is."

"When I was sixteen, she had red hair."

"She still does, and she's still rather beautiful, actually. The marriage was not a happy one, but she is full of life and passion for the theater. Her husband, Turgay, died after they separated. So it's clear she's not making this claim to humiliate him but to secure some kind of income for her struggling son. She must have heard about DNA tests and the repeal of the old statute of limitations . . ."

"And the boy, what has he been doing?"

"This Enver, the man who claims to be your son, holds an accounting degree from some obscure university. He is single, runs a small accounting firm in Öngören . . . He's also involved with nationalist youth organizations, hates Kurds and leftists. He has a real chip on his shoulder about his father and about life."

"When you say 'his father,' do you mean Turgay?"

"Yes."

"Necati, what would you do in my position?"

"You know much better than I do what happened thirty years ago, Mr. Cem, so I can't put myself in your shoes. But since you do recall being with the lady in question, I'd suggest arranging a blood test . . . I'll request one at the first court session, no need to waste time. I'll also petition the judge to impose a gag order, otherwise the press will get wind of it and turn you into tabloid fodder."

"Let's not tell Ayşe, for now. She'd be devastated if she found out. Why don't you meet with this Enver first? Maybe we can find an amicable solution outside the courts."

"The lawyer says his client does not wish to meet you."

I was surprised at how much these words stung and realized that, deep down, I wanted to find out more about this "son" of mine.

Did we look alike? Did he walk the way I did? How would I feel if we were to meet? Was he really colluding with a bunch of semifascist nationalists? Why had he settled in Öngören? What did the Red-Haired Woman think of all this?

38

Two months later, I had my blood tested at the university hospital in Çapa. Necati received the results in advance, and called me before the judge was due to read them out in court. The next week, the judge ruled that Enver was to be registered officially as my son. I'd spent each stage of the process, from the initial court proceedings to the blood test, the judge's ruling, and finally the time in the registrar's office, secretly hoping that I might run into my son in some corridor. How would we react when we first saw each other?

According to our Necati, my son's refusal to see me was a good sign. Whatever their age, sons who found themselves in this position were inevitably bitter. As soon as their true paternity was officially registered, they and their mothers earned the right to sue the father for damages suffered from years of living in penury. We should be relieved that neither had done this so far. Perhaps they weren't interested in getting anything more out of us after all. But when he saw how relieved I was by his words, the lawyer warned me not to let my guard down; for ultimately, paternity cases were always about money. Never in history had a son gone to court to claim that his father was that impoverished nobody over there, rather than this distinguished, prosperous gentleman over here. Thinking of Sohrab's investments, Necati reiterated that it would be wise to delay no further in arranging that company presentation in Öngören.

I had to break the news to Ayşe first, so one evening I said, "There's something I need to tell you, but it's important. We should sit down and talk it through."

"What is it?" said Ayşe, already imagining the worst. I knew this was not a secret I could keep from myself and from the rest of the world as I'd kept Master Mahmut at the bottom of that well for all those years.

"I have a son," I blurted out at dinner after two glasses of *rakı*. I told her everything exactly as it had happened. As swiftly as the weight was lifted off my shoulders, it settled onto Ayşe's.

"I suppose you have a responsibility toward the child," said Ayşe after a long silence. "This is very painful news. Do you want to meet him?"

Faced with my silence, my wife began to ask her further questions: Did I want to see the Red-Haired Woman again? Did I want to befriend my son? Did I expect Ayşe to do so, too? Did this explain why we'd spent our lives poring over various versions and interpretations of *Oedipus the King* and the story of Rostam and Sohrab?

We both got completely drunk that night and soon turned to the crucial matter we couldn't help but think about: since we had no other children, and Turkish law did not recognize wills, this son of mine would automatically inherit two-thirds of Sohrab after I died. If Ayşe were to die before me (certainly possible, considering she wasn't much younger than I was), this child we'd never even seen would receive the *whole* of Sohrab after I was gone.

"Last night I dreamed that your son was murdered," said Ayşe the next morning.

We were discussing inheritance law, attorneys, and trust funds another night when she went even further: "I can't believe I'm saying this, but sometimes I just want to kill him. Imagine the irony if that bastard's name had been Sohrab."

"Don't use that word," I told my wife. "It's not the child's fault. Besides, we know who the real father is now."

Seeing me siding with the boy hurt my wife's feelings, and she fell silent. She tried to get me to admit to having met up with my son without her knowledge. "He doesn't even want to see me," I reassured her. "I think he may be a little strange."

"What about you? Do you want to see him? Do you wonder what he looks like?"

"No," I lied. I'd decided that I couldn't tell my wife the truth: that I had begun to feel an irrepressible, fascinated sympathy for my son.

Three months had passed when Murat called me up from Athens with a proposal. Having remembered how much I enjoyed our trip to Tehran years ago, he said I should come and join him at the Hotel Grande Bretagne, where the British had set up their military headquarters during the civil war that engulfed Greece after World War II. When we met in Athens two days later, he announced breathlessly that Greece was about to go bankrupt. As we sat in the stylish hotel lobby, Murat informed me that property prices in the city had tumbled by half and that a fair number of people lounging around us right now were foreign businessmen—mostly Germans—come to snap up some property on the cheap. He had color photographs of some of the buildings on sale in the heart of the capital.

I spent the next two days viewing properties with Murat and his estate agent in Athens. One afternoon I hired a taxi to take us to the city of Thebes, an hour away. Here, too, we saw abandoned railway lines, old carriages crawling with vines and spiders, empty factories and depots. King Oedipus's city stood on a steep hill, just as Ingres and Gustave Moreau had painted it. Over a cup of coffee, Murat confessed he needed cash and offered to sell me the land he'd bought in Öngören.

Our lawyers in Istanbul, whose minds worked more swiftly and meticulously than mine, confirmed that we could go ahead and advised that Murat's asking price was reasonable. This acquisition was bound to make Sohrab a tidy profit, but before we moved forward, it was past time we arranged that neighborhood meeting we'd been talking about to remind the locals of my Öngören days, put their minds at ease about Sohrab's intentions, and prove that I, too, treasured the memory of Master Mahmut.

Unbeknownst to Ayşe, I authorized Necati to hire a private detective if need be to find out how Gülcihan and Enver would react if we were to announce such a meeting in Öngören.

Two weeks later, my lawyer reported back. The Red-Haired Woman and her son, having always been inseparable, had grown apart after the paternity suit. When Necati had approached the red-haired Ms. Gülcihan, she had initially said she wouldn't come to the meeting, and though she briefly relented, on the condition that we not "tell anyone," she'd later changed her mind again and decided against attending. She lived in the Bakırköy neighborhood of Istanbul, in an apartment left to her by her husband, Turgay, and earned a modest living dubbing foreign TV series.

According to Necati, my son, Enver, wouldn't attend the meeting either, partly out of disgust at our advertising campaign, and partly to avoid anyone else's finding out that I was his father. My son's accountancy skills were average at best, but local shopkeepers trusted him and let him handle their bookkeeping and tax returns. Some thought he hadn't married yet because he was too attached to his mother, and others blamed it on his temper. He mixed with a group of young men and women who shared his mother's love of the theater and wrote poetry which was published in conservative journals like *The Crescent* and *The Spring*. Necati had found some copies, and as I read them at home, concealing them from Ayşe, I wondered what my father would have thought of a grandson of his writing poetry for religious magazines.

I instructed Sohrab's marketing department to organize the meeting in Öngören. I told Ayşe I wouldn't be attending. I was intimidated by the prospect of returning to Öngören, and I didn't want to upset my wife, who would have preferred there to be no meeting at all.

I scheduled a trip to Ankara on the day of the presentation. But toward noon that Saturday, as I was making my way to the office, I decided to cancel that plan. The team was getting ready to make their way to Öngören, and their anticipation was contagious. I asked Necati not to tell Ayşe that I'd be joining them after all. I told my employees that I wanted to make the journey by train—as I'd been planning in the back of my mind for thirty years. On the way out, I grabbed my Kırıkkale pistol and the gun license that the government issued on request to oil barons and construction magnates. Two weeks before, I'd tested the Kırıkkale in one of Sohrab's empty building sites, shooting bottles I'd lined up on bags of cement. Naturally, I was worried there might be trouble.

39

AS THE TRAIN to Öngören shuddered alongside the old city walls and the Marmara Sea, past ancient and crooked buildings and new parks, concrete hotels, restaurants, ships, and cars, I grew increasingly nauseous. Necati had seen me off with assurances that Enver would not be present at the meeting, wouldn't be in Öngören at all today, but I couldn't help thinking there was a chance my son would come to see his father. Thirty years on, the fear of facing up to my crime against Master Mahmut had transformed into the thrill of meeting my son. As the train slowly pulled into Öngören, I couldn't distinguish our plateau for the countless concrete buildings, yet I had the distinct feeling that there was someone here I was meant to meet.

The moment I walked out of the station, I knew that the old Öngören was gone: the building I used to stare at looking for the Red-Haired Woman's window had been demolished, and in its place a bustling shopping mall filled the whole square, drawing a young crowd eager to eat hamburgers and drink beer and soda. Banks, kebab vendors, and sandwich stalls had opened on the ground floors of the buildings defining the square's perimeter. Retracing the same steps I followed so frequently in my memories, I started walking automatically from the Station Square to where the Rumelian Coffeehouse had stood, and specifically toward the spot on the pavement where our table had been, but I found nothing to remind me of all the cups of tea we'd had in that place. All the people who'd once been here, and all the homes in which they'd lived, had since disappeared, replaced by new buildings inhabited by new people—rowdy, cheerful, inquisitive, and eager to find ways of amusing themselves on a Saturday afternoon.

Walking through Diners' Lane, I was struck that even on a weekend there were no soldiers around, or any gendarmes to keep an eye on them. The hardware store, the blacksmith, and the grocer where Master Mahmut had bought his cigarettes every night weren't where they used to be, but sometimes I wasn't even sure that I was searching for them in the right places, without the reference points of all the old low-rise homes, each with its private garden, which had given way to indistinguishable apartment buildings.

I decided I needn't be so apprehensive about this return to Öngören. The town I'd known was now a run-of-the-mill Istanbul neighborhood, crammed with concrete structures like any other. I did, however, manage at last to find some of the people who used to live here. I was reunited with my apprentice friend Ali, who greeted me with an affable smile. I visited Sırrı Siyahoğlu and his equally rotund wife for a cup of tea, soon to be joined by Necati and the other Sohrab directors. I was introduced to a cake-shop owner said to be a relation of Master Mahmut's, and at the behest of a crowd of onlookers, we were made to shake hands, much to our mutual embarrassment. As I climbed the hill leading to the cemetery where Master Mahmut was buried, I concluded that aside from those with a stake in the local property market, nobody in Öngören knew who I was anymore, and so there was nothing much to fear.

"Our plateau" at the top of the hill had also transformed from the vacant plot it had been thirty years ago into a concrete labyrinth of six- to seven-story apartment buildings, warehouses, workshops, gas stations, and a wide array of street-side diners, kebab stalls, and supermarkets. With all these structures in the way, the road whose turns we used to avoid by cutting through the fields was no longer discernible, making it difficult to find the spot where we'd dug the well.

Sohrab's diligent marketing team led me through the town's backstreets to the wedding hall they'd hired out for the company presentation and the banquet that would follow. Looking through the hall's wide windows, I tried to figure out what part of our plateau we might be standing on, and which way to look for the army garrison and the blue mountains that had framed our view in the distance. Our well had to be about half a kilometer away in that direction. What I wanted most of all, now, was to forget everything else and go there.

Soon to connect Öngören and the highways leading to the new airport and to the Bosphorus Bridge, a four-lane asphalt road was set to approach the old town center from the direction of our well rather than from the train station. Consequently, the value of land and houses on our plateau was rising. Most of those attending the presentation weren't Öngören locals but members of the new, motorized rich contemplating a home purchase in this rapidly developing area. I was so restless that I could hardly tell whether these prospects were duly impressed by the plywood models brought by Team Sohrab, by the dazzling views guaranteed from our upper-floor units, or by the large swimming pools and children's playgrounds we had planned. Our team had also brought in couples to offer testimonials on how happy they were in their apartments in Sohrab's Beykoz and Kartal developments. Their talk of a so-called Sohrab lifestyle piqued the curiosity of those seated toward the back, who seemed to be idlers with nothing better to do rather than serious sales prospects. Hearing a number of sarcastic questions, I concluded that those in the back had a hidden motivation; perhaps they were orchestrating ways to embarrass me—insult me, even—and thus undermine our sales effort.

Though my presence had not been announced, the Öngören old-timers were expecting me. I gave a brief speech, mentioning how I'd come to this charming corner of Istanbul thirty years ago to join my master in digging a well. I paid tribute to Master Mahmut, whose successful quest for water had brought this dusty stretch of land to life, making possible the influx of new people and industries now settled here. The future buildings, whose models were being presented today, were but the natural continuation of that move toward civilization first undertaken thirty years ago.

As the hecklers in the back were making no effort to conceal their contempt, I thought they must be harmless, mostly there to amuse themselves. I craned my neck to scan the whole crowd of about a hundred; any real danger was likelier to come from those sitting in silence.

Like those who'd spoken before me, I was peppered with questions before I'd even had the chance to say, *Any questions?* I let the project manager answer one about payment plans. The same manager was responding to another couple wondering when they could expect to receive the keys to their apartment if they were to buy today, when—looking at the middle of the room—I caught sight of a mature woman with her hand aloft, and I felt my heart speed up.

My mind took longer, somehow, to grasp what my eyes had instantly recognized: it was obvious from the color of her hair that this lady in the middle of the room was the Red-Haired Woman. Our gazes met as she kept her hand raised amid the buzzing all around her. She smiled good-naturedly and I called upon her to speak.

"We congratulate you on the success of Sohrab, Mr. Cem," she said.

"And we hope you will consider making room for a theater in one of these buildings."

A few of those around her applauded politely. I didn't notice anyone unusually interested in our exchange or reading very much into her words.

The crowd began to thin out once they ran out of questions, and as people went over to examine the models, I came face-to-face with the Red-Haired Woman for the first time in thirty years.

Time had been kind to her; it had only enhanced the beautiful, inscrutable expression on her face, the shape of her nose and mouth, and the distinctive set of her full, round lips. She seemed neither weary nor hostile; on the contrary, she looked relaxed and upbeat. Perhaps that was how she wished to appear.

"You must be surprised to see me, Mr. Cem. I'm helping to set up a youth theater here with some of my son's friends . . . I wanted you to meet them. They never said you would come, but I knew you'd be here today."

"Is Enver here?"

"No."

The youths she'd mentioned were standing in a group apart from everyone else. Necati discreetly led me and the Red-Haired Woman toward a more secluded part of the room, where he had some tea brought over and left us alone.

"For years I wasn't sure whether our son Enver's father was you or Turgay . . . I didn't dwell on it too much. I did always wonder . . . But I wouldn't have been able to prove anything even if I'd gone to court, and that would have done nothing but upset everyone and bring shame on you and me both. I'm sure you know I would never want that to happen."

I drank in every word that came out of her mouth and meanwhile kept an eye on those still milling about in the hall, should anyone suddenly become too interested in what we were doing. Everything she said surprised me. It seemed impossible that she was sitting before me now, her delicate hands still moving nimbly through the air, her outfit the same sky blue as the skirt she'd worn thirty years ago on our walk through the Station Square, her face and her fingernails so wonderfully smooth.

"Of course neither of them ever suspected my doubts about who the father was," she continued. "Turgay was often mean to us, perhaps because I'd been married to his older brother before him. He passed away some time after we separated, and it wasn't easy having to explain to Enver that his biological father might actually be someone else, someone so successful and talented, and to persuade him to file the lawsuit. He did it in the end, but not before putting up a fight. Our son has yet to make his mark on the world, but he's a proud, sensitive, creative boy. He writes poems."

"So I've heard from Mr. Necati. I know he's had some of them published—I've even found copies of the magazines. They're good poems. But I'm not sure how I feel about his political views and those of the journals he's published in. And unfortunately they didn't include any photographs of the young poet."

"Oh, of course! I must send you a picture of our son," said the Red-Haired Woman. "I wouldn't worry about his politics, though. Today it's a religious magazine, tomorrow he might be composing odes to the army and the flag . . . He's obstinate and he knows his own mind, but it's all bravado. What he needs is a solid father figure to show him the way." A few people were walking toward us now. "Enver must get to know and love his father," she said. "I asked him to come here today, but he refused. I'm the one who taught these young folk here today about the theater. We get together on Sundays and go down to Istanbul to see plays. Some of them are Enver's friends."

As more people approached us, the Red-Haired Woman assumed a more formal air of a potential buyer inquiring punctiliously about apartment features and then continued sipping elegantly on her tea.

I got up and wandered through the crowd for a while before finding Necati. I asked him to invite the Red-Haired Woman and her young theater aficionados to the banquet that evening.

"That went well," he said, euphoric with relief. "Sohrab shouldn't have too much trouble in Öngören anymore."

"I wouldn't be so sure," I said. "This isn't Öngören now; it's Istanbul."

40

IT WAS THE marketing department's idea to follow the meeting with dinner and drinks in the wedding hall. Liberation Restaurant, the caterer, was still in business in Diners' Lane. I met the elderly owner, a man from Samsun, and as we reminisced, I thought of how I'd shared a table in that restaurant with the Red-Haired Woman one night thirty years ago. I decided to avoid her and her young troupe of actors and head back to Istanbul as soon as the meal was over. All I wanted before I went home was to see the well I'd dug with Master Mahmut. "That's easy," said Necati, but I became concerned when I saw that rather than asking one of the locals, like my apprentice friend Ali, to show me the way, he sent the Red-Haired Woman and one of her young friends over instead.

"Serhat is the brightest of my young thespians, and the most mature," said the Red-Haired Woman. "His dream is to stage Sophocles in Öngören one day."

"How do you know where the well is?" I asked Mr. Serhat.

"That well became famous as soon as it sprang water," said Mr. Serhat. "When we were kids, Master Mahmut used to tell us stories about it, as well as old fairy tales."

"Do you still remember any of those fairy tales?"

"I remember most of them."

"Join me, Mr. Serhat," I said. "Perhaps we can take a quick break from dinner later and you can show me to the well."

"Of course . . ."

There was a glass of Club Rakı before me, some fresh cheese, a few cold appetizers, and the Red-Haired Woman sitting at the other end of the table, just as on that night thirty years ago. In the interim, I'd learned to love *rakı* as much as my father had. I refilled my young companion's glass, gulped down my own, and looked anywhere but at the Red-Haired Woman and her protégés.

I asked courteous, *rakı*-loving Mr. Serhat which stories he remembered best from among those he'd heard as a child from Master Mahmut.

"The one I remember most vividly was about a warrior called Rostam, who killed his son by mistake . . . ," said the sensitive young man.

Where had Master Mahmut heard that one? Though he'd been to the yellow theater tent before me, it would have been difficult to piece together the plot from that patchwork of a show. It must have been the Red-Haired Woman who'd explained it to him. Or perhaps he'd heard it as a boy.

"How come Rostam's story stuck with you? Did it scare you?"

"Master Mahmut wasn't my father," said logical Mr. Serhat. "Why would I be afraid?"

"He was like a father to me, one summer thirty years ago . . . ," I said. "My real father left us. So while I was digging that well, you might say I found a new father in Master Mahmut. How is your relationship with your father?"

"Distant," said Serhat, lowering his eyes.

Was he wishing he could go back to sitting with the Red-Haired Woman and his actor friends? Had I pried too much into this taciturn young man's life? The alcohol had galvanized the other guests. The hall rang with the ceaseless chatter of *rakı*-soaked hometown reunions and sports bars filled with soccer hooligans.

"How did you know Master Mahmut?"

"He used to sit all the neighborhood kids in a circle around him and tell us stories. I just happened to go over to his house one day. I was so scared when I saw his shoulder."

"Would you mind taking me to Master Mahmut's house, after we've seen the well?"

"Of course . . . They moved a few times, some of the places where he used to live have been demolished. Which one would you like to see?"

"I used to be scared of Master Mahmut's stories . . . ," I said. "They always ended up coming true . . ."

"What do you mean they came true?" he asked.

"The things he told me in his stories happened to me in real life. And I was also scared of Master Mahmut's well. I was so terrified that one day I just left him there and ran away. Did you know that story?"

"I did," he said, looking away.

"How did you know?"

"Ms. Gülcihan's son, Enver, told me. He is an accountant here in town. You could say Master Mahmut was like a father to him. They used to be very close."

There was no hint of malice or duplicity in his expression. He didn't seem to be aware of the truth. I fell silent. The night smelled of *rakı* and cigarette smoke, and I felt its grip deep inside my mind.

"Is this Enver here tonight?" I asked eventually.

"What?" said Serhat. He seemed astounded by my question, as if I'd said something brazen or absurd. I hadn't seen anyone that day, neither at the presentation nor among the guests at the dinner, whom I would have been proud to call my son.

"Enver isn't here," said Serhat. "Did he tell you he would be?"

I said nothing, but he'd sensed my agitation.

"He would never come here!" he said.

"Why not?"

Now it was Serhat who kept quiet.

41

I PUZZLED OVER why my son might be reluctant to show up. Perhaps he disapproved of his father. The thought made me indignant. But recognizing that my anger might be unjustified, I wanted to meet him anyway, even as I knew it would be better to leave Öngören immediately, before I could get into any sort of trouble. "It's getting late, Mr. Serhat, shall we go and take a look at this well?" I said.

"Of course."

"You go ahead and wait for me at the bottom of the slope. I'll come and find you in five minutes; that way we won't draw too much attention."

He swallowed his last morsel and rushed off. The Red-Haired Woman was surveying me from the other end of the table. After a few more sips of *rakı* and another bite of white cheese, I left to meet Serhat at the foot of the black hill.

We paced silently through the shadows, darkness, and echoes of the past. I couldn't work out where the slope was in relation to our plateau, or which way the well was, but instead of blaming this on the concrete blocks, walls, and warehouses that had sprung up everywhere, I put it down to the *rakı* clouding my mind. And if my mind was clouded, that had to be because my son didn't want to see me.

We walked along a pale wall, passing a warehouse and a gray courtyard dotted with trees that shone pink under the neon lights. I saw myself and my young guide reflected as silhouettes on the dark windows of a barbershop that had closed for the night, and I noticed that we were the same height.

"How long have you known Enver?" I asked the young thespian Serhat.

"For as long as I can remember. I've always lived in Öngören."

"What is he like?"

"Why do you ask?"

"I used to know his father, Turgay," I said. "He lived here for a while, thirty years ago."

"Enver's problem isn't his father; it's his lack of one," said clever Serhat. "He's an angry introvert, a peculiar sort of guy."

"I never had a real father, either, but I'm neither angry nor introverted; in fact, I'm not so different from everyone else," I said, enlightened by *rakı*.

"Of course you're different; you're rich," said quick-witted Serhat. "Maybe that's what bothers Enver."

I was silent for a time. What exactly had this haughty young man meant? That Enver suffered because he was poor? Or that he didn't approve of people whose lives were all about money, and that's why he hadn't come to the meeting today?

Tormented by the thought that he might have meant the latter, I soon noticed the slope leveling out and realized we must be getting closer to our well. I saw the same weeds and nettles from thirty years ago growing on empty lots and in the cracks in the pavement. I thought briefly of being reunited with that wrinkly-necked tortoise and of venturing, as in the old days, some musings on life and the nature of time. *Here we are, thirty years on!* the tortoise would say. *An entire, wasted life for you. A blink of an eye for me.*

Had the Red-Haired Woman told our son, Enver, that his grandfather was a romantic idealist who'd gone to prison for his political convictions? It was mortifying to think that my son might picture me as some superficial and morally corrupt version of his grandfather. I was growing increasingly irate at this supercilious Serhat for plunging me into this state of mind when I saw a familiar stretch of road. "Here it is," I exclaimed. "This was the last turn before we got to our well."

"Really? What a coincidence. For a while Master Mahmut lived right over there," said sharp-eyed Serhat.

"Where?"

I watched the dim outline of his hand gesturing toward a cluster of depots, factories, and apartment blocks barely visible in the darkness. I saw the walnut tree where I used to take my afternoon naps. It had grown taller but was now enclosed within the walls of a factory. I saw a dull light through the windows of an old house nearby.

"They were here for a while," said Serhat. "Enver and his mother, Gülcihan, used to drop by to wish him well on religious holidays. I met Enver in Master Mahmut's garden."

It should have seemed suspicious that Serhat had mentioned Enver again, but I was preoccupied taking in all the concrete and walls that had piled up on this patch of land that had been empty and barren only thirty years ago and by the sheer numbers of people and animals (such as the menacing mud-brown stray that loped up to us for a sniff) now living here; my priority in that moment was to assimilate this new reality as quickly as possible. Would I be able to find even a brick or a window or catch even one familiar whiff to summon a memory from those days?

"This is the house where Master Mahmut first told us that story from the Koran about the prince who left his father to die at the bottom of a well," said pushy Serhat.

"There's no such story in the Koran, or in the *Shahnameh,* for that matter," I said.

"How do you know?" said Serhat. "Are you religious? Have you read the Koran?"

I stood silent in the face of his aggressive demeanor, which I ascribed to my son Enver's influence. I was heartbroken and had to concede that coming here had been a bad idea. "I was fond of Master Mahmut. He was like a father to me, during that summer I spent here," I said.

"If you want I can show you where Enver lives," said my guide.

"Is it close?"

I followed Serhat into a side street; as we walked past apartment blocks with unlit porches, vans and minibuses parked haphazardly on both sides of the road, a small first-aid clinic and pharmacy, a garage, and warehouses with morose, chain-smoking watchmen, I wondered how it was possible that all of this had somehow been squeezed onto our plateau.

"Enver lives here," said Serhat. "Second floor, the windows on the left."

My heart beat to an odd, shallow rhythm. I knew I would never be able to disregard this longing to know my son.

"Mr. Enver's lights are on," I said, with drunken disinhibition. "Shall we try his doorbell?"

"Just because his lights are on doesn't mean he's home," said quick-thinking Serhat. "Enver has chosen to be alone. He leaves his lights on when he goes out at night so thieves and foes will think there's someone home, and so that when he gets back, he won't remember how lonely he is."

"You seem to know your friend well. Surely Enver wouldn't mind your showing up at his door."

"You never know what Enver will do."

Did he mean that my son was fearless? Should I be proud? I walked toward the door. "But why would he be lonely when his mother loves him so much and he can count on a friend as close as you?" I said.

"He isn't close to anyone . . ."

"Is that because he grew up without a father?"

"Perhaps, but if I were you I'd think twice about ringing that bell . . . ," said my son's prudent friend. But I ignored his warning, and as my eyes roamed down the list of names and numbers on the buzzer, the size and style of handwriting changing with each entry, I froze, spellbound, at the following label:

6: ENVER YENIER

(FREELANCE ACCOUNTANT)

I pressed the bell three times.

"Enver's door is always open for uninvited guests who show up in the middle of the night," said Serhat. "He'll let you in if he's home."

But the door stayed shut. I became convinced that my son was at home and refusing to let me in out of sheer stubbornness, even though I'd come all this way to see him. My frustration with him and with Serhat's insinuations grew.

"Why are you so keen to meet Enver?" asked intrusive, irritating Serhat. Perhaps he'd caught wind of the gossip after all.

"Show me this well so I can go home before it gets any later," I said. I figured I could always sneak back here another day to see my son.

"When you grow up without a father, you think there is no center and no end to the universe, and you think you can do whatever you want . . . ," said Serhat. "But eventually you find you don't know what you want, and you start looking for some sort of meaning, some focus in your life: someone to tell you no."

I did not reply. I sensed that we were getting closer to our well, and that I was nearing the end of the quest I'd spent my life on.

42

"YOUR WELL IS IN THERE," said Serhat, peering into my face as we stood before the rusty gate of a derelict factory.

"After Hayri Bey died, his son outsourced all of the dyeing, washing, and stitching to Bangladesh, and production here stopped altogether. They've been using this place as a storage depot for the past five years, but ultimately they plan to get someone like you to tear it down and build high-rises on the land."

"I didn't come here to scout new construction sites; I came for my memories," I said.

As Serhat approached the guardhouse, I spotted on the bare wall a Perspex panel that said ENDEAVOR TEXTILES LLC. I looked around trying to remember what the place had been like thirty years ago. The only indication that this was indeed Hayri Bey's land was the way the factory walls seemed to stretch on endlessly, and that feeling I'd first had at age sixteen that I was much closer to the sky than usual.

I heard the furious barking of a dog. Serhat returned.

"There's no one there, but I know the watchman," he said. "He's left the dog on its leash; he'll be back soon."

"It's getting late."

"If I remember, there's a low spot further along the wall. I'll go and take a look," said Serhat, dissolving into the night.

It wasn't completely black beyond the wall, and despite the dog's relentless bark, I was reassured by the reflection of the neon lights off the low roofs and metal poles on the opposite side, so I decided I would just take a quick look at the well and come straight back. Serhat, meanwhile, seemed to have disappeared. I was beginning to lose patience with my young guide when the phone rang in my pocket. It was Ayşe.

"They told me you're in Öngören," she said.

"I am."

"You lied to me, Cem. And you're making a terrible mistake."

"There's nothing to be afraid of. Everything went fine."

"There's a lot to be afraid of. Where are you now?"

"My guide has brought me to see the well I dug with Master Mahmut."

"Who is he?"

"A young man from Öngören. A bit arrogant, but he's been extremely helpful."

"Who introduced you?"

"The Red-Haired Woman," I said, and for a moment, I was able to think clearly through the fog of *rakı*.

"Is anyone with you now?" said Ayşe, almost whispering into the phone.

"Do you mean the Red-Haired Woman?"

"No, I mean the man she introduced you to. Is he there right now?"

"He's not, he's gone to look for a way through the wall. He's going to sneak me into the empty factory."

"Cem . . . listen . . . come back immediately!"

"Why?"

"Get away from that boy and make sure he doesn't follow you."

"What are you so worried about?" I said, but already the fear I could sense through the phone had begun to affect me, too.

"Have you simply forgotten the stories we've been reading all these years?" said Ayşe. "Of course you went to Öngören to find your son. That's why you didn't want me to come along. Who introduced you to this guide of yours? The Red-Haired Woman! Do you realize now who he is?"

"Who? Serhat?"

"He's probably your son, Enver! You've got to get away, Cem."

"Calm down. People here are all right. Master Mahmut was barely mentioned."

"Now listen to me very carefully," said Ayşe. "What if they had someone stab you under the pretense of a political squabble, what if they got someone to shoot you and say it was some sort of drunken brawl?"

"Then I'd be dead," I said, with a chuckle.

"And Sohrab would end up belonging to the Red-Haired Woman and her son," said Ayşe. "These people wouldn't hesitate to kill a man for that."

"Are you saying someone's going to kill me tonight to get their hands on my estate?" I asked. "No one knew I was going to come here today; not even me."

"Is that young man with you?"

"I told you he isn't!"

"I'm begging you, please just go somewhere he can't find you."

I did as my wife said. I hid on the gloomy porch of a shop on the other side of the road.

"Listen to me," said Ayşe. "If it's true, everything we've always believed about Oedipus and his father, and about Rostam and Sohrab . . . then if that young man is your son, he is going to kill you! He's a textbook case of the rebellious Western individualist . . ."

"Don't worry. If he tries anything, then I'll be the authoritarian Asian father, like Rostam, and kill the brat myself," I said lightheartedly.

"You would never do anything of that sort," said Ayşe, taking her drunk husband seriously. "Stay where you are. I'm taking the car. I'll be right there."

In the dark, oppressive Öngören night, ancient books, myths, paintings, and civilizations seemed so remote that I could not understand why my wife was so anxious. But I stayed where I was, and, hearing nothing from my guide, Serhat, I too began to worry. Could he really be my son? The silence stretched on, and I grew annoyed with the young man who'd forgotten me here.

"Mr. Cem, Mr. Cem," he finally called from the other side of the wall.

I stayed silent, feeling suddenly tense. The young man kept calling out to me.

Presently, he reappeared in the very spot where I'd lost sight of him earlier. He began to amble toward me. He was roughly my height, and there was something about his bearing that was reminiscent of my father. It scared me.

When he reached the point where he'd left me, he called out twice: "Mr. Cem!"

I yearned for another look at him from up close; from where I stood I couldn't see his face. There was a dreamlike quality to how I was hiding from this young man, all these years later, because he might be my son. Emboldened by the gun in my pocket, I stepped out toward him.

"Where were you?" he said. "Follow me if you want to go inside."

He turned around and continued along the wall. The street was completely dark now. It occurred to me that he might be trying to lure me to some desolate, unlit corner in which to cut my throat. How I wished I'd had at least one good look at his face! I marched into the darkness to the sound of his footsteps.

When we got to the lower section of the wall, Serhat sprang like a cat and vanished over the side. Grabbing hold of his clammy hand (and wondering briefly whether it could really belong to a son of mine), I too climbed over the wall. The empty factory's guard dog was straining on its chain and barking madly. This was definitely our plateau.

I thought I'd shoot the dog down if it managed to break free of its chain, so I maintained my composure as I walked among the industrial buildings. Evidently, once water had begun to come from the well, Hayri Bey and his son—who'd been wearing new soccer shoes the day I met him—had set up a washing-and-dyeing operation even more extensive than the one they'd first proposed. Scattered throughout the complex were also a number of more rudimentary constructions, which must have been built before the textile industry migrated to China, Bangladesh, and the Far East over the past ten years. Some—like the administrative building with the marble staircase—had since been abandoned and now served to store surplus construction materials, empty crates, and dusty rust-covered junk. Some had been reduced to ruins.

Our well had been engulfed by the cafeteria, which Hayri Bey had always promised he'd build during visits to our dig site. The windows were all broken, so the place had no use even as a warehouse. I followed my guide in the faint light from a neon lamp on the other side of the wall, past spiderwebs, corroded sheet metal, loose pipes, and formless furniture, until we reached the concrete rim of what had been our well.

“This lock never works,” said my guide, crouching as he fiddled with the padlock fastening the lid on the well.

“You seem familiar with this place,” I said.

“Enver used to bring me here all the time.”

“Why was that?”

“I don’t know,” he said, still fussing with the lock. “Why did you want to come here?”

“I’ve never forgotten how I worked here with Master Mahmut,” I said.

“Trust me, he never forgot, either.”

Was he driving at how I’d crippled Master Mahmut?

When my young companion straightened up to gather his strength for a last attempt at the lock, a beam of light caught his face, and I inspected it carefully. A parched tenderness lay dormant inside me, ready to bloom at the first sign of moisture.

But I was disappointed. While it was true that the young man’s features, gestures, and build were similar to mine, I disliked his personality—what our elders would have called his temperament. Ayşe was wrong. This couldn’t be my son.

My shrewd guide perceived immediately that something about him had rubbed me the wrong way. There was a silence. Now he was looking back at me with unveiled hostility.

“Let me have a go at it,” I said, getting on my knees in the semidarkness to try and force the lock.

43

KNEELING BY THE LOCK helped temporarily relieve the guilt inflaming my conscience. Why had I come here? The lock snapped open.

I stood and handed the padlock to the young man. "Now open the lid," I said, like a German tourist instructing a peasant to show him the Byzantine-era well in his back garden. I was disenchanted with my guide and troubled by his disdain.

He heaved against the rusty metal lid but couldn't get it to budge. I watched him struggle, and when I couldn't resist any longer, I grabbed hold of the lid myself. It creaked open under our combined efforts, like the gate of a Byzantine dungeon.

In the faint light of the distant neon lamp I saw a spiderweb and the flicker of a lizard. A dense smell of rot stung my throat, and the words *Journey to the Center of the Earth* rose up from the recesses of my memory.

The foot of the well was so far down that we couldn't even see it at first. But my eyes soon adjusted to the dark. Finally, I could see light reflected in a pool of water or mud at the bottom. The distance was startling.

We stared into the abyss, dumbstruck. The well was so deep that one couldn't help feeling terror but also admiration for the person who'd dug it using nothing but a spade and pickax. I pictured Master Mahmut thirty years ago, scolding me from the depths below.

"I'm getting dizzy," said my young guide. "It would be easy to fall. It's so deep it pulls you in."

"Don't ask me why, but just now I've thought of God," I whispered into his ear, as if it were a secret, and for a moment I felt a sense of communion with the young man. "Master Mahmut wasn't the type to pray five times a day. Even so, when we were digging this well thirty years ago, it felt not as if we were burrowing into the ground but ascending toward the sky and the stars, to the kingdom of God and His angels."

"God is everywhere," said cocky Serhat. "Above and below, north and south. Everywhere."

"That's correct."

"Then why don't you believe in Him?"

"In whom?"

"In Allah the Almighty, Creator of the universe," he said.

"How do you know whether I believe in God or not?"

"It's pretty obvious . . ."

We studied each other wordlessly. He certainly seemed angry enough to be my son, and I was gratified to discover his strong, combative nature. But I was also afraid of what might happen were his anger turned on me here by the well.

"Rich Westernized Turks always say 'My relationship with God is none of your business!' when they're defending secularism," said Serhat. "But they couldn't care less about God; they're only set on secularism so they can dress up their wickedness as modernity."

"What have you got against modernity?"

"I don't have anything against anyone!" he said, sounding calmer now. "But I won't have my enemies define me, and I won't be caught in false dichotomies like left and right, or godly and modern. I just want to be myself. So I avoid people and concentrate on my poetry. Someone rang my doorbell earlier, but I was working on a poem, so I didn't let them in."

I was confused. But I also sensed that the young man's anger might be diluted if the conversation were to take a more academic turn. "Do you think modernity is a bad thing?" I asked with drunken guilelessness.

"The modern man is lost in the chaos of the city. He is, in a way, rendered fatherless. But his search for a father is effectively pointless. For if he is an individual in the modern sense, he will never find a father in the tumult of the city. And if he does find him, he will cease to be an individual. Jean-Jacques Rousseau, the French pioneer of modernity, knew this to be true, so he abandoned each of his four children just to ensure they would be modern. Rousseau never showed the slightest interest in his children, nor did he ever seek them out. And you? Is that why you left me here, so that I would be modern? If so, then you were right."

"What?"

"Why didn't you answer my letter?" he asked, stepping closer.

"What letter?"

"You know full well what I'm talking about."

"I'm sorry, it must be the *rakı* making me forget things. Why don't we head back to the dinner, and you can remind me on the way?"

"I sent you a letter signed 'your son.' Why didn't you write back to me? I left my e-mail address at the bottom."

"Forgive me, please, but what letter do you say you signed?"

"Don't pretend to be formal all of a sudden," said Serhat. "You must have figured out by now who I am."

"I'm not sure I understand, Mr. Serhat."

"My name is not Serhat. I'm your son, Enver."

We didn't speak again for a long while. Even the factory dog had gone inexplicably quiet. The silence that reigned was profound, and it reminded me of the time when my father abandoned us years ago, that feeling of forgetting even what his face looked like. It would feel like being in a room when the lights go out or like going momentarily blind.

As I looked at Enver, he looked at me, trying to read my thoughts. I felt a building disillusionment. Our reunion would be nothing like those emotional scenes from Turkish melodramas, with tearful embraces and cries of "Father!" and "Son!"

"It seems you're the one who's been pretending," I said eventually. "Why would my son, Enver, try to pass himself off as Serhat?"

"To decide whether he's even going to like his father . . . To see whether I'll warm to you. Fatherhood means a lot to me."

"What is a father to you?"

"A father is a doting, charismatic figure who will until his dying day accept and watch over the child he sires. He is the origin and the center of the universe. When you believe that you have a father, you are at peace even when you can't see him, because you know that he is always there, ready to love and protect you. I never had a father like that."

"Neither did I," I said impassively. "But if I'd had one, he'd have expected me to obey him, and he'd have suppressed my individuality with his affection and the force of his personality!"

Enver's eyes widened with the realization that his father had clearly given the question some prior thought. He seemed genuinely, even respectfully, interested in what I had to say; that was encouraging.

"Would I have been happy if I'd bowed to my father's will?" I wondered aloud. "That might have made me a good son, but I would have fallen short of being a true individual."

He bluntly put a stop to my musings: "Our wealthy, Westernized classes are so obsessed with individualism, they've forgotten how to be themselves, let alone how to be individuals," he said. "These Westernized Turks are too conceited to believe in God. Their individuality is all they care about. Most choose not to believe in God just to prove they're not like everyone else, though they won't even acknowledge that's the reason why. But faith is precisely about being like everyone else. Religion is the haven and the consolation of the meek."

"I agree."

"So you're saying you do believe in God. That must be hard to admit, for a rich and Westernized Turk."

"Yes."

"If you really believe in God and you've read the Koran, why did you leave Master Mahmut in this bottomless well? How could you? True believers have a conscience."

"I've thought about that a lot. I was a child, back then."

"No, you weren't. You were old enough to sleep around and get women pregnant."

I was stunned by the sharpness of his response. "You know everything," I murmured.

"Yes, Master Mahmut told me everything," snarled Enver. "You left him at the bottom of the well because you are vain, and you thought your life was worth more than his. Your school, your university dreams, and your life were more important to you than the existence of that poor man."

"But that's normal. Everyone thinks that way."

"Some people don't!"

"You're right," I said, backing away from the well.

There was a long silence. The dog began to bark again.

"Are you afraid?" asked my son.

"Of what?"

"Of falling into the well."

"I don't know," I said. "People must be wondering where we are. Let's head back . . . This kind of impertinence is not what I would expect of a son . . ."

"Oh, and how should I have addressed you, dear Father?" he said, derisively. "If you want me to be an obedient son, I can't be a modern individual, can I? If you want me to be a modern individual, then I can't be an obedient son. You have to help me out here."

"My son can obey his father of his own volition, and still remain a fully formed individual," I said. "Our character is forged not just by our freedoms, but also by the forces of history and memory. This well is history and memory to me. I'm grateful to you for bringing me here, Mr. Enver. But this conversation is over now."

"Why do you want to go back? Are you afraid?"

"Why would I be afraid!"

"You're not worried about falling into the well by accident; you're scared that I might push you in," he said, looking into my eyes.

I looked right back at him. "Why would you do something like that to your father?" I said.

"To avenge Master Mahmut . . . ," he began. "To make you pay for abandoning me, for seducing my married mother, for not even bothering to write back to your own son after all those years . . . Or perhaps just to be the Westernized individual you want me to be. Oh, and of course to inherit your fortune . . ."

I was alarmed at the length of this list. I tried to talk him—my son—out of it. "You'd be dragged through the courts and end up rotting in jail," I warned him tenderly. "You'd spend the rest of your life in prison waiting for your mother's next visit. Things like murdering your father or protesting the government are only celebrated in the West. Over here, everyone except your mother would hate you for what you'd done. Besides, patricidal sons are not entitled to their father's inheritance; it's the law."

"Nobody does something like this thinking of the consequences," said my son. "If you think of the consequences, you can't be free. Freedom requires forgetting about history and ethics. Have you ever read Nietzsche?"

I decided to keep quiet.

"Anyway, if I were to push you into the well right now and tell everyone you fell in by accident . . . no one would be able to prove me wrong."

"You're right."

"Sometimes my anger at you is so intense that the thing I want most is to gouge out your eyes," said my son meditatively. "The most unbearable thing about fathers is that they can always see you!"

"A father's regard is something to be cherished."

"Only if he's a real father! A real father is a just father. You're not even a real father. I'd definitely start by blinding you."

"Why is that?"

"I'm a poet; playing with words is my calling. At the same time, I know that what we really think can't be expressed in words, only in pictures. I can't ever put the essence of what I'm thinking into words, but I can visualize it as an image. And the only way I can imagine becoming the sort of independent individual you want me to be is to blind you right now. Do you know why? Because if I do that, it'll mean I've finally become my own self; I'll have written my own story and created my own legend."

It was hurtful to hear all his animosity and hostility directed at me.

I should have embraced him and kissed him as a proper father would have done. But in the grips of disappointment and remorse, I said something I shouldn't have said:

"You're not a real son, either. You're both too resentful and too submissive."

"Submissive? Tell me how!"

I took a step back, flinching at the furious gesture punctuating his words. He stepped closer.

My second mistake was, at this point, to draw the Kırıkkale pistol from my inner pocket and to make a show of cocking it, half in jest.

"Stop right there, Son. Don't make me do this. It might go off!" I said.

"You don't even know how to use that," he said, lunging at the Kırıkkale.

We toppled over in the obscurity, father and son, and wrestled on the musty earth near the well. We'd rolled around several times until he pinned me down, grabbed my arm, and started smashing it against the side of the well, trying to release my grip on the gun . . .

• PART III •

THE RED-HAIRED WOMAN

ONE NIGHT around thirty years ago, in the earlier half of the 1980s, a few members of our theater troupe were having dinner and drinks with a group of political activists from the provincial town where we were performing, when a red-haired woman appeared at the other end of the table. Everybody started commenting on the remarkable coincidence of having two redheads at the same table, saying, "What are the odds" and debating whether we were in fact harbingers of good luck or of some other kind, when suddenly the red-haired woman at the far end of the table declared:

"I'm a natural redhead."

She seemed at once apologetic and proud. "Look, I have freckles on my face and on my arms. My skin is fair, and my eyes are green."

The whole table turned to me, eager to see how I would respond.

"You may have been born a redhead, but I chose to become one," I replied immediately.

Now, I'm not normally one to have such ready answers in life, but I'd given the matter a lot of thought previously. "God blessed you with red hair; what was destiny for you was a conscious decision for me."

I left it at that, not wanting my drinking companions to think I was too full of myself. I could already hear them scoffing. But had I held my tongue, it would have been like saying, "Yes, guilty, my hair color is fake," and my silence would have been taken for capitulation. They would have come to the wrong conclusions about my character and labeled me an impostor with unsophisticated aspirations.

For those of us who become redheads later in life, choosing the color is equivalent to selecting a personality. After becoming a redhead, I spent the rest of my days trying to stay true to my choice.

In my midtwenties, I was active in reviving the open-air folk theater tradition for modern audiences and hadn't yet begun spinning morality tales out of ancient myths and fables. Though I was full of righteous liberal sentiments, I was basically content. My lover at the time—a handsome militant ten years my senior—had just left me after a secret affair lasting three years. Oh, how romantic, how blissful, we'd felt all those hours we'd spent poring over books together! Though I was angry at him for leaving me, I couldn't really blame him; our affair had been discovered, and our comrades wouldn't stand for it. They insisted that the romance would poison the group and end in tears for all those involved. Then before we knew it, it was 1980, and there'd been another military coup. Some of us went underground; some crossed over by boat into Greece and from there on to Germany, where they became political exiles; some were arrested and tortured. My old lover Akın went back home to his wife, his son, and his pharmacy. Turhan, whose attentions had always annoyed me, and whom I'd always resented for bad-mouthing my lover, now treated me with great kindness. One thing led to another, and we decided to get married, thinking it would also be good for our leftist group, the National Revolutionaries.

But my new husband couldn't get over my old relationship. He was convinced my past was undermining his authority with the organization's rank and file, though he stopped short of blaming me for being "easy." He was nothing like my married lover Akın, who forgot as fast as he loved. For Turhan there was no pretending that nothing was wrong. He started hearing veiled gibes and insinuations in the most innocent comments. Pretty soon he accused his National Revolutionary comrades of ineffectiveness and went off to Malatya to marshal an armed resistance. But when those very people my husband was trying to muster alerted the authorities to the presence of a rabble-rouser, the gendarmes cornered him in a ditch somewhere. I'm sure you can guess what happened next.

Having suffered a second major loss in such a short space of time, I felt even more alienated from politics. I considered going back home to live with my parents (my father had been involved in local government before retiring), but I could never commit myself to doing so. Going home would mean both a defeat and giving up acting—and it would have been a struggle to find another theater company willing to let me join them. I had reached a point in life where I wanted to be involved in the theater for its own sake—not because of politics.

So I stayed within the organization and eventually married my late husband's younger brother, just like those wives of Ottoman cavalrymen sent to the Persian front never to return, the only difference being that it was my idea to marry Turgay. I was also the one who encouraged him to set up a traveling theater. In the early days, our marriage was thus unexpectedly harmonious. I had already loved and lost two men, and Turgay's boyish youth seemed like a guarantee that he would last. We spent winters in big cities like Istanbul or Ankara, performing in the auditoriums of left-wing organizations and in meeting halls you could hardly call theaters, and during the summers we followed our friends' recommendations, taking our tent to provincial towns, holiday resorts, military garrisons, and newly built plants and factories. We'd been living like this for three years when I met that other red-haired woman at the dinner table, and it had been only one year before that I'd decided to dye my hair red.

It wasn't a deliberate decision. One day, I just went into some nondescript salon in Bakırköy and told the middle-aged hairdresser: "I want to change my color." I didn't even have a specific one in mind.

"Your hair is already rather light; blond would suit you."

"Dye it red," I said instinctively. "That'll look good."

He chose a shade somewhere between an orange and a fire truck. It really stood out, but neither Turgay nor anyone else I cared about complained. Perhaps they thought I was preparing for a show. I knew they also put it down to the unfortunate run of love affairs I'd suffered through. "Can you blame her?" they might have said, before looking away.

The reactions I received helped me realize the full import of what I'd done. Turkish people are singularly preoccupied with the distinction between authentic and artificial. After that other redhead's pompous dinner-table affirmation, I stopped relying on hairdressers and their chemicals and started dyeing my own hair with henna bought from the market. I suppose this was the upshot of my encounter with the natural redhead.

Onstage, I always paid particular attention to the high-school boys, university students, and lonely soldiers in the audience, keeping my heart wide open to their dreams and longings. They are much better than older men at distinguishing what is real from what is fake, between affected and genuine emotion. If I hadn't been dyeing my hair with my own henna recipe, perhaps I would never have caught Cem's eye.

I noticed him because he noticed me. He looked so much like his father that it was a joy to look at him. I realized he had fallen for me when I caught him looking up at the windows of the building we were living in. He was shy, which I also appreciated. Shameless men scare me, and we certainly have plenty of those to go around. Of course shamelessness is contagious, and so widespread that this country can sometimes feel suffocating. Most of these men expect you to be as shameless as they are. But Cem was gentle and timid. I worked out who he was during our stroll around the Station Square the night he came to see our show.

I was surprised, but perhaps some part of me had known who he was all along. Theater has taught me not to dismiss anything in life as mere coincidence. It's no coincidence that both my son and his father dreamed of being writers; that I was reunited with the father of my boy here in Öngören thirty years later; that my son experienced the agony of fatherlessness just as his own father had before him; and that, after years of shedding tears onstage, I now have real reason to weep.

In the wake of the coup of 1980, our folk theater group shifted its political stance to stave off any run-ins with the government. We diluted our leftist rhetoric. Trying to appeal to the widest audience possible, I picked speeches from Rumi's *Masnavi* and old Sufi stories and fables, as well as emotional scenes and dialogues from familiar tales like "Farhad and Shirin" or *Asli and Karam*. But by far our most popular piece was the monologue I'd adapted from the story of Rostam and Sohrab at the suggestion of an old screenwriter friend who used to write melodramas for the Yeşilçam films and who assured us that this particular story never got old.

After a few spoofs of popular television commercials, I would break into a belly dance, at which point the catcalling lechers in the audience, driven wild by my long legs and short skirt, would either fall in love on the spot or else lose themselves in elaborate sexual fantasies; but the moment I stepped back onstage as Sohrab's mother, Tahmina, and shrieked at the sight of what my husband had done to my son, every single one of them—even the perverts who'd just been howling, "Take it off!"—would fall into a ponderous, unnerving silence.

I would start to cry, softly at first, but building quickly to full-throated sobs. As I wept, I would revel in my power over them and rejoice in having devoted my life to the theater. Standing onstage in my long, revealing red dress, the costume jewelry, the broad military sash around my waist, and an antique bracelet on my arm, I cried with a grief only mothers can know, and looking at those men seated before me, feeling their souls tremble, seeing their eyes well up, I'd recognize the guilt stirring in them all. From the way they all sided with him as soon as the fight began, I could tell that most of the angry, young provincial men identified with Sohrab, not his powerful, overbearing father, Rostam. It was therefore essentially their own deaths they were mourning. But they would not allow themselves to weep at their fates until their red-haired mother led the way with her uncontainable grief.

Even in the grip of such excruciating emotions, my adoring fans couldn't help but let their eyes roam over my face, neck, cleavage, legs, and of course my red hair, in keeping with how abstract suffering is commonly joined with sexual arousal in the old folktales. In certain rare and glorious moments, I was able with every glance, every turn of the neck, and every measured step to engage those men in their minds and hearts at once, appealing to their youthful sensuality. Sometimes one of them would burst into noisy tears, his sobs quickly infecting others around him. Someone else, feeling uncomfortable, might start clapping in the middle of the piece, drowning me out and provoking a scuffle. On several occasions, I witnessed the entire audience inside the tent lose its collective mind: the loud bawlers tangled with the buttoned-up weepers; the swearing hecklers taking on both those who cheered us and those who watched quietly. Normally this kind of energy and intensity from the crowd is something I crave, but the threat of violence could make me nervous.

Trying to find something to balance the scene with the weeping Tahmina, we introduced a reenactment of that moment when the prophet Abraham prepares to cut his only son's throat to prove his submission to the will of God; I played a woman crying in the background and later the angel who walks onstage carrying a toy lamb. In fact, there was no real room for women in this story, and I wasn't making much impact. So I reworked Oedipus's exchange with his mother, Jocasta, for my monologue. The notion that a son might kill his own father by accident was met mostly with emotional detachment, but at least it stimulated the audience intellectually. That should have been enough. How I wish I'd left out the bit about the son sleeping with his red-haired mother . . . Today I can see what an ill-fated choice that was. Turgay had warned me. But I ignored him, just as I ignored the boy who brought us tea during rehearsals and exclaimed, "What the hell?" when he heard the speech, not to mention our manager Yusuf's anxious response: "I'm not sure about this one!"

In 1986, in the town of Güdül, I played Jocasta with red hair, shedding genuine tears as I spoke of how I'd inadvertently slept with my own son. We received a number of threats after the first performance, and after the second, the tent was set ablaze in the middle of the night, and we barely managed to extinguish the flames. I performed the same monologue again a month later in Samsun, where we'd set up near the shanties on the coast, and the next morning, local kids pelted our tent with rocks. In Erzurum, angry young nationalists accused us of peddling "Greek plays"; cowed by their threats, I had to hole up in our hotel while troops of brave and honorable policemen stood guard around our tent. We had begun to think that perhaps our art was too explicit for the hinterlands, but even when we went to the Progressive Patriots' Society of Ankara, in a tiny auditorium stinking of coffee and *rakı,* we were ordered to stop after just a couple of performances for "offending the sensibilities and susceptibilities of the public." It was hard to disagree with the judge in a country where every man's favorite curse starts with "your mother."

I used to discuss these matters with Akın, my son's future grandfather, back in my twenties when we were in love. He was always astonished to recall all the profanities boys learned in school and military service, swear words I'd never even heard of when he mentioned them, commenting how "disgusting" they were and launching into a tirade on the "oppression of women," which always ended with his assurances that no such obscenities would survive the establishment of a working-class utopia. I had only to be patient and stand behind our men while they prepared the revolution. But this is neither the time nor the place to broach the age-old debate about sexism in the Turkish left-wing movement. My closing monologues are never just angry; they are lyrical and elegant, too. I hope my son's book can match that tone and convey to its readers as full a range of emotions as I used to convey from the stage. It was in fact my idea that Enver should write a book about our experiences, beginning with his father and grandfather.

When he was still a child, I considered schooling Enver at home rather than sending him to a place where he was bound to lose all the goodness and the humanity he was born with and pick up all the foul habits boys seem to acquire as they grow. But Turgay dismissed my idea as fantasy. By the time we enrolled our son in elementary school in Bakırköy, we had both quit the theater and started working as voice actors on those foreign TV series that were appearing on every channel. What kept us coming back to Öngören was Sırrı Siyahoğlu. Our leftist and socialist enthusiasms may have faded, but we still kept in touch with old friends. It was Sırrı in fact who would reunite us with Master Mahmut all those years later.

Our Enver delighted in Master Mahmut's stories. We would visit him in his house, where he had a beautiful well in the back garden. He had made a lot of money digging wells there during the flurry of construction projects that had followed his first one, and having also bought, early on, a good bit of local land that had since appreciated, he was living rather comfortably. The locals arranged for him to marry a beautiful widow whose husband had abandoned her and their son and gone to Germany, never to be seen again. Master Mahmut adopted the boy as his own; he was a good father to him. Enver became good friends with this boy, Salih. I tried, without luck, to get Salih interested in the theater. But most of my youth theater group was composed of Enver's friends as well as other boys and girls from Öngören. I had started spending more time there because of Enver. The love of theater can be infectious. Most of these kids were frequent visitors at Master Mahmut's house. He'd padlocked the lid on the well he'd dug in his honeysuckle-scented garden so none of the children would fall in while playing in the yard. But watching them from his second-floor balcony at the back I'd still call out to warn them: "Stay away from the well." The things you hear in old myths and folktales always end up happening in real life.

I played a central role in rescuing Master Mahmut from the well. The night before, I had been seduced by my clumsy teenaged lover—who would leave me pregnant, an outcome neither of us could have even remotely envisaged—and as he'd gulped down yet another glass of Club Rakı, he had confessed to me *absolutely everything* (those were his exact words): his master was putting far too much pressure on him, he'd had enough and just wanted to go home to his mother, he didn't believe they'd ever find water, but he didn't even care anymore; his only reason for remaining in Öngören was me.

So when around noon the next day I saw him sprinting toward the train station with his little valise, I was perplexed. The men who fell in love with me (however fleetingly) after watching me perform weren't often content with seeing me once; usually they were intensely jealous.

I was probably just disappointed that I'd never see Cem again. He'd told me so little about his father; had he suspected something from the outset? My colleagues and I had planned to take the next train out of town, but I could not understand why Cem had fled Öngören like a bandit. The station was swarming with children and villagers bearing baskets of produce for the market. The night before Cem's visit, Turgay had enlisted apprentice Ali to bring Master Mahmut to our tent, where he saw our show in respectful silence. We discovered that Ali was no longer helping him and that the landowner who'd commissioned the dig had stopped financing it. Burning with curiosity, we sent Turgay to the plateau to find out more, and since our train came and went in the meantime, the rest of us soon headed up the hill to the well like a gang of characters in an old fairy tale. After we lowered Ali down, he came back up carrying a semiconscious Master Mahmut.

They took Master Mahmut to the hospital, but as we later discovered, he returned to his well before giving his broken collarbone a chance to heal properly. We never knew whether he found another apprentice; we'd left Öngören by then. To be honest, I was eager to forget how I'd slept with a high-school boy there one night in a moment of theatrical abandon, not to mention having been in love with that same boy's father before him, only for that flame to burn out. I wasn't yet thirty-five, and already I'd discovered how proud and fragile men could be, the sense of self that courses through their veins. I knew that fathers and sons were capable of killing each other. Whether it was fathers killing their sons, or sons killing the fathers, men always emerged victorious, and all that was left for me to do was weep. I thought perhaps I needed to unlearn everything and begin a new life elsewhere.

Never mind Turgay; even I hardly suspected that Cem could be Enver's father. It did cross my mind as I was working out when he could have been conceived, but I didn't give it much more thought. Yet as Enver grew up and I saw clearly that his eyes and especially his nose looked nothing like Turgay's, I began to think once more that perhaps my young lover was indeed the father of my son. Did Turgay ever wonder?

Enver and Turgay never got along. It seemed that every time he looked at our son, Turgay remembered that I had originally been his brother Turhan's wife. He also shared his brother's opinion that having previously had an affair with a married man, I must have been unfaithful to Turhan, too. I knew this was how he felt, though he never said as much. He couldn't stand my red hair because it reminded him of my past—though he never admitted to that, either.

I brought Turgay translations of plays and novels originally written in French or English to show him that the West portrayed red-haired women as fiery, assertive shrews, but he was unimpressed. I read an article entitled "Women According to Men," which a women's magazine had lifted verbatim from an English one. There was a painting of a beautiful red-haired woman with the caption: "Fierce and mysterious." Her expression and the shape of her lips were comparable to mine. I clipped the picture out and stuck it on the wall, but my husband ignored it. Turgay's horizons had always been much narrower than his leftist and internationalist pretenses implied. According to him, in our country, a redhead was a woman of easy virtue. If she'd chosen to color her hair red on purpose, it was tantamount to choosing that identity. Only the fact that I was an actress mitigated my offense by turning it into a kind of theatrical spectacle.

Thus, in our years working as voice actors, Turgay and I grew apart. We lived in an apartment in Bakırköy that my husband had inherited from his parents, but Enver didn't see much of his father at all. Turgay was busy dubbing commercials and adding in those jobs he took on the side, and he always got home late, if at all. Sadly, I know what it's like to raise a child whose father may or may not be back for dinner.

So Enver and I became very close. I was there to witness the evolution of his shifting moods, of his delicate soul and sensibility. I felt his fury, his loneliness, and his hopelessness as clearly as I observed his terrors, his silences, and his little anxieties. I loved running my fingers over the smooth skin on his arms and his neck, and I was gratified by the sight of his shoulders and ears spreading out. The development of his sexual organs was no less gratifying than the burgeoning of his intelligence, his powers of reason, and the survival of his childish silliness.

Some days we were just as he wanted us to be, best friends chatting, laughing, playing hide-and-seek at home, solving crossword puzzles, and shopping together. But sometimes a veil of melancholy and loneliness would descend upon us, and we would take refuge even from each other, terrified by the sheer size of the world and fed up with our place in it. I understood in those moments how difficult it is to empathize with anyone, to truly know another and commune with their soul—even when the person in question was Enver, the one I loved most in life. I would take him by the hand and show him the whole world: streets, houses, paintings, parks, oceans, ships. I wanted him to play out in the street with his friends in Bakırköy and Öngören, also to learn how to fight for himself and stand on his own two feet, but I wanted just as badly for him to steer clear of those delinquents who called one another motherfucker, lest he should turn into one of those men who used to jeer us in the theater tent.

Enver spent much less time than the other children playing outside.

But to my dismay, he was also an average student and never top of his class. Sometimes I wondered why this upset me so much. After all, more than I wanted him to have a successful career—or even to be rich—I wanted my son to be compassionate, to value justice, and to be at peace. But I felt he could be happy and a hero both! I had such high hopes for him. I used to pray that he would never be the kind to fill his head with trivial concerns. When, as a little boy, he would bawl his eyes out with his pink mouth hanging wide open, I would chant, "May life be kind to my darling son."

I would look earnestly into his liquid eyes and tell him that he was different from everyone else, that there was something special about his spirit. We read children's books, old fairy tales, and poems together. We watched cartoons and children's theater shows on TV. I could see that he was more thoughtful and sensitive than his father and grandfather. I told him he would write plays one day. He liked the idea of writing but rejected the theater.

After his elementary-school years, an angrier and pricklier side to Enver started to emerge; I'd never seen it in either his father or his grandfather. I made allowances for his rages, thinking he might have inherited them from me. He'd been such a serene child. As a baby, my Enver used to love bath time, when I rinsed his graceful, delicate little body with warm water, carefully soaping up his slender arms, his sweet, melon-shaped head, his little bean of a penis, and his strawberry-pink nipples. The bathroom would be nice and warm, and sometimes I would wash myself after washing him. In the house in Bakırköy the bathroom always took forever to warm up, so we bathed in the tub together until he turned ten. Afterward, I taught him how to bathe on his own, how to wash his head, his hair, and his legs without opening his eyes.

My son didn't like that at all, and I've come to believe that his fits of rage, which grew more protracted and severe as he grew older, took root at this time. During his high-school years, when Turgay stopped coming home altogether, Enver became miserable, his sorrow exacerbated by failing to get into a decent university and by my disappointment, which I couldn't hide despite how much I adored him. He seemed to relish arguing with me and contradicting me just for the sake of it. When I criticized his comic books or changed the TV channel he was watching, he would snarl, "What would you know?" He would shave his head like a fugitive or grow a beard like a religious fanatic or leave his cheeks unshaven for days like a lunatic, and taking a twisted satisfaction in my alarm, he would pick a fight. We would end up screaming at each other until he stormed off, slamming the door behind him.

At the university, he started going often to Öngören to see his childhood friends. He had fallen in with a bunch of unemployed idealists he'd met at Master Mahmut's place. He went through a phase of gambling on the horse races at the Veliefendi track near our house in Bakırköy, but quickly repented, and never once asked me for money. During his military service in Burdur, he was so lonely that he would spend his weekend leave on the phone with me, crying. When he came home to Istanbul, my eyes would well up with tender tears to see him with such short hair, so sunburned, and so skinny, his neck like a cherry stalk. We were always on the verge of another shouting match, after which we could sometimes go several days without speaking. He would retaliate by staying out late or, worse, not coming home at all, and I would spend sleepless nights waiting for him. I was terrified that he might fall for some half-witted girl or a damaged, aggressive older woman. But no matter how much we argued and sulked, and in spite of all our heavy silences and snide remarks, at some point we would hug each other tight and make up. In those moments, I would realize that I could not endure being separated from my son, or survive without him.

Since we were already estranged from his father (or the man he thought was his father), Enver was unaffected when Turgay and I formally divorced and even when Turgay eventually passed away. I ascribed the boy's fits of rage, his irrational furies, his increasingly taciturn and judgmental ways to his sensitive nature and to the absence of a father figure. But the chief cause, I also believed, was poverty. So when I saw Cem and his property developments in newspaper ads, and read in those same papers how Western medicine had worked out fail-safe ways for anyone to determine the true identity of their father, even to the satisfaction of the Turkish courts, it got me thinking.

In my youth, I would never have dreamed of filing this kind of lawsuit. Using the police and the laws of the state to corner a man into accepting his responsibility for a child he would otherwise never have acknowledged; dangling the threat of another lawsuit to extract more money; showing up at the public meeting he'd organized . . . My son was appalled at the things I was doing. But he also knew that it was all for his sake, and once the flurries of rage abated, he was mollified.

For months I'd begged and cajoled him into filing the suit; we yelled and quarreled endlessly. Obviously it was asking a lot for him to accept that his mother had had an extramarital affair that had produced a child, let alone that she'd kept it a secret for all these years. He would ask me again and again, with furious embarrassment, "Are you sure?" and as many times I would answer, "Would I have said anything if I wasn't?" He would look away—or perhaps I would—and we would both fall silent.

But mostly, we screamed at each other. "It's for your own good!" I'd tell him. That was the strongest case I could make. During one row, he pulled down the picture of the red-haired woman on the wall and ripped it in half. He told me he'd learned on the Internet that she was as bad as I was. So I looked her up, too. The picture I'd taken from a magazine was of a painting by Dante Gabriel Rossetti. Struck by his model's alluring eyes and her full lips, he fell in love and married her. I repaired the picture with tape and put it back up on the wall.

My son could only ever broach the subject of suing his father when drinking *rakı,* whose influence fortified him with the confidence to discuss anything while also exacerbating his stern irritability and causing him to address his mother in language befitting a sailor. As when he first moved to Öngören after university, now too he would curse me after every row, vowing not to waste another moment's thought on a whore like me (or horrible words to that effect). But then, unable to cope on his own, he'd take the train from Öngören and show up in Bakırköy for dinner a day or two later.

"I'm glad you came," I used to say. "I made meatballs."

We'd chat about this and that as if nothing had happened only two days before. After dinner, we would sit side by side on the couch, just a mother and her son watching television, as we used to do every evening when he was still in school and we awaited his father, who never came home. When the show was over, he would be too proud to admit his reluctance to go back home and spend the night on his own, so he would instead start switching channels looking for another program to become engrossed in.

He would soon curl up and fall asleep in front of the television, and I would quietly watch over him and blame myself for not having found him a suitable girl to marry. But I suspect I would have disapproved of any girl he liked, and that he was perfectly capable of refusing, out of sheer spite, any girl I might pick for him. Besides, my son had neither the financial means nor the social standing to guarantee him a good match.

I have never regretted any of my decisions after the day I dyed my hair red. My only regret is my hopeful insistence that my son meet and get to know his father. Enver was scathing about the idea, though he never dismissed it entirely. Mostly, though, he accused me of being a fantasist or of doing it all for the money. It's no coincidence that all the newspapers wound up accusing him of the very same thing after Cem's death. But my son didn't mean to kill his father. He is certainly no murderer, despite the liberal use the press has made of that slur, tainting his name forever.

My son was merely trying to defend himself against the blind rage of a man with a gun, who happened to be his father. Enver's only hope coming to the meeting that night was to be finally reunited with the father he'd never known. It was I who stirred that need in him; it is all that I regret now. I don't for a second regret all the stories I told him as a child about Rostam and Sohrab, Oedipus and his mother, or Abraham and Isaac. As for the youths, the students, the angry men who came to our yellow theater tent . . . No one had ever told them these stories, but somehow they knew them anyway, just as people can sometimes still know, deep down, things they've forgotten.

Whatever the prosecutor may have claimed, my son's familiarity with these old stories, and with life's occasional tendency to imitate myths and fables, does not prove his guilt. Enver would have dearly wished to leave that well without causing the death of his father. But was there even a moment to think as he tried to wrest the gun out of his father's hand? My son killed his father by accident. This much was clear to me as soon as I heard his own sincere account of what had happened. It should have been clear to most journalists, too, had they not preferred to deceive their readers for the sake of a good story.

The success of Sohrab, Cem's incredible wealth, the technology that now allowed Enver to prove who his father was . . . It all made for irresistibly titillating copy. Countless paragraphs described how I'd wept upon reaching the scene of the crime. Well-meaning columnists who enjoyed wallowing in melodrama wrote lengthy pieces on the tribulations of the "former stage and voice actress" who'd witnessed her son killing his father. Other more malicious hacks, whose newspapers sold advertising space to Sohrab, published disgraceful slanders about how my tears should fool no one, for this was no accident but a murder plot we had been hatching for years, and how we'd acted solely because we couldn't wait to get our hands on childless Cem's inheritance. They presented my red hair as proof of my disreputable character. Never mind that it wasn't my son but his father who'd brought a gun to Öngören and drew it in a fit of rage by the well . . .

The gun was registered to Cem, and the judge will take this into account when assessing my son's integrity, together with the lack of any proof of premeditation on our part. I am sure of it. But of course the newspapers have ignored these facts. And now my son and I will go down in Istanbul history as the evil red-haired mother and her conniving son who killed the father out of greed. I can't bear to think of it. Every time I visit my son in Silivri Prison, there is always some brazen inmate staring daggers at me or taunting me with gibes based on lies in the papers; even the more helpful wardens sometimes give me such looks that I want to die. These stares and accusations are so much worse than anything I experienced in all those years' of hearing shameless hecklers yelling, "Strip! Strip!" I asked Enver to write down a complete account of how he'd come to kill his father by mistake. When he reads it, the judge will surely have no choice but to acquit him on the grounds that he acted in self-defense. But to present the story in its full context, he must start from the very beginning, with the summer his father went to dig that well—and that has made it necessary for me to help him discover everything that happened before and since. The fruit of all those efforts is the text you are now holding, offered as a statement for the defense to the criminal court of Silivri. The whole thing—and not just the next few pages—can be regarded as the investigative report of a murder, with every piece of evidence subject to and withstanding legal scrutiny. Just as in Sophocles's *Oedipus the King*.

That day, I'd introduced my son to everyone as Serhat, so it would be easier for him to approach his father, but somehow this has been presented as evidence of our delinquency. The press has also published a series of allegations about the paternity suit, all unfounded. But the account you will find here is complete and unequivocally true. So I'll pick up where I left off:

When I realized that my son and his father weren't coming back to the banquet hall, I rushed to the well myself. A few witnesses came with me.

The night watchman directed us to the old cafeteria building. As we stepped inside, an ugly, unruly cur was barking as if his life depended on it. I saw my son sitting alone on the floor a few steps from the open mouth of the well, and I realized immediately what must have happened. My son had accidentally killed his father. I ran to his side and held him close. I cried just as profusely as I used to cry in the theater.

But my misery was far more complex than the stage version. As I let out each piercing wail, hoping for some release from the anguish, I became aware of why even the most insolent soldiers, the most foulmouthed drunks, and the most shameless perverts were always silenced by the sight of a woman weeping: the logic of the universe turns on the tears of mothers. That explained why I was crying now. I was crying about everything, and it was comforting to do so, for it seemed to free my mind to think about other things.

The drunken busybodies who'd followed me from the banquet hall were trying to determine the whereabouts of their boss when my son announced that Mr. Cem (he did not refer to him as his father) had fallen into the well.

Someone from Sohrab called the police. Cem's wife, Ayşe, arrived before they did; she was led to the well, and like all the others, she too refused to believe that her husband could be all the way down there. I wanted to embrace her as one woman reaching out to another, I wanted to mourn with her for the dead father, for the son who'd killed him, and for our lives. But they wouldn't let me anywhere near her.

The newspapers later wrote in ominous tones about the depth of the well, the murky waters inside, and the surreal notion that anyone could have dug a hole so deep in the ground all those years ago with nothing more than a shovel and a pickax. They started talking about fate, and although I wasn't much convinced, I too liked the idea nonetheless.

I would have dearly loved a chance to talk to Ayşe in the days following my son's arrest, to console her for her loss and try to assuage the hatred she must have felt toward us. I wanted to tell her that, as women, we were not responsible for what had happened, for it had all been dictated by myth and history. But understandably, she was more interested in what she read in the newspapers every day than she was in ancient myths and legends. We were disheartened to discover that Sohrab's employees were feeding gossip to the same journalists who were writing that my son had killed Ayşe's husband for his estate and that I had masterminded everything.

The police found a single spent cartridge near the well. But there was no sign of the gun. A diver who was accustomed to the depths and strong currents of the Bosphorus was secured to a rope and lowered into the muddy hole, from where he emerged with Cem's wretched corpse, already unrecognizable just two days after his death. My son's father was then subjected to a brutal autopsy in which every one of his organs was extracted and dissected. Since no trace of the dirty well water was found inside his lungs, it was clear that he must have died before falling in.

The same autopsy also revealed the cause of death. The coroner's verdict was splashed across the next day's front pages: "He shot his father in the eye!" But no one wrote about their tussle by the well or mentioned my son's court statement, in which he explained that he'd acted only to defend himself and that the gun had gone off by accident while he was trying to disarm his father.

The judge sent the diver into the well again, and this time he surfaced with the Kırıkkale pistol. It helped our case that it was registered to Cem and that the bullet that had entered his left eye came from its barrel, according to the ballistics analysis. We were therefore confident that the judge would rule that my son had acted in self-defense and that he wasn't a murderer. It hadn't been a case of an embittered son who'd brought the gun to the well, but of a father who feared his own child.

Ms. Ayşe's and Sohrab's conduct toward me changed after the retrieval of the weapon. When it became clear that my son hadn't planned to kill his father and that he might even be acquitted—free therefore to inherit Cem's estate after all and become Sohrab's biggest shareholder—their animosity lessened considerably.

In our first meeting at the Sohrab offices, I found Ayşe poised and dignified. Did she believe any of the tabloid gossip about me? I could tell from the look in her eyes that she was suppressing all her bitterness and anger in the effort to remain composed. It was obvious that she'd decided to bury her grief over the loss of her beloved husband for the time being and was willing herself to get along with me.

I tried to reassure her: though I couldn't speak for Enver, who was still in prison awaiting the conclusion of his trial, she could be sure that neither of us had any intention of dismantling the construction empire on which my son's late father had expended all his wits and creativity, much less of leaving its hundreds of employees out in the cold. In fact, we hoped to do the very opposite: we wanted Sohrab to reach even greater heights. I told her I believed Sohrab was born on that day in 1986—thirty years ago—when my son's late father began to dig that well with Master Mahmut.

Having made this delicate point, I described how, during that same year, Master Mahmut and the father of my son had each visited the yellow tent of the Theater of Morality Tales, only a day apart, and how struck they had both been by the tragedy of Rostam and Sohrab. The tears I'd shed in the tent that night were thus related to those I'd shed by the well thirty years later by the same inexorable bonds between myth and life.

"Life follows myth!" I said, electrified. "Wouldn't you agree?"

"I do," said Ayşe politely.

I could sense that neither she nor Sohrab's board of directors was prepared to do anything that might antagonize me and my son.

"Don't forget that I was right there in Öngören when our company was digging its very first well. And even its name, Sohrab, was taken from what was my closing monologue at the time."

Ayşe blinked as if to dispel her disbelief at what she'd just heard. Of course, the name Sohrab didn't come from my monologue, but from Ferdowsi's thousand-year-old *Shahnameh*. She had been studying "these matters" (she couldn't bring herself to say the words "filicide" or "patricide") with her husband for years, during which they'd examined untold paintings and ancient manuscripts in museums across Europe and the rest of the world. She looked out of the windows of the Sohrab headquarters, her eyes roaming over Istanbul's skyscrapers and its sea of roofs and chimneys, and started describing scenes from a happier past, as though she had a point to prove. She spoke of a museum in Saint Petersburg, of a house in Tehran, of Athens, of signs, symbols, and artworks scattered over a huge geographical expanse, and though her tone was enigmatic, her satisfaction and enjoyment at recalling these moments were palpable. This woman had been a companion to my son's father, and they'd been happy together. Now, due to a series of legal quirks, there was a chance my son might end up owning most of the company they had surely worked so hard to build, for alongside my son's father, it was this woman who'd raised and nurtured Sohrab.

Taking care to ensure that her tone would not offend me, provoke my imprisoned son, or reveal how much she loathed us, Ayşe told me the story you have been reading in this book, starting all the way back to when she met her husband at university and they used to visit the Deniz Bookstore together. Watching her closely as she spoke, I got the unmistakable feeling that she was using her blissful memories to exact some sort of revenge on me. But I didn't let that get to me and listened humbly to her account; after all, both the child and Sohrab belonged, in a sense, to me.

Over my next few visits to Silivri Prison, I began to tell my son some of the stories I'd heard from Ayşe. Despite how far it was from home, and all the buses I had to take to get there from Bakırköy, I still made it to the gates every time, asking myself what it could mean that my son was being held here, just five kilometers from where his father and Master Mahmut had dug their well, in this prison whose warden and guards proudly proclaimed was not only the biggest in Turkey but "in the whole of Europe." Once I was through the gates, there was the endless merry-go-round of metal detectors, female guards never without a snide remark about my red hair as they searched me, waiting rooms, doors opening and doors closing, locks clicking open and locks clicking shut, halls and hallways, until I would lose all sense of time and place. As I waited for my son to appear beyond the soundproof glass of the visiting room, I would daydream, mistaking other inmates for him, and growing either sleepy or restless in my barely contained fury, and when my son finally arrived, it was as if the figure behind the glass wasn't him but his dead father—no, his dead grandfather.

If our lawyer happened to be present, we would talk through the latest developments in our case, the nonsense peddled by the press, and any particular difficulties my son might be suffering in his cell block. There was the abuse from those who believed he'd killed his father for money, the awful prison food, and the frustration of hearing about a new wave of pardons that proved to be merely rumor. Enver'd tell us harrowing stories of pro-opposition journalists and Kurds now being held in the same cells once occupied by coup-plotting generals, and he'd have us write yet another useless petition asking for privacy, a little more fresh-air time, or the review of an unjust verdict. This would all take so long that usually our allotted hour would pass before the two of us, mother and son, even had the chance to exchange a few tender words in private.

But there was usually nobody but the prison guard monitoring our conversation. Remembering the stories I had heard from Ayşe and read in books she'd mentioned, I would try to explain everything to my son as if the ideas and the fantasies had been my own. Enver didn't like hearing about ancient myths, since they reminded him of his crime, and often he would pretend not to understand the point I was trying to make. He didn't believe me when I told him I had once heard these stories from Master Mahmut himself, but he listened anyway. For what really mattered wasn't the myth itself, but the fact that we were here together, talking face-to-face. Sometimes I would stop talking and just reflect for a while, struggling to hold back tears at the sight of how much bulk my son had put on, how he was steadily taking on the appearance of a prison thug.

The hardest thing was parting when the hour was over. I could manage somehow to leave that room, but my son couldn't bring himself to say goodbye, just as he couldn't as a child, and though he would valiantly stand when the guard warned him that our time was up, he couldn't face the thought of walking out. He would stand by the door staring helplessly as I left, and I would recall how before he was old enough to go to school, he used to beg me not to leave him alone even for a five-minute trip to the grocery store. I'd tell him, "I'll be back before you know it," but he never believed me. He would follow me to the door, pulling on my arm and my skirts, crying, "Don't leave," and refusing to let go, as if he were convinced that whenever I walked out the door it would be the last time he would ever see me.

Our greatest consolation was that they allowed physical contact between prisoners and their families during the monthly social visits. The whole block was attuned to these occasions, waiting patiently for the next one, feeling crushed if one happened to be postponed as a punishment of some sort, and rejoicing when new ones were added by ministerial decree during religious holidays. Because there were so many leftist and Kurdish militants in the prison, we were not allowed to bring any food, books, or mobile phones. But with a little gift to the warden, I managed to slip my darling son the notebook he'd kept in Öngören, his pens, and a few of his favorite poetry anthologies. I realized that writing might be an effective therapy for his suffering and rage. That's how I came to suggest that he start an account of his life, perhaps even working the entire story, now nearing its end, into the form of a novel. I made sure to check on his progress during those social visits.

In the visiting room in the felons' block, the two of us would embrace in some secluded corner, sitting apart from the hordes of common smugglers, killers, armed robbers, thieves, and swindlers huddling with their own families and friends. From the moment I touched my son again, that same luminous look would dawn on his face that used to appear whenever I bathed him as a child. He would then launch into cheerful descriptions of his fellow prisoners, the corrupt wardens, and all the dirty business he'd witnessed inside, concluding that things really weren't so bad, even though he knew I would never believe him. And then full of courage, he would recite for me a poem he'd written about the view from his cell window or the sky above the courtyard.

After expressing sincere admiration for my son's poetry, I would lead the conversation back to the book I knew he must write, not only to convince the judge of his innocence, but also as an act of moral witness for people generally. I would give him my latest thoughts, talk to him about Oedipus and Sohrab (neither book was to be found on the shelves of the prison library, but I managed to smuggle those in for him, too) and his late father's momentous trip to Tehran, or about my life in the theater, about the summer I met his father, the plays we used to stage in our yellow tent, and the meaning of the monologue I would deliver at the end of every performance. "Those shows I did were all for the sake of that final monologue," I told my son, looking fervently into his eyes.

Sometimes we would sit quietly and simply gaze at each other as if we'd just met for the first time. I would pick off a piece of lint from his woollen sweater, or touch a button that was about to fall off his shirt, or gently comb his messy hair with my fingers. So many times I wanted to ask him how much he remembered of his childhood, why he'd been so angry all the time, why he'd put a bullet in his father's eye, and why he seemed so peaceful now, but I always resisted the urge. I would just hold his hand, and caress his arms, his shoulders, his back, his neck. He, in turn, would cradle his sixty-year-old mother's hands in his and kiss them as fervidly as a lover.

On the day of the last Feast of the Sacrifice, we sat together again and looked into each other's eyes before embracing without a word. It was a sunny autumn day. He told me he would finally start working on the novel in which he would explain "everything." There were, he said, as many thoughts in his head right now as there were stars in the sky beyond the window of his cell at night. It was difficult to comprehend all those stars, no less difficult than to put all his emotions into words. But he would turn to other books for inspiration. Political books weren't allowed in the prison library, but he'd found Jules Verne's *Journey to the Center of the Earth,* Edgar Allan Poe's short stories, old poetry collections, and an anthology called *Dreams and Life.* He was going to read them all just as his father had done as a young man, and once he understood how they'd influenced him, he would be able to put himself in his father's place. He asked me to tell him about his father. I answered his questions enthusiastically and gave him a joyful hug, upon which I was ecstatic to notice that his neck still smelled as it had when he was a child: a mixture of plain soap and biscuits. As the end of the visit approached, I pleaded with God to comfort my son at our parting on this holy day.

"I'll be back on Monday," I said with a smile. I pulled out the taped-up picture of the red-haired woman by Dante Gabriel Rossetti and handed it to him. "I'm so happy to hear you're going to write your novel now, my darling boy!" I said. "You can put this picture on the cover when it's finished, and perhaps there may even be some room in there for you to write about your beautiful mother when she was young. See, this woman looks a bit like me. Of course you know best how your novel should start, but I think it ought to be sincere and mythical at the same time, like the monologues I used to deliver at the end of our performances. It should be as credible as a true story, and as familiar as a myth. That way, everyone, not just the judge, will understand what you are trying to say. Remember: your father had always wanted to be a writer, too."

January–December 2015